2 Tim 1:7

FAR
FROM
GOOD

FAR FROM GOOD

A NOVEL

THE TRIAL

OF

SAM CRAY

STEPHEN VAN ZANT

WinePressPublishing
Great Books, Defined.

ISBN 13: 978-1-60615-050-4
ISBN 10: 1-60615-050-2
Library of Congress Catalog Card Number: 2010926712

I will send you the prophet Elijah ... [and]
he will turn the hearts of the fathers to their children,
and the hearts of the children to their fathers;
or else I will come and strike the land with a curse.
—Malachi 4:5–6

Perhaps the reason he was separated from
you for a little while was that you might
have him back for good—no longer as a slave,
but ... as a dear brother.
—Philemon 15–16

To Kelli, the girl of my dreams.
You are by far the finest thing about me.

CONTENTS

ACKNOWLEDGMENTS

Rick Walts, Darrell Bramer, Julie Law, and Jenny Houlton read long-suffering early drafts of this book, as did Jenny's son, Alex. I am indebted to their encouragement and insight. I am grateful to my family—my wife, Kelli, and our children, Zack, Katie, Abbey, and Adam—for their wonderful support. I know my scattering of little scraps of paper all over the house often reminded you of Russell Crowe's depiction of a schizophrenic in *A Beautiful Mind*. I also thank my mom, Marian, for her unconditional encouragement of all the crazy things I do.

To all my friends at WinePress Publishing, including Athena Dean, Mike Owens, and Abigail Davidson, thank you for your kindness, expertise, and professional dedication to your craft. To freelance editor, Adam Blumer, thank you for your meticulous work in honing the story.

I am indebted to my grandmother, Virginia (Ginny) Van Zant, for preserving a portion of my grandfather's writings and speeches, and for granting permission to use them here. My grandfather, Albert W. Van Zant, was the youngest judge ever elected to the bench in Kentucky when he became the county judge of Metcalfe County in 1941 at the age of twenty-six. He also served as the editor of the local paper, the *Edmonton Herald-News*, which still exists today. The speech Judge Graves gives in this novel is taken from one my grandfather gave to graduates of Edmonton Elementary School in 1971. The obituary in the book is also modeled after one he wrote.

All legitimate historical facts contained in the book are drawn from Professor William A. Withington's *Kentucky in Maps* and my notes from his class taken in the spring of 1989 at the University of Kentucky. The poem on the Civil War monument in the story is from "The Bivouac of the Dead" by Theodore O' Hara (1820–1867), Kentucky poet and military officer. All other historical-looking information is the product of my imagination.

AUTHOR'S NOTE

I'm not a real writer. I will explain. On the morning of June 12, 2008, I was drinking coffee in the lobby bar of the Galt House Hotel in Louisville, Kentucky. I was between hearings at the Jefferson County Courthouse during my fourteenth year of practicing law as the fourteenth lawyer in my family. At the time I was struggling to find satisfaction in my career, and also feeling the intense financial strain of simultaneously owning a struggling sports facility.

I decided to spend some time that morning writing and penciled in my journal, "Write the book." This was a peculiar idea because the only writing I'd done since obtaining an English degree was crafting little deeds and wills for my law practice. Accordingly, my initial response to this suggestion was, "What book?" However, as I gazed at the gray Ohio River flowing by me, a flood of ideas for this novel came to mind. Now, one year later, during moments stolen here and there, I have completed this draft.

My hope for this book is to tell a simple tale set in imaginary Kidron County, Kentucky. My desire is that you, the reader, may in some way go back in time and experience life in that small Kentucky community in 1975.

Stephen W. Van Zant
Elizabethtown, Kentucky
May 15, 2009

PROLOGUE

Colgate, Kidron County, Kentucky
Two hours south of Louisville
Population: 3,702

Monday, August 26, 1974

I t was only football practice at Colgate Junior High, but to Sam Cray it felt more like torture.

The sharp crack of shoulder pads crashing together echoed in his ears on this sun-scorched Kentucky afternoon. Behind the redbrick science building lay the football field, a well-used stretch mostly comprised of dirt and patches of tawny grass. There the seventh-grade offense scrimmaged the eighth-grade defense beneath an azure sky.

Sam and his buddies sweated in the scalding heat while clouds of dust trailed their cleats like clumsy, elongated shadows. Black grime clung to their arms and faces, their skin glistening under the glaring, unforgiving sun. Salty sweat dripped down to the corners of their mouths.

Each boy wore the school colors: gray practice pants and maroon jerseys. The school's mascot, a southern colonel, was emblazoned on the front of each jersey. Stickers advertising "Colgate Pride" adorned the sides of their helmets.

Sam winced at the harsh barks that burst from the lips of Ray Bedford, who ran the joyless practice. Coach Bedford oversaw the football program at the junior high and was the eighth-grade coach.

Sam's coach, George Hicks, was gone today, so Coach Bedford was in charge.

From his position as seventh-grade quarterback, Sam could see Coach Bedford now. Hands on his hips, he stood like an angry bull just beyond the line of scrimmage, the steamy air filled with his occasional bursts of profanity and angry running commentary on the practice.

From his creased, swarthy face he barked commands with crisp authority. He wasted no words, and everybody knew better than to question him. Meanwhile, his intense, black eyes darted from player to player, a clipboard in hand as he meticulously recorded his observations. His slicked-back, dark hair gleamed with the shellacked look of too much Brylcreem.

Coach Bedford wore light-gray elastic shorts and a dark-gray golf shirt with "Colgate Colonels" embroidered in maroon on his lapel. He was of average height with a slim build one might underestimate. His large hands and muscular arms, on the other hand, radiated athleticism and discipline.

Sam dropped back to pass. The outside linebacker sprinted toward him untouched on a weakside blitz. Sam spun away from him and looked for daylight through the oncoming traffic of defenders. He ducked under the arms of another tackler only to be sandwiched between two defensive tackles who took him down with body-slamming intensity that knocked the wind out of him.

Sam tried to suck in a breath. Cold fire sizzled up his hand. He cried out in pain.

While players began rolling off him, Sam peered up at the clear sky, head groggy, and tried to catch his breath while he held his hand. He gritted his teeth through spasms of stabbing pain.

Someone yelled at him. He stiffened when he recognized Coach Bedford's voice.

"Boy, get up! You get up now!"

Sam grimaced, pulled himself out of the dirt, and stood unsteadily to his feet. His head swam. "But Coach, my finger's broken!"

Sam struggled against a sudden rush of lightheadedness and held his right hand high. There his right pinky protruded at a ninety-degree angle from the rest of his hand.

"Man, that's sick!" said Nick Walker, one of his teammates, turning his head away from the grotesque hand.

"Let me see that." Coach Bedford examined Sam's hand. "Your finger's not broken. Just dislocated."

Sam stared at him. *Just dislocated?*

The coach clamped his left hand around Sam's wrist and pulled the boy's arm under his own before tightening it.

Sam grimaced. It felt as if Coach Bedford had placed his arm in a vice. Before he knew what was happening, the coach snapped his dislocated pinky back into place. The stabbing pain faded to a dull ache.

Coach Bedford slapped his hands on Sam's shoulder pads and shoved him toward his huddled teammates. "Get back in there, Cray!" he said, irritated by the delay.

Sam jogged toward the seventh-grade offensive huddle while staring at his hand in disbelief. To his amazement he could wiggle his stiff, throbbing pinky.

Coach Bedford's angry voice jerked Sam back to attention. "This is the worst scrimmage I've ever seen. You're playin' just like a bunch of sissies. You don't wanna play football?" He threw up his hands, face reddening, and slammed his clipboard into the dirt. "We're gonna stop right now and run. In fact, we're gonna run 'til somebody quits."

Sam groaned. *Please, not more running.* He joined his teammates, who were lining up on the goal line.

"To the fifty and back!" Coach Bedford said.

Sam longed to remove his helmet and shoulder pads—he felt like he was in a furnace—but knew Coach Bedford would never allow it. Sam just needed to hunker down and do as he was told. Or suffer the consequences.

Fifteen grueling minutes later, Sam pounded the ground with weary, aching feet that felt like dead weights. Sweat poured down his arms and face, stinging his eyes.

Nearby, five teammates were puking along the fencerow. Dewayne Webb, a slender, black, wide receiver with long, curly, black hair, had taken off his helmet. He was on his hands and knees, retching into the thicket. Spittle and other matter Sam didn't want to contemplate hung from his mouth.

Sam knew enough about Dewayne Webb to know he was trouble. Another seventh grader, Dewayne had a bad reputation as an agitator who frequently argued with his teachers. He was also sweet on Coach Bedford's daughter, Meredith. The rumor was that their relationship made the coach furious.

Simon Puckett, the skinny, red-headed manager in thick glasses, was trying to provide some comfort. He bent over Dewayne and wiped the back of his glistening neck with a wet towel.

Simon always wore a ready grin and rarely knew how to hold his tongue—a quality that often got him into trouble. Simon was an only child like Sam, and his mom was church secretary at Kidron Valley Church, the town's largest and most prominent church.

Sam almost tripped on his aching legs when Coach Bedford's angry voice bellowed across the field.

"Get away from him, Simon!" he said. "Who told you to do that? You worthless piece of crap."

Simon backed away from Dewayne, head lowered, and lifted his hands and towel in surrender.

"Boys, get your helmets back on and get on the line!" Coach Bedford said.

Four of the five sick players grabbed their helmets and stumbled toward their teammates, but Dewayne Webb didn't budge. He sat with his back against the barbed-wire fence. His eyes narrowed on his sweaty face. "Coach, I need some water!" he said.

Coach Bedford stiffened. He turned and stared at Dewayne. "Water? Webb, you ain't earned water." He marched toward Dewayne, nostrils flaring with each inhalation. "Get your helmet back on and get on the line! We're runnin' 'til somebody quits. Maybe, Webb, that's gonna be you."

Webb grabbed his helmet and flung it toward Coach Bedford's feet. "Yeah, it's me, all right! This ain't worth it. I'm outta here!" He pushed himself to his feet, using the fence for support. He held Coach Bedford's stare for a long moment before plodding toward the locker room.

"Well, that's just fine!" Coach Bedford said at Dewayne's retreating back. "In fact, it's the best news of the day." He flashed a wide grin at the remaining players. His mood had obviously improved.

"Okay, bring it in!" he said. "Take a knee." The team formed a circle around him and removed their helmets. Sam sighed in relief as the cooler air caressed his head.

Coach Bedford looked at each boy in turn. "Good riddance to Webb. Let me tell you somethin' about Dewayne Webb. The God's honest truth is that he's a talented athlete. He's got great hands, great speed, and he can block like a Buick when he wants to. But ... how do I put it?" He hesitated, his eyes glittering in the light. "He's got a million-dollar body but a dime-sized heart."

A pause followed.

"Come here, Williams," Coach Bedford said.

Bates Williams stood and hustled to Coach Bedford's side. As the best athlete in the seventh grade, he played running back and line-backer. Bates was another black player, but his skin was a lighter shade than Dewayne's.

"I want you to look at Bates," Coach Bedford said. "Just look at him."

Eyes downcast, Bates endured the stares at his muscular, wide shoulders and the thick, pronounced muscles in his arms and legs. To Sam he looked less like a boy and more like a little man. His jersey was ripped at both shoulders, and dirt plastered his pants. Blood glistened on his forearms and stained his knuckles.

Bates was like a soldier ready for battle, his chiseled profile regal against the blue sky. Sam couldn't help sensing his own inadequacy. How could he possibly measure up to Bates?

"You want to play for me?" Coach Bedford said to the team. "You need to be like Bates. He's tough. He gives everything he's got on every play. He does everything I ask him to." He paused. "Football's a man's sport. You want to play for me? You want to be a man? Then be like Bates."

Sam spied Dewayne Webb out of the corner of his eye. Dewayne had paused outside the school and was staring at them, hands on his hips.

Something in Sam's gut told him that this feud was far from over.

PART ONE

HOUND'S CREEK

CHAPTER 1

Tuesday, June 3, 1975

(Nine months later)

Thirteen-year-old Sam Cray bounded down the rickety, seventy-year-old steps so hard that they sounded like they might splinter. Four steps from the bottom, he launched himself into the air and achieved a solid landing on the hardwood floor with a resounding thud. He paused and inhaled the stale, musty smell in the foyer, nose wrinkling.

Too much furniture crowded the small living room to his right, which included, of all things, a salon hair dryer chair. He turned left, took two strides across the dining room, and thrust his open hands against the swinging door, bursting into the kitchen.

His mom sat at a small table in a flowered bathrobe. She blew on her steaming cup of coffee while reading the morning paper.

With a frown he let his gaze wander around the less-than-appealing room. The aged, sputtering florescent lights, which kept the room only dimly lit, depressed him. Years of traffic had worn away the pattern on the yellow linoleum, which had turned up in the corners under the cabinets. White paint peeled like dead skin on the hood above the stove and above green metal cabinets, where two drawers were missing handles.

At the sink Sam turned on the cold water in a torrential blast and took a swallow of tepid water, not caring that the water splashed all over his face and T-shirt. He turned the faucet off and wiped his face on his shirttail, ignoring the towel on the counter beside the sink.

He turned on his heel and paused at the stove before grabbing two strips of bacon from the black, cast-iron frying pan. "See ya, Mom," he said over his shoulder and headed toward the door.

"Stop right there, Sam Cray, or I'll take a yardstick to ya."

He stopped and turned, worried to see dark circles under her weary eyes. He wondered if she was sleeping okay or working too hard. Maybe a little of both, now that their lives had completely changed.

"Now you march right over here." She favored him with a lopsided smile. "Graduatin' from the seventh grade today doesn't make you too old or too cool to hug your mama."

Sam studied her pretty blonde hair, her slender build, her graceful neck. He couldn't for the life of him figure out why his dad had chosen to walk away from someone so pretty.

She looked small and vulnerable to Sam as she hunched over the lifestyle section of the newspaper. Even though she smiled at Sam, he didn't miss the drawn expression on her face and knew the cause. Exactly one week ago she'd been sitting in the bright, airy kitchen at their much nicer home in Kidron Heights subdivision, surrounded by freshly painted walls and new appliances. Now they lived in this dump. Why did it have to happen? He wished someone would just tell him why.

Sam crossed to the table and gave her a halfhearted, one-arm hug. But that gesture must not have been enough. She wrapped both arms around his neck and pulled him close. Yet something about her clinging manner suffocated him, and he jerked away.

He dashed out of the kitchen, stepping around unopened cardboard boxes they still hadn't unpacked after their move. Backpack in hand, he stepped out the front door.

As he walked, he reflected on how strange his mom's hug had made him feel. Only a few years ago he'd enjoyed cuddling with her. She'd run her hand through his hair, and he'd pull her close. But now the same display of affection revolted him in a way he couldn't explain.

Maybe the problem is me.

Mary Cray sipped her coffee, her heart aching. Why had Sam pulled away? Why couldn't he just stay her little boy a while longer?

She got up and crossed to the dirty window, watching him scurry down the sidewalk. How quickly he was growing up. She loved the way his face tanned in the summer, his brown, wavy hair flopping down over his brown eyes and covering his ears like the little Dutch Boy paint character. Today he wore his usual—cutoff jeans, white T-shirt, and tube socks with three blue stripes pulled to his knees. Later, when he returned home, red clay would crust the edges of his gray Chuck Taylor canvas tennis shoes.

She shook her head. *He'll bring half the dirt in Kidron County inside this old house with those shoes.*

Nine months ago Mary was married to her high school sweetheart, Dan Cray. He had been the star quarterback on the football team in a town which revered its football, and she had been on the cheerleading squad. Four years after graduating from Colgate High, they married.

After high school, she took a few classes from a community college outside the county before quitting to take classes at a beauty school. Her husband landed a job at a local rubber plant in town that made automotive belts and hoses. He quickly received promotion after promotion, until a year ago he was made assistant general manager.

Although Colgate was a small town, it held certain undeniable classes, and she had known that her family was near the top of the town's social food chain. Her husband earned a good salary, which afforded them a comfortable lifestyle. They were members of Kidron Valley Church— the largest and most prominent in town. They had decided to have only one child and had been blessed with a happy, healthy son whom they named Sam.

Then, in October, Dan filed for divorce. It came to her as a complete surprise. He did not break it to her in person, but left a note for her and Sam. Her friends told her there must be another woman in Dan's life, but he denied it. He moved out of town and settled in Louisville. Mary and Sam stayed in the house in Kidron Heights for as long as they could, but Mary could not make the mortgage payments, and the county judge ordered that it be sold.

Mary now worked at a local grocery store. She felt somewhat humiliated by having to go back to work as a cashier when she had been a stay-at-home mom for thirteen years. Since quitting his job at the rubber factory, Dan now made considerably less money and, as a result, the monthly child support he paid was meager. She believed herself to be an object of universal derision in the town, and as a single mom living in a modest home and working as a cashier, she wasn't sure how she fit in anymore. She knew she was in a different social strata and felt anxious about how she was perceived by others. She sensed awkwardness whenever she saw her old friends in town, especially when they shopped at the grocery store and she was forced to wait on them. She struggled with bitterness toward Dan and what he had left her to deal with. In fact, most mornings she struggled to get out of bed.

For her, the one relationship in which she desperately wanted to maintain a close bond seemed strained even to her. In her mind, she knew Sam felt smothered by her attention, but she could not stop clinging to him.

Sam jumped off the four-step stoop and strolled down the ancient sidewalk, where stray blades of grass sprouted between the cracks. Almost to the road, he glanced back at the old, tired house, a far cry from the beautiful house they'd left in Kidron Heights.

Drainpipes were rusted through in several places, and window screens were torn. Several of the windowpanes were cracked, and the soffit above the door was rotting. The roof gaped with missing shingles, and wild honeysuckle twined its way up one half of the house. Overgrown juniper bushes covered the base of the house, and a holly tree flanked the right corner. To add to the rundown impression, a plant he couldn't identify lay dying in a clay flowerpot on the front stoop. From where he stood he glimpsed the dented metal shed in the backyard, which was overrun with heather and scrub.

At Kidron Heights, large yards complemented the spacious houses. But the front and side yards on Dixie Avenue were small, the narrow backyards offering little more than sparse grass. Sam shook his head, wishing he knew the magic words to repair his parents' marriage and take him back to Kidron Heights. It wasn't fair. Most of his friends' parents were together, and they didn't have to leave their nice houses and move into ugly, old shacks. Why had this happened to him?

Sam glanced left and peered through the branches of the magnolia tree at the home of Coach Ray Bedford. Painted brick pillars framed a screened-in porch. Like the Crays' new house, the Bedfords' once white exterior had faded to a drab gray.

Suddenly, a pit bull across the street yanked on a chain and growled an obvious challenge. Sam made a face at the dog before shuffling down the sidewalk.

CHAPTER 2

Coach Ray Bedford peered out the window just as Sam Cray was crossing the street. He needed to have a talk with that boy.

He took a seat at the kitchen table with his son and daughter and picked up the newspaper, perusing it while he sipped strong, black coffee and waited for his breakfast. His wife, a thin, frail woman with blonde hair and a long face, clattered pots and pans behind him at the stove.

He set down the newspaper and glanced at the portrait of his father on the wall. Pride swelled in his heart as he viewed the face of the man who served as sheriff of Kidron County for many years before dying in 1969 while in office. He pushed aside a tinge of guilt that he hadn't followed in his father's footsteps and gone into law enforcement, but people found him to be a rigid, demanding enforcer of rules at the junior high school. So in one sense he *had* gone into law enforcement, just not the same kind.

He glanced at his daughter, thirteen-year-old Meredith, a graduating seventh grader like Sam. She wore her dark brown hair in a boyish bob, and between her high, sculpted, and freckled cheekbones perched a pencil-straight nose. Natural color radiated from her face like a flower, and her slender body was beginning to show curves and a certain roundness befitting her age.

"What do you know about the Cray boy who moved in next door?" he said to her.

9

"Why do you ask me?" Meredith was absorbed in the comics page. She pushed black-framed glasses up her nose, shielding her intelligent blue eyes. "You should know him from the football team."

"I just want to know who my neighbors are—isn't that reasonable? Why is everything so difficult with you?"

She smirked, a mischievous look in her eyes. "Because you always have a hidden agenda."

"No, I don't."

"Do too."

He realized the argument was pointless. "I don't know what you're talkin' about. I'm a laid-back kind of guy."

"Sure you are, as long as everything goes exactly the way *you* want it."

Coach Bedford was about to correct her sassy tone when Larry, his sixteen-year-old cocksure son, said, "Sam's a dorky kid if you ask me."

Coach Bedford smirked when he noticed a short strand of wiry hair protruding from Larry's chin. "Did you know that his dad was one of the best quarterbacks we've ever had at Colgate?"

"Well, that was his dad," Larry said. "The only reason the seventh-grade team was any good last year was because of Bates Williams. Now, that guy's good."

Coach Bedford measured his broad-shouldered son, deciding that he stood at least a head taller than Sam. As a sophomore, Larry had been the starting quarterback during the last football season at Colgate High School.

"Football's such a waste of time." Meredith sighed and turned a page. "It's gotta be the most Neanderthal of all sports."

Larry's devious, gray eyes drilled into her. "How can you say that? Dad is a football coach and your brother"—he puffed out his chest—"well, your brother is a football star."

"Not a star," Coach Bedford said. "At least not yet. Let's say you've got the potential to be good if you work hard enough. Nothin' comes free in this world. You've gotta be self-disciplined and love hard work."

Coach Bedford eyed Meredith, unable to understand how she could be a member of this family and have such an utter lack of interest in sports. All she liked to do was hang around her room and read poetry by Emily Dickinson, watch birds from her bedroom window, possess an odd desire to protect endangered species, and volunteer her free time at the Kidron County Dog Pound. He'd never had any use for pets, so he found her interest in the pound a total waste of time.

Coach Bedford glanced at his wife, who seemed to be listening to the conversation but not contributing, not that she could anyhow. Five years earlier, a stroke had affected her speech. Though she could say any number of things, she tended to repeat the same phrase—"far from good"—over and over, altering its cadence depending on the situation and her response to it. No one knew where the phrase had come from, but she said it loudly and quickly when she was angry, or slowly and remorsefully when she was sad. She said it with the shake of her head when she disagreed or with a nod if she agreed.

Finally, just when Coach Bedford was weary of waiting for his rather late breakfast, she set a plate of scrambled eggs, a plate of homemade biscuits, and a bowl of gravy on the table.

"Hey, these biscuits are burned," Coach Bedford said.

"Far from good," Mrs. Bedford said. "Just brown."

"Well, they look burned to me."

"Me too," Larry said.

Mrs. Bedford sighed and dropped her chin. "Far from good," she said in an irritated voice.

Larry shook his head. "She's such a freak job," he said to his dad.

Meredith chose a biscuit and took a bite. "Mmm. They taste great to me, Mom. Thanks for makin' breakfast."

Mrs. Bedford smiled at Meredith and patted her shoulder. "Far from good," she said in a pleased voice.

"Anyway, I hope that Cray boy's a respectful kid." Coach Bedford heaped scrambled eggs onto his plate before assaulting them with pepper. "I liked the Hamiltons when they lived next door, at least when they could keep up with their yard work. They were just the kind of neighbors I like: quiet, respectful, and—"

"—nearly dead," Larry said. "What was Mr. Hamilton? Ninety-five when he died?"

Coach Bedford poured a generous dollop of gravy on his three biscuits. "I'll have a talk with the Cray boy as soon as I can. There's no substitute for bein' proactive about this sort of thing. The last thing I want is a little hellion livin' next door with nobody but a single mom to discipline him."

Larry flashed a crooked grin at his dad. "I'd be happy to take care of Sam if you want me to."

"Hey, Sam's a good kid." Meredith wiped her mouth on a napkin. "Both of you, just stay away from him. After all, he's been through a tough time—with his parents' divorce and all. The last thing he needs is you two gettin' into his business."

Coach Bedford frowned at her. "Meredith, the fact is, any boy left without a strong male influence is destined for trouble. Believe me, I know from experience. I've been shapin' the lives of boys in this town for many years. Sam's essentially fatherless now that his dad lives in Louisville. He's gonna need some manly instruction, especially if he's gonna be our neighbor."

Meredith's face tightened. "It's presumptuous of you to think Sam needs anything from you."

"'Resumptious' or not, I agree with Dad," Larry said over a mouthful of biscuits and gravy.

"Oh, you're so dense."

"And, Meredith, *you're* naïve—that's what *you* are," Coach Bedford said. "You don't know people the way I do."

He wiped his mouth and glanced out the window at the Cray house. *Yep, that Cray boy needs some instruction, and I think I'm just the person to give it to him.*

"Far from good," Mrs. Bedford said in a worried voice.

CHAPTER 3

A three-minute walk would take Sam to downtown Colgate, but he had another destination in mind. He turned left on Dixie Avenue and began the half-mile trek to Colgate Junior High School. While he strolled, he pulled a wrinkled photograph out of his front pocket and studied it with mixed emotions.

The photo was of him and his dad on a South Carolina beach. He climbed onto his dad's back for a piggyback ride just before they both grinned at the camera.

Someone on the sidewalk behind Sam began whistling *The Tears of a Clown* by Smokey Robinson. Sam stuffed the photo back into his pocket just as the muscular frame of Bates Williams drew abreast of him. Bates was also graduating from the seventh grade.

"Whatcha' hidin' there?" Bates eyed Sam's pocket.

"Oh, nothin'."

"It's all right—you don't have to show me. We've all got our secrets, don't we?"

Sam glanced at his friend and realized something. Though he'd known Bates most of his life, he hadn't known him well until the seventh grade. His quiet, mild nature always surprised Sam when he considered Bates' fierce manner on the football field.

Bates pulled a plastic bag out of his backpack. The bag bulged with Jolly Ranchers and other hard candies. "Want one?" Bates always offered him the bag.

Sam helped himself to a grape piece. They crossed the street and moseyed down the sidewalk.

"You ready for summer?" Bates asked.

"Guess so."

"Congratulations, by the way. You lived an entire week next door to Coach Bedford and his maniac son, and you're still in one piece." Bates patted Sam on the back and shook his head with a chuckle. "I'm sorry you and your mom had to move. Guess the house in Kidron Heights was too big, huh?"

Sam hated whenever this topic came up. "Sellin' it was part of the divorce settlement."

"But of all the houses in Kidron County, why'd y'all pick the one next to Coach Bedford and Larry?"

Sam shrugged. "Mom said the house came at the right price."

"Yeah, I bet it did. That's because nobody wants to live next door to the Bedfords."

"I'm gonna just ignore 'em. They can't bother me if I don't pay 'em any mind."

Bates raised his eyebrows. "I wouldn't be so sure 'bout that."

The boys walked in silence for a few minutes, passing the town's largest building, the monolithic home of Kidron Valley Church. The church's three-story education building was attached to the sanctuary, which seated up to two thousand people. Above them towered the gigantic white steeple that Sam could see anywhere in Colgate, regardless of where he was.

In one of his history classes, Sam had heard that the church, established in 1789 and named after the valley outside Jerusalem, was actually older than the town. "The prominence of the church in the Kidron County community cannot be overstated and gives Colgate a strong sense of shared values and beliefs," the teacher had said.

Sam knew that most of the town attended church here, as did most of the town's businessmen and elected officials, including the mayor and most of the city council members. The church's membership was also all white. Immanuel Temple, on the other hand, was located in the Bottoms and had a membership of three hundred blacks.

As Sam and Bates passed under the shadow of the Kidron Valley Church, Sam heard a car's engine approach from behind. He turned in time to see Coach Bedford's dark-gray Chevrolet El Camino pull alongside the sidewalk. Coach Bedford was driving, with Larry riding shotgun and Meredith in the middle.

As the vehicle passed by, Larry scowled at them. Bates shook his head as the car pulled away. That's when Sam noticed the maroon bumper sticker:

COLGATE FOOTBALL COLGATE PRIDE

The sight of Larry Bedford soured Sam's mood. He wished they could talk about something other than the Bedford family, but Bates said, "Now that y'all are neighbors, do you talk to Coach Bedford much when you're at home?"

"I tried saying 'Mornin' Coach' to him last week when we moved in when I saw him in his yard. He told me I could say 'Good mornin', *Coach* Bedford' or 'Good mornin', *Mr.* Bedford.'"

Bates shook his head. "You know what the older football players say about him? The man gargles with gasoline—"

"—and flosses with barbed wire. Yeah, I know. Coach Bedford also told me, 'Don't think that because you live next door to me that you're gonna get any extra privileges at school or on the football team.' Yesterday I saw him but didn't say a word. He said, 'Don't give me that brook-trout look, son. If you're gonna live next door to me, you can at least say good mornin' to me.'"

"He's a nut. I bet he'll be worse this summer when it gets really hot. Mama says people are meaner in the summer. She says that a fist fight is bound to break out in the Bottoms on a hot summer day."

"Coach Bedford doesn't need a hot summer day," Sam said. "He's a beast in all seasons."

As they drew closer to Colgate Junior High, Sam wondered if Bates felt proud to be the first black student ever elected as a class officer at Colgate Junior High. Racial tension had always been part of this town, and Sam couldn't help reviewing it in his mind.

While Sam and his friends had attended Eventide Elementary School, an all-white school located on the same campus as Colgate Junior and Senior High Schools, Bates had attended Booker T. Washington Elementary School, an all-black school on the south end of town beyond the railroad tracks. Most of Colgate's black families lived on the other side of the proverbial tracks—either on Colgate Hill, known as "the Hill," or in the flat area near the Hill, known as "the Bottoms." Bates lived in the Bottoms.

Prior to 1972, Booker T. Washington School had offered education through the twelfth grade. The Kidron County Board of Education had faced mounting pressure from civil rights groups, however, and decided to close the school's upper grades and integrate the junior and senior high schools. When the upper grades at Booker T. Washington were closed, the superintendent had avoided any discussion of race by saying that the integration of the upper grades would provide better use of limited school resources. He'd said the move was motivated purely by finances, but no one believed him.

Sam's mom had told him about the social unrest that occurred at that time in Louisville. A federal judge had ordered the school system to integrate by way of forced busing to achieve strict racial quotas at each school. The protests from white families in Louisville had been especially long and loud, and police officers had escorted the school buses.

On the first day of integration in Colgate, white protestors picketed the offices of the board of education, but the protest waged by the gentle citizens of the town had been mild, and they'd soon lost their passion. What helped appease them was the fact that the lower grades would remain segregated except for a few handpicked exceptions. Therefore, by 1975 all black and white students in the upper grades attended Colgate Junior and Senior High Schools; only the two elementary schools were still segregated. Though most white residents were unenthusiastic about this change, they accepted it as inevitable.

Sam and Bates reached Colgate Junior High and merged into a mob of students in a surge of color and noise. Some students were on foot, while others zipped by on bikes. Three smaller children sped by, chasing each other.

"Say, Bates," Sam said. "Some of us are gonna head over to Hound's Creek after school and celebrate the end of the school year. You wanna come?"

Bates hesitated before answering. "That sounds pretty good."

Sam was about to tell him who else was coming when he noticed a crowd gathered in front of the school marquee. He and Bates waded into the throng of bustling pupils. When they reached the front of the marquee, they froze. Someone had spray-painted red words on the marker:

BITE ME COACH BEDFORD

They stepped back into the crowd of gawking students. Sam remembered last fall when Dewayne threw his football helmet down in anger and stalked off the football field. "I bet Dewayne Webb did this," Sam whispered. "He and Coach Bedford hate each other."

Bates shook his head, eyes serious. "Dewayne's so busted."

"Uh-oh." Sam tensed. "Look. Coach Bedford's coming."

Coach Bedford crossed the teacher's parking lot, working his way through the crowd to the front of the marquee. The graffiti was impossible to miss, and his face reddened.

He turned and faced the crowd, hands drawn into fists. "Who did this?" he said. "I want to know, and I want to know now."

"Coach Bedford, th-th-th-that will be enough!" said a loud voice.

Robert Sheridan, the principal, emerged from the crowd and faced Coach Bedford. He was a thin, short man and a fastidious dresser. He parted his light brown hair on the side and always kept it neatly combed. He spoke with a stutter, a problem a lifetime of effort couldn't fully correct.

Principal Sheridan and Coach Bedford had been classmates at Colgate High School, and Sheridan was president and valedictorian of their class. Coach Bedford was captain of the football team and its star linebacker. Since their youth, tension had often flared between the two men, and five years ago the school board had added more fuel to fire when they'd decided to make Sheridan principal of the junior high instead of Coach Bedford.

Coach Bedford thrust his face toward Principal Sheridan until their noses were almost touching. "There's chicken crap on somebody's shoes here, Bob, and I intend to find out whose. I want to interrogate the whole lot of 'em."

Principal Sheridan shook his head, maintaining control. "Th-th-that won't do. We can d-d-discuss this inside."

He turned to the crowd and raised his arms for order. "S-s-students, it's time for you to go to your f-f-first period class."

Coach Bedford grabbed Principal Sheridan's arm. "Believe me, Bob," he said, "this will be more than a discussion. I'm going to deal with this."

CHAPTER 4

In Colgate Junior High's central hallway, Sam and Bates passed a large trophy case, where a caption read "OUR COLGATE HEROES." On display inside were trophies the school's victorious athletic teams had won over the years, along with various photographs and autographed footballs. Banners in maroon and gray announced "Colgate Pride." In one photo, Coach Bedford glowered at Sam and Bates from where he posed with one of his championship teams.

Making the football team was a prize every boy in town coveted. Each year most of them tried out for the squad, but according to the math, the coaching staff cut one out of every two boys who tried out.

Sam and Bates reached a wide staircase off the central hallway. Last year Coach Bedford designated it as the "up" staircase in an effort to improve traffic flow. During school hours students reached the second floor using only these stairs. To reach the first floor from the second floor, students used the "down" staircase at the other end of the building. Sam knew the regulation wasn't to be taken lightly. Coach Bedford patrolled the halls and kept his eye out for staircase offenders.

They ascended to the second floor and reached Mrs. Legg's homeroom with a few minutes to spare. Bates found his seat near the front of the room next to Meredith and Dewayne, while Sam parked himself at the back near his best friends, Simon, Nick, and Josh. Born and raised in Colgate, they'd attended school together since the first day of kindergarten.

As Sam took his seat, Nick poked—or "frogged"—him in the arm, instantly making his entire arm numb. Sam just gave Nick a groan of annoyance. He knew there was no point in getting upset.

Simon Puckett spotted a penny on the floor. When he bent over to pick it up, Nick kicked him in the rear, knocking him to the floor. While Simon pulled himself to his feet, his face red, Nick roared with laughter, his hand covering his mouth. Several other students gathered around to join in the fun.

"Nice move, retard!" Nick said.

Josh helped Simon to his feet.

"You know, it's not the kick that hurts," Simon said to Josh and flashed him one of his perpetual smiles. "It's the humility of bending over to pick up a penny."

Josh clapped Simon's shoulder with a chuckle.

Sam smiled, glad to have a friend like Simon, whose vivid personality was always full of fun. Though he was thirteen like Sam, Simon was much smaller; in fact, he could have barely passed for ten with his tiny feet and hands, narrow shoulders, and lithe frame. His coarse red hair was blinding against a complexion as pale as alabaster, and thick, horn-rimmed glasses perched on his nose. Due to his asthma, his mother refused to let him play competitive sports.

"Boys and girls," Mrs. Legg said from the front of the classroom, "let's come to attention so we may get started."

When Sam had met Mrs. Legg at the beginning of the school year, he'd liked her instantly. Her soft eyes communicated warmth, and he heard a sort of splendor when she spoke. He enjoyed her good-humored face and graceful attitude. He liked the way she hummed along to the classical music she played on a record player behind her desk. Though she had a slow, methodical manner about her, he liked the fact that she laughed often, usually without restraint. He liked her melodious voice, even while teaching mundane subjects. Though Sam couldn't explain it, her elegance, grace, and generosity of spirit drew him to her. Completion of today's classes, she told them recently, would mark her twenty-fifth year as a dedicated schoolteacher.

Sam also liked Mrs. Legg because she took him and his classmates on more field trips than they'd ever been on before. Colgate prided itself in the quality of services it provided its citizens; therefore, Mrs. Legg took them on trips to the town's water treatment plant, landfill, hospital, cemetery, and sewer treatment plant.

"First, this morning we have a few housekeeping matters to take care of," Mrs. Legg said. "I received a note from the library saying we've returned all of our books except two." She picked up a piece of paper from her desk and held it in front of her. "Does anyone still have William Golding's *Lord of the Flies*?" Over the top of the page, she scanned the faces expectantly, her gray-brown eyes twinkling.

"You got me!" Nick grunted as if shot. He clasped his hands over his heart, a look of pain on his face, and rolled out of his chair and onto the floor.

Mrs. Legg rolled her eyes. "Without the drama please, Mr. Walker."

Nick got up with a sigh and dug into his backpack. He retrieved the book and placed it on Mrs. Legg's desk.

Sam shook his head. *What a ham!* Everybody knew Nick was her most troublesome student.

"Very well," she said. "Now, does anyone have R. M. Ballantyne's *The Coral Sea*?"

"I do." Josh brought the book to the front and placed it on top of *Lord of the Flies*. "Sorry about that."

"Good. Thank you, boys." Mrs. Legg surveyed the class, looking at each student in turn. "Now, if you haven't learned anything else during this academic year, I hope you'll remember what I have been constantly reminding you about—to begin applying deodorant as part of your daily routine. This practice is a gift to yourselves and others, and I hope it is something you are practicing today."

The classroom chuckled in unison while her expression remained serious.

Since it was June, the temperature in Colgate would be stifling by day's end. Though the summer heat came early each year, swamping the whole town, the Kidron County Board of Education hadn't yet approved air-conditioning for any of its schools. When the temperature rose and the humidity spiked, the thick air inside the schoolrooms became oppressive. Though the school provided a box fan for each classroom, these only churned the hot air and did little to provide real relief from the bath of torrid temperatures.

Sam grinned and exchanged glances with Simon, Josh, and Nick. He knew what they were thinking—that other classmates needed this lesson in hygiene when in fact they all smelled foul by noon each day. By early afternoon, the classroom usually smelled like a locker room. To Mrs. Legg's continual chagrin, the students seemed oblivious to this fact.

For their midmorning health class, Mrs. Legg sent the girls to the other seventh-grade classroom while the boys stayed in hers. After the girls left, Mrs. Legg smiled at the boys. "Today we're going to conclude our discussion about the reproductive system by taking questions from the class. Now, boys, I don't want you to be shy. This morning I want us to have a nice question-and-answer time together. Understood?"

Sam exchanged knowing looks of dread with his buddies.

"This is your last chance to ask any questions you want," she said. "Before we begin, bear with me while I repeat something I've said before. As we've discussed, sex is only for marriage. When you're in high school, your teachers will explain to you—in horrific detail, I might add—all of the bad things that will happen to you if you have sex before marriage. I will leave that discussion to them, but those things are really bad."

Simon's face paled, but Nick laughed and put his hands over his face.

"Within marriage sex is a wonderful thing." Mrs. Legg glanced out the window with a small smile. "Mr. Legg and I enjoy it very much." Sam felt like throwing up. Disgust covered his classmates' faces, but they remained respectfully quiet.

"Now, I need to go to the office for a minute." Mrs. Legg checked her watch. "When I return, I want to hear your questions." She narrowed her eyes, a fist on one hip, and shook her head. "Boys, we're not going to move on this morning until I hear them."

After she left, Nick whispered, "Mrs. Legg is the last person on earth I want to talk to about sex."

"I'm not sayin' anything," Josh said.

"Me neither," Sam said.

"But we have to ask somethin', or else we're stuck," Simon said. "Oh, no! Here she comes."

Mrs. Legg stood in front of the boys and waited patiently. After a pause, she said, "Well, boys?"

Simon leaned forward and raised his hand. Sweat dampened his shirt where he'd rested against the back of the chair, and his leg bounced under his desk. Sam wondered if he could ever be still.

Mrs. Legg smiled at him, eyebrows raised. "Yes, Simon?"

Simon pushed his thick glasses up the bridge of his sweaty nose. "Do girls fart?"

The room erupted in laughter. Though Mrs. Legg's mouth didn't laugh, her eyes did.

"What? I'm serious," said Simon.

Nick leaned toward Simon, smirking. "Just for the record, Simon, you're an idiot."

Mrs. Legg cleared her throat to restore order. "Well, Simon, that question's not related to this section of our human health studies," she said in a patient tone, "but yes they do; however, not as much as boys and they are more discreet when they do."

Mrs. Legg put her hands on her hips as if to show that she was waiting for a better question.

Josh raised his hand, a slight blush rising in his cheeks. "What I want to know is, if … if we're … if it's best to … you know … wait and all until we're married, why do we get these … um … urges now … instead of later? How does that make any sense, I guess is what I'm askin'."

"Now *that's* a good question," Sam whispered to Josh.

Mrs. Legg hesitated, her face puzzled as if she were hunting for the right words. Finally, she said, "Boys, sex is like a fire you want to use. Fire is useful. It's good, it heats your home, it cooks your food. But if you put fire in the middle of your livin' room, then you might burn your whole house down."

Sam glanced at his friends, confused. They looked as bewildered as he felt.

"Here's another way to look at it," Mrs. Legg said. "Sex is like takin' a long hike and gettin' thirsty. You pass by a stream, and the water in that stream looks good to you, but it's not. It's bad. Polluted. Harmful. If you wait until later, then you'll find good water."

"What?" Simon said. "Fire in the livin' room? Water in a stream? What in the world are you talkin' about, Mrs. Legg?"

Mrs. Legg sighed in frustration. "I'm tryin' to … what I'm tryin' to say is that the longer you wait, the better. And—"

The noon bell rang before she could finish her thought, and the boys bolted out of her classroom like calves released from their stall.

After lunch Mrs. Legg took her class to the school library's theater room, the only carpeted room in the school. The students sat on the floor while Josh readied the projector. Mrs. Legg sat on a metal chair at the back of the room.

When Josh was finished, he said, "Mrs. Legg, it's ready."

With her arms crossed she said in a frustrated tone, "The Kidron County Board of Education requires that I show you this film. The school board insists that every seventh-grade teacher expose her students to this subject matter. Boys and girls, for most of you this will introduce you to the theory of evolution. Josh, please start the projector. Sam, turn off the lights."

The projector came to life and flickered white light onto the screen before the film caught hold. In a deep, baritone voice the narrator described Charles Darwin's trip aboard the *Beagle* and his observations while on the Galapagos Islands. He discussed Darwin's book, *The Origin of Species,* and the film, running about twenty minutes, contained various photographs of the Galapagos Islands and illustrations of reptiles, monkeys, and humans.

While the film played, Sam ran fingers through hair plastered to his sweaty forehead. He whispered to Josh, "I've heard only negative stuff about this Darwin guy, but some of this makes sense to me."

"Yeah, me too," Josh whispered back. "But I don't know if I go all the way with him."

The film ended with the narrator stating, "As we have seen, British naturalist Charles Darwin has made a solid case for his theories of diversification and origin of species through variation and natural selection."

"Sam, turn the lights back on," Mrs. Legg said from her chair. "Josh, turn that thing off!"

Her irritated tone made everyone turn and stare.

Mrs. Legg said, "As I mentioned, the board of education requires that I expose you—as able-minded seventh graders—to Mr. Darwin's views prior to your graduation. As you can see, I have delayed showing you this film until the last day of school."

She paused, as if considering what she should say next. Finally, she shook a finger at the projector. "You can believe those lies if you want to. As for me, well … I believe God created our world in six days just like the Bible says."

Mrs. Legg stood, trying to regain her composure. "Let's get back to class."

Puzzled, Sam said to Josh, "I guess we'll have to sort this out later."

Josh nodded. "Yeah, I guess so."

CHAPTER 5

Later, Sam sat with Simon, Nick, and Josh on the forest-green, tiled floor of the lunchroom. At the front stood a small stage with a podium and microphone. On the stage sat Principal Sheridan and Judge Albert Graves.

Principal Sheridan stood, stepped up to the podium, and said into the microphone, "Now s-s-students, your attention, p-p-please."

He waited until the room had quieted before proceeding. "As is our t-t-tradition at Colgate Junior High, we close this school year with a g-g-guest speaker. I want all our s-s-students to give their c-c-complete attention to our s-s-speaker."

He cleared his throat and looked down at a piece of paper. "Judge Graves was b-b-born and r-r-raised in Kidron County. Since he obtained a d-d-degree in history from the University of K-K-Kentucky and a law degree from the University of Louisville, he has practiced law in Colgate for f-f-fourteen years. Five years ago this county elected him to be our county judge, and he is running for reelection this fall. P-P-Please join me in welcoming J-J-Judge Graves."

Judge Graves rose and took Principal Sheridan's place at the podium. The student body clapped politely, but without enthusiasm.

Sam leaned back against the lunchroom's concrete wall and studied the judge. He knew Judge Graves because of his parents' divorce case; he'd had to appear before him in a visitation hearing. Grateful for the patience and kindness Judge Graves had shown during that difficult time, he couldn't think of a more honorable man in all Colgate.

The judge's deep-set brown eyes swept over the student body as he stroked his white-streaked black beard. His face bore the wrinkles of a man in his mid-fifties. Though he was six-four, his high-pitched voice practically squeaked.

"Boys and girls, I have it on good authority that Principal Sheridan heard the speech I gave to the graduating class at Colgate High School last year. Apparently he was so impressed by its brevity that he thought it appropriate for me to speak to you today."

Only a few teachers in the audience picked up on the judge's intended humor and chuckled.

Sam listened intently while others fidgeted on the floor or in their plastic seats around cafeteria tables. For the most part they remained quiet as Coach Bedford and others patrolled the lunchroom, looking for disrespectful students.

Judge Graves continued. "I do not have any advice to give. I won't tell you that these are the most carefree of your carefree days and to enjoy them while you can. I do know that some of you have real problems now, but I also know they will become very different problems when you reach the adult world with its obligations and opportunities. But it is about these opportunities that I wish to speak to you for a few minutes."

He paused and cleared his throat. "Every worthwhile boy or girl wants to make good. He wants to tackle something and succeed at it. Whether he grapples with a football opponent, diagrams a sentence, or engages in the making of money, he wants to finish what he sets out to do. He wants to be able to say rather proudly, 'I did it.' But too often he feels his opportunity is found elsewhere, certainly not in a little, old town like Colgate.

"I want to talk to you this afternoon about geography. Where we live is not important in making good. If you have what it takes—reasonable intelligence, honor and integrity, perseverance, and the element of good luck—you can make good just about anywhere. And since this is so, it may be that a place like Colgate is the place for you."

Simon muttered something in Sam's ear, but Sam didn't hear him clearly and decided to ignore him. Simon turned to Nick, and the two shared a private joke and chuckled, though not loudly enough to get Coach Bedford's attention.

Judge Graves continued, "Many of you may have goals that will take you away from our town, and many may long for the day when you can leave. But our town does afford a certain way of life that millions in a big city would grasp if they could. Take personal acquaintances, for instance. Knowing the people of our town is one of the finest things I can think of, but in a large city apartment building, many do not even know the names of those who live next door—or even care.

"Greatness takes many forms. Some people who span rivers with massive steel structures are acclaimed as great, while others play beautiful music. Some hit home runs, while others minister daily to the needs of the people in their community. Build a big building, win a war, plant a small tree—I cannot separate one from the other. Greatness is a lot of little things added up over a lifetime of service. And so much that is great goes unrecognized simply because it is not spectacular."

A commotion to Sam's right disrupted the speech. Coach Bedford collared two eighth-grade boys clowning around at the back of the cafeteria. With one hand clamped around the back of each neck, Coach Bedford led them into the hallway.

Judge Graves continued, unfazed. "To give you one more reason for staying here or coming back home after you have completed your education, I want to tell you about a few people who have lived in this community, which I consider a cut above the average."

"This is too long," Nick whispered to Sam before yawning with great show. "I wish he'd shut up and sit down."

Sam ignored him. He was enjoying the speech. As to whom he wanted to be when he grew up, his dreams included a blend of professional athlete or mystery novelist. To do anything worthwhile or to be anyone special, he'd assumed that he would need to leave the confines of Colgate. But maybe he didn't need to leave home after all.

"I'll always recall the time when the late Judge Harry Wilcox gave his approval to the kids of the town to play baseball in the courthouse yard," Judge Graves said. "There was some opposition to this decision because we kids tore up the grass. 'But,' the judge said, 'when they're in the courthouse yard playing baseball, I know they're not in the

Campbell Field shooting craps.' And to this day, kids play baseball in the courthouse yard.

"Or take Dr. R. D. Gardner. Although he's been dead for a few years, his name isn't a strange one to you since he brought a great many of you into the world. You may not meet a person like him if you go to New York or Chicago or San Francisco. They may not grow them that big just anywhere.

"He'd give you a cussin' while he was sewing you up if he figured you needed it, but he'd also give you five dollars on your way out of his office if he figured you needed it. And this building you're in, incidentally, came about largely through the efforts of Dr. Gardner.

"Then there is Fanny Goodman. The Lord loves a cheerful giver, and if He looked for her, he'd know she would be somewhere giving of her time and talent. He'd know that she might be at the Beta Club Convention in Louisville or at the Kidron County Fair or at a fundraising campaign or at a dozen other places she might be needed. Or she might be at her beauty shop, giving a nighttime perm to a 'busy' person. She is without guile and has no idea of the depth of her contributions to this community."

Judge Graves paused and took a deep breath. "In closing—" the judge began before being interrupted again.

A student to Sam's left started clapping his hands, and a smattering of laughter broke out. Coach Bedford stifled the rebellion by striking his right hand against the back of the concrete wall with a smack.

"In closing," Judge Graves repeated, "I want you to understand that you are living in a community that has known many great people who have contributed to the greatness of rural America. I challenge each of you to rise to the greatness of our past and present. I have mentioned several wonderful people who have become great in their own right. Learn from them that to become worthwhile you must serve and serve, and give and give. If you want to set your sights on high, pick out one of the outstanding people of our community and out serve them if you can—and I hope you can."

Judge Graves stepped away from the microphone and peered out over the sea of faces as warm applause echoed off the walls. Principal Sheridan said something to the judge and patted him on the shoulder;

the men turned to leave. The applause faded, and Judge Graves ambled toward the exit.

Sam watched him go and kept thinking about the speech, filing it away in his mind for later contemplation. Then Judge Graves turned, as if remembering something he'd forgotten, and strode toward Sam. When he reached Sam, he offered his hand with a warm smile. Sam accepted the judge's hand and shook it, surprised to be singled out.

Judge Graves' eyes were warm and kind. "It's good to see you, Sam."

Sam had no idea that he'd soon see the judge again, but on a much more serious occasion.

CHAPTER 6

After the assembly, Sam and his classmates had just returned to the seats in Mrs. Legg's room when a voice over the school's public address system said, "All graduating seventh-grade boys are encouraged to attend a meeting with Coach Bedford at this time. This meeting is for all seventh graders interested in playing eighth-grade football next fall. Please report to the gym for a brief meeting with Coach Bedford."

Sam rose with Nick and Josh.

"If I didn't have asthma," Simon said, "I'd go out next year."

"Yeah, right," Nick said. "And if my grandma had a mustache, she'd be my grandpa."

"No, seriously," Simon said. "I'd play if my asthma cleared up."

Nick peered down at him with a scowl. "Simon, just face it—you're a weenie. You aren't big enough to play football, and you know it."

As Nick swept past him, Sam saw the hurt look on Simon's face.

Sam followed Josh, Bates, and Dewayne out of the room and down the hall to the gym, which was set apart from the main school building, and accessed by means of two tunnels. It contained wooden bleachers all the way around the basketball court. Painted in deep maroon, the words "Colgate Colonels" appeared in two places along the wall and included the drawing of a white-bearded rebel colonel wearing a white suit and a black string necktie. The words "Colgate Tradition," also in maroon lettering, appeared in other places along the wall.

The boys entered the south tunnel and were boisterous until they bumped into Coach Bedford. Just the sight of him quieted them down.

33

"We're meetin' in the locker room," he said, his voice stern. "Head on down."

Sam descended the steps with his friends to the boys locker room, which was located in the basement beneath the stands and court. Muted light glimmered from opaque, uncurtained windows above. At their right, green, metal mesh surrounded the coach's office on two sides. Beyond the coach's office, a long room provided several sinks and toilets, showers in the back, and dented lockers lining both walls. Sam remembered that the room, which was large enough to accommodate most of the school's boy population, had been built to serve as an underground shelter for the entire junior high in the event of a tornado.

"Everybody settle down and have a seat," Coach Bedford said. To Sam his tone suggested a joyless meeting was coming.

The boys sat wherever they could find a spot—on the benches and along the concrete floor. Sam took a seat near the showers next to Josh and Simon. He noticed that most of the black students sat along the opposite wall.

Chatter faded, and the students sat with rapt attention. Coach Bedford's dark eyes scrutinized them for a full minute before he spoke again. He was no longer dressed in his morning attire. Light-gray elastic shorts and a dark-gray golf shirt summed up his afternoon look. From where he stood, Coach Bedford partially eclipsed another rebel colonel drawing on the wall. This one had a caption—"Take Your Stand for Colgate!!"

"Before we get started, I need your help with something," Coach Bedford said. "Somebody at this school committed a cowardly act of vandalism last night." His fierce black eyes flicked to each boy in turn. "Somebody spray-painted graffiti on our school's marquee. This person had the audacity to attack me personally."

His voice echoed off the walls, and Sam squirmed. Coach Bedford had a way of making everybody feel guilty, even those who were innocent.

"I need your help discoverin' this person. Anybody who has knowledge of this act or the guilty party should see me after we finish today." He thrust a finger toward them. "Let me tell you this. If I find out later that you knew something and didn't tell me, you'll be punished. Mark my words."

Sam glanced at Dewayne, who stared straight ahead. Dewayne might have been feeling fear, guilt, or even smugness—but his face betrayed nothing.

Dewayne's upbringing had been less than ideal. His older brother raised him, he didn't know who his father was, and his mom struggled with drug and alcohol addiction. His aunt had welcomed him and his brother into her meager home.

Coach Bedford cleared his throat and rubbed his hands together. "Okay, I'll get right to it. First, we play football at Colgate to win. Let me say it again—we play football at Colgate to *win*, not just to *play*."

He frowned in the dim light. "Secondly, there are too many of you here to make the team next year. I'm only dressing thirty-five players."

Sam glanced around and guessed maybe fifty boys filled the locker room.

"In fact, except for a few positions," Coach Bedford said, "I already know who the starters will be."

Many of the boys murmured and shook their heads.

"Now, wait a minute—there's still hope for some of you. You've got the whole summer ahead of you. You can run and lift weights, and we'll see what happens when tryouts begin in August. I can tell you what I'm lookin' for—we need more help in the speed positions."

He studied the black students. "You can't teach speed—you've either got it, or you don't. There are certain skill positions that require speed, and some of you naturally have that. For example, I can already tell you that Bates Williams is gonna be our startin' runnin' back and linebacker next year."

No big surprise there. Several boys near Bates smiled and patted him on the back. Bates ducked his head as if oversensitive to praise.

The coach turned back to the main group. "Let me make a few things clear. I oversee this football program—I don't own it. I oversee it for the benefit of the school and for this town. I want to put every one of you in the position I think you should be in to best help this football program. As you know, we receive a great deal of fan support from this community, and no less than a thousand fans will attend each home game." He punched the air with his fist, his voice rising. "I'll do whatever I have to do to put the best football team on that field for those fans and this community. Do you understand me?"

A few boys nodded, wide-eyed, while others mumbled, "Yes, sir."

The passion in his voice went up a notch. "I ask, do you understand me?"

"Yes, sir!" voices rang out.

"You boys are older now. You'll be eighth graders next year—no longer children. I'm not here to hold your hand or wipe your nose. I'm here to make you into good—in some cases, great—football players."

He paused, hands on his hips, at ease when he was the center of attention. "I run a tight ship here. We do things *my way* on and off the field." His eyes swiveled to the black players again, his finger stabbing the air. "I demand respect from every single one of you. Some coaches want to be your friend, but that's not me—no, sir. We'll practice the way *I* want to practice."

His looked at Dewayne, who kept his head down. "We'll run the offensive plays and the defensive sets *I* want to run. You'll get water when *I* think you've earned water, and don't ever tell me that you're hot or thirsty."

He glanced away from Dewayne. "Do you understand me?"

"Yes, sir," they said in unison.

"You see, playin' football isn't for everybody. There's no other sport quite like it, and that's why this school's football tradition means so much to this community. And that's why I wanted to have this meetin' on the last day of school. I want each of you to ask yourselves a few questions. Do you want to play football? If so, do you want to play football *for me*? This summer some of you need to think long and hard about those questions."

He paused, and his voice turned mocking. "Some of you might be better playin' in the band next fall or maybe joinin' one of those nice clubs we have at the school, like the chess club or the debate team."

The boys snickered at these references.

"Football is serious, guys. Don't try to play for me next year if you're lookin' for a way to make new friends or to get to know the coaches a little better." He paused and took a breath, scanning their faces. "Now, does anybody have any questions?"

Dewayne's hand shot up.

Sam flinched. Everybody knew that no love was lost between Dewayne and Coach Bedford. Why Dewayne had even bothered coming to the meeting was a mystery to him.

Coach Bedford eyed Dewayne, his voice dripping with sarcasm. "What do *you* want?"

"Coach, will we have any fun?" Dewayne asked.

Several students near Dewayne burst into nervous laughter.

Sam tensed. This showdown might not be pretty.

Coach Bedford folded his arms across his chest. "Excuse me?"

Dewayne lifted his chin and met Coach Bedford's gaze. "That was a pretty heavy speech you just laid on us, man. I mean, c'mon! It's not like we're goin' to war or somethin'." He studied the faces of the boys around him. "Football's a sport, right? It's supposed to be fun, ain't it?"

Laughter rippled across the locker room. Sam was glad that some-body had the guts to challenge the tone of Coach Bedford's talk, though Dewayne's challenge was rather like watching a moth defy an eagle.

"Are you tryin' to sass me, boy?" Coach Bedford's face reddened, nostrils flaring.

The room grew quiet.

Sam swallowed. *Dewayne's in big trouble now.*

Dewayne shook his head. "No, man. I guess I'm just tryin' to figure you and this whole thing out."

Coach Bedford pointed at Webb, his face rippling with anger. "Let me tell you what you can figure out, boy. You can figure your way right out of this locker room. Webb, you quit on me last season, and I hate quitters. You shouldn't even bother tryin' out again next year. You'd only be wastin' your time and mine. Get out of here, you sissy."

Dewayne rose and faced the coach. His fists were clenched, but Sam thought he saw moisture in his eyes. "You got it, old man! I don't want nothin' to do with this no way! Forget you!"

Dewayne made his way through the seated boys and stormed out of the room without looking back. Sam heard the echo of his feet as he marched up the steps. The slam of the door echoed through the locker room before Coach Bedford asked, his voice low, "Any more questions?"

No hands went up this time.

CHAPTER 7

In their homerooms students waited for the final ring of the school bell that would mark the end of another school year and usher in the summer of 1975. Sam sat at his desk and stared at the clock, counting down the minutes. Mrs. Legg startled him when she called his name.

"Sam, would you come here? I'd like to speak with you."

Sam stood and crossed the room to her desk, wondering if he'd done something wrong.

"Come closer, Sam—over here." Mrs. Legg pointed to a spot behind her desk next to her. Sam obeyed, but he glanced over his shoulder to see if other students were watching him. Thankfully, nobody appeared to be paying any attention to him. They were all counting down the final minutes.

Mrs. Legg remained seated and studied him. Her voice was low, almost as if she were sharing a secret. "I want to know how you're doin', Sam—really doin'." She wasn't using her teacher voice this time; she was asking as a friend, her gray-brown eyes betraying an earnestness Sam had rarely seen before. Stands of her white-streaked, black hair had loosened from a bobby pin and poured over her shoulders.

Sam couldn't suppress his feelings of affection for her. Once, while his mom was driving on the outskirts of town, she'd pointed out Mrs. Legg's house—a small, white farmhouse with an expansive garden out back. Mrs. Legg had told the class about how she loved to spend countless hours weeding her flowers and cultivating her vegetables. Mr. Legg was a pole climber for the Kidron County Rural Electric Cooperative. Their two children, a son and daughter, had moved away.

"I'm fine, thanks." Sam averted his eyes and stared at the black-and-pink pattern on the rug under her desk.

"You've changed this year, Sam." She bit her lip, then shook her head. "You don't seem as happy and confident as you used to be. Are you sure there's nothin' I can help you with?"

He raised his eyes to hers for a second before veering them back to the floor. "I'm okay."

"How's your mama doin'?"

"She's fine."

"I heard she got a job at the Good-N-Handy."

"Uh-huh."

"How's your daddy?"

"Fine."

"How often do you get to see him?"

Sam shrugged. "I talk to him on the phone some. I saw him at my grandparents' farm over Memorial Day weekend, and I'll probably see him a lot this summer." That last part wasn't exactly true. He doubted he'd see his dad much at all now that he lived in Louisville.

Mrs. Legg tugged on her lower lip. Finally, she gave him a gentle smile. "How do you like your new house? I heard y'all moved over to Dixie Avenue."

"It's an older place. The appliances and plumbing are old, but I like it all right, I guess."

"Coach Bedford lives next door to you, doesn't he?"

The way she said this, he could tell she and the coach weren't exactly best friends. "Yes."

"Ray and I went to school together long ago. When I was growin' up, his daddy, Bull Bedford, was the county sheriff. He was a stern man and awfully hard on Ray."

She lowered her voice, her eyes passing over the classroom to see if anyone noticed. "Just between you and me, I think Ray Bedford is crass, and he can be downright cruel, especially to his football players. I think he mistreats them when he makes those good, churchgoin' boys play like devils." She paused to catch her breath. "Principal Sheridan doesn't like Ray either and would fire him if he could—that is, if the board would let him. But he's such an institution in this town."

Sam tried not to smile when she pulled her hands into fists, clearly riled. "I don't care how many football championships his teams win. He thinks he's so all-important to this school and this town. The same goes for his boy, Larry." She rolled her eyes, sarcasm in her voice. "The big, budding football star. He's been raised to think just like his daddy." Then, as if wondering if she'd said too much, she blinked and sighed. "Now, you don't let either of them bother you none, ya hear me?"

"Yes, ma'am. I won't."

She held his gaze as if to be sure he meant what he'd said. "Now Meredith here"—she gestured toward the front row—"She's as good as gold, and so is her mama, the dear soul. But I wouldn't trust either of those Bedford boys as far as I could throw 'em."

Sam had never seen Mrs. Legg so worked up before. She suddenly gripped both of Sam's shoulders and squeezed them. He feared she was about to hug him. But instead, she let him go and patted his back.

She took a deep breath. Then in a pleasant, gentle tone, her voice returned to regular volume. "Sam, you can go back to your seat now. I hope you have a good summer."

Sam retreated to his desk. As he passed by, Meredith Bedford turned her head with a small smile and pretended she hadn't heard the conversation.

When the bell rang, students poured down the school's front steps like the rush of water down a slope. Smiles covered their faces and the happy spring of youth was in their steps. Sam followed Simon, Nick, and Josh to the flagpole and waited.

"Let's go already." Simon's tone was impatient.

"Wait a sec," Sam said. "Let's see if Bates and Dewayne want to go with us."

"Not Dewayne Webb!" Nick spat on the ground. "Bates is fine, but I don't want Dewayne comin' along. He's a pain in the neck. He's constantly arguin' with me. Why, he's the most stubborn person I know."

Nick was always like that. Nothing delayed quick decisions or actions on his part. He always knew his own mind, and internal moral struggles never hindered him.

Just then Sam spied Dewayne heading out of the building. He always wore worn clothes, hand-me-downs from his brother; and the clothes hadn't even been new when his brother wore them.

Dewayne met Meredith Bedford at the bike racks, and the two chatted.

Nick spat again on the sidewalk. "Besides, he's a troublemaker and a quitter. He's no friend of mine. You heard him at the football meetin' today." He shook his head and blew a sigh out of his ballooned cheeks. "Sheesh! To be honest, I wouldn't pee in his ear if his brain was on fire."

Sam chuckled at Nick's weak attempt at humor.

"Hmm. I recall seeing a different troublemaker at the football meetin' than you did," Josh said. "Seems to me that Dewayne was just sayin' what he thought. Coach Bedford's the one who kicked him out of the meetin'."

Sam nodded. "There's bad blood between those two—that's for sure."

Simon shook his head. "Did y'all hear what happened on Valentine's Day? Dewayne gave valentines to *all* the girls in our class, even the white ones."

"I know." Nick grinned. "I 'bout busted my gut when the girls gave the valentines back to him. Some people just don't get how things are supposed to be."

Josh said, "Why don't we give Dewayne a chance and invite him to come?"

"No way, Josh!" Nick shook his head, his mind made up. "He ain't goin' with us, and that's final. Bates is fine, but not Dewayne."

CHAPTER 8

Sam followed Nick, Josh, Simon, and Bates across town toward Hound's Creek. The sun was high in the sky, and his shirt stuck to his sweaty back.

They cut across backyards instead of using roads and sidewalks.

When the boys reached the backyard of a small, brick ranch house, Nick and Simon paused. "Check this out!" Nick said. "This is Tracy Wollum's house." Tracy was captain of Colgate High School's cheerleading squad.

Sam spotted the clothesline strung out behind the Wollums' house. A light breeze made the clothes on the line dance like invisible people.

"Those at the end have to be hers," Nick said. "Simon, I dare you to go touch 'em."

Simon grinned. "Just watch. I'll do better than that."

Simon glanced around to see if anybody was watching. Then he scampered toward the clothesline and yanked a cream-colored bra free, its clothespin flying.

The creak of a backdoor shoved Sam's heart into his throat. Mrs. Wollum was coming out of the house and carrying a clothes basket full of wet clothes.

Sam didn't give her a chance to see him. He sprinted to a neighboring yard, hid behind a bush with his friends, and crouched to see. Their eyes were wide as they watched Simon move the bra behind his back.

"He's so busted," Nick whispered.

Mrs. Wollum looked surprised to see Simon. Then she studied him, her forehead creased in puzzlement. "Simon Puckett, what're you doin' in my backyard?"

"Oh, hi, Mrs. Wollum." Simon began backing away while still holding the bra behind him. "I noticed that some of her … I mean, your … clothes had fallen. I was just … um … puttin' 'em back up for ya."

Mrs. Wollum frowned. "I see."

"Well, I gotta get goin' now." Simon continued backing away. "I'll see ya later. Tell Tracy hey for me, okay?"

He dashed to join his friends and rounded the bush, gasping for breath.

Mrs. Wollum just shook her head and began hanging the wet clothes on the line.

When the boys were sure she hadn't seen them, they rose from their hiding place and continued on their trek to Hound's Creek.

"That was close!" Simon said.

"I can't believe you took it," Nick said. "You've got more nerve than I've given you credit for."

Simon shrugged. "Well, you dared me. What else was I supposed to do?"

"You're crazy." Sam shook his head. He glanced at Bates to see what he thought. Bates was smiling but keeping his thoughts to himself.

"So, why'd you do it?" Josh asked.

"I know why." Nick flashed a knowing grin. "He needed it to go along with the blue one he's been hidin' under his bed."

"Hallelujah!" Simon waved the bra through the air as if it were a flag. Then he draped it over his arm as if he were a merchant displaying fine wares for sale.

"You're nuts," Josh said.

Simon unzipped his backpack and stuffed the bra inside

Nick stared at him in disbelief and shook his head. "Tell Tracy hey for me?"

To reach Hound's Creek, the boys needed to cross Kidron Heights subdivision at the edge of town. Sam's stomach churned when he saw his old neighborhood. Well-maintained landscaping adorned the center strip between the lanes, and a marker at the development entrance announced that visitors were entering "Kidron Heights, the County's Finest Community." The boys passed through a grove of fruit trees and strolled under a tree laden with mulberries. Each boy plucked a handful for a snack and kept going.

"Didn't this used to be a dairy farm?" Josh said between bites.

"Yeah." Nick nodded. "Stinky cows everywhere."

"Hey, let's check out the shelter," Simon said.

The Broadman brothers developed Kidron Heights in the 1960s by turning their eighty-acre dairy farm into Colgate's first planned subdivision with forty-five lots. Prior to its development, all the residences in Colgate had spread out in rows from the town square.

Like others in Kidron County at the time, the Broadman brothers feared the Russians and their intercontinental ballistic missiles aimed at the U.S. Treasury's gold vault in Fort Knox. Because Fort Knox was located about an hour from Colgate, the residents believed they would be among the first targeted if nuclear war broke out between the United States and the U.S.S.R. Therefore, when the Broadman brothers developed the subdivision, they decided that a bomb shelter, big enough for all subdivision residents, would be a desired amenity and increase the value of their lots.

Nick led the way to the old bomb shelter, where large cedar bushes failed to completely hide the entrance. Cedar needles littered the spot where the metal entrance protruded above the ground like a sandwich cut diagonally. A wave of relief swept over Sam when he saw the brass padlock locking the entrance. He didn't want to go in there anyway.

Last summer he, Nick, and Simon had explored the shelter after some teens cut the lock. With flashlights in hand, they'd opened its metal doors on rusty hinges that squealed in protest. Sam descended dirty concrete steps with trepidation and reached the shelter's dank floor, eager to see what was inside.

The place felt like a tomb, musty and dead. The strong aroma of mold and damp concrete hung in the air. Row after row of iron bunk beds lacking mattresses lined the walls of the central room.

Sam clutched his flashlight, certain that a deranged person was going to jump out at them from the shadows. His search of the room's confines revealed little more than rat droppings, empty glass bottles, and candy wrappers littering the floor. Simon drew their attention to a smaller room at the back where crude, steel toilets lined the walls.

Nick suggested that they make the shelter their new hangout. "We could put our own padlock on the door." But after their brief escapade in the shelter, none of them really wanted to go back.

Now, Sam stood beside the locked shelter. That night last summer he had left it with a pledge never to return to the subterranean world below. Sometimes at night he lay awake, unable to sleep, thinking about those Russian missiles falling near Colgate with ear-splitting explosions. He would think about himself being trapped in the bomb shelter and trying to get out. The shelter, in fact, scared him more than the thought of bombs exploding nearby.

CHAPTER 9

Sam followed the sidewalk across the subdivision and paused with his friends near his old house, where a large moving van was parked in the driveway.

A young couple stood in the front yard. The woman watered flowers she just planted, and the man pointed at the shrubbery. Even from where he stood, Sam could hear his voice. He didn't like the shrubs and wanted to tear them out and plant something else. The squeals and laughter of children rose from the back yard.

Sam thought it strange that he couldn't just walk into the house, find his bedroom, and crash into bed. But this place didn't belong to his family anymore. What were he and his friends doing here? He didn't want to see this place again; it only reminded him about the rundown house on Dixie Avenue.

Nick gripped Sam's shoulder. "Sam, I'm sorry your dad ran off and left you and your mom."

Sam's throat was tight. He hoped the couple would take good care of the lawn. His dad had spent a lot of time making sure the grass was weed free. "Thanks."

Sam felt relieved when his friends moved on, leaving the former Cray residence behind. They meandered through another backyard near Nick's house.

"Hey, Nick," Simon said, "got any food we can take down to the creek with us?"

"Great idea!" Nick said. "C'mon, let's check."

The Walkers' house, one of the largest in town, was a sprawling, two-and-half-story colonial with a gabled roof. The boys headed up the semicircle driveway, and Nick's dog, Crum, a black-and-white beagle with floppy ears, greeted them on short, stubby legs. The beagle had been named after the University of Louisville's successful basketball coach, Denny Crum.

"Go Wildcats!" Nick said to Crum, referring to the mascot of the University of Kentucky, the University of Louisville's biggest rival.

As if on cue, the hair on Crum's neck bristled. He snarled and crouched as if ready to attack a University of Kentucky Wildcat fan.

Nick laughed. "Not bad, you mongrel." He smacked Crum on the head a little too hard and almost knocked the dog over.

"I should report you to the dog catcher for abuse," said Sam, a University of Kentucky fan. "Poor dog doesn't know the good guys from the bad."

Nick led his friends up the walk. A fountain threw beads of water into the air, and they tumbled into a terracotta bowl. On the other side of the walk, which was bordered by a curbed stone bench, lay an ornamental pond, where yellow and red fish swam amid the water lilies.

"Take off your shoes, guys," Nick said.

They trooped into the foyer, where a blast of arctic air blew down from above.

"Man, you guys keep your house cold!" Simon folded his arms across his chest, shivering.

Sam took off his shoes and glanced around the place, his eyes widening. The diamond-shaped tiles in the well-scrubbed floor were white with blue inlay. The gilded table stationed at the base of the curved staircase supported an emerald-blue stone vase. Like the tile, the wainscoted walls were also white, and an expensive crystal chandelier hung from the high ceiling.

On his way to the kitchen with his friends, Sam glanced into another room. Two plush easy chairs, stationed in front of a large chest of hammered brass, sat beside an oversized ivory fireplace. A thick Persian rug lay in the center of the room, and green-and-red embroidered curtains framed the windows.

To the sound of socked feet shuffling down the marble floor toward the kitchen, Sam followed his friends. Each jumped to reach the molding above the kitchen door. He slapped the molding without difficulty and turned in time to see Simon try but fail. He missed by several inches.

The mouth-watering aroma of freshly baked rolls filled every corner of the room. Stoop-shouldered Regina, the Walkers' thin, elderly housekeeper, stood at the stove, basting a chicken with its fat drippings. Nick's dad worked long hours at the car dealership, and his mom stayed preoccupied with so many social activities, he saw Regina more than he saw his own parents.

"Nick, what's you doin' here?" asked Regina, her white hair bright. Though she was up in years, she was still spry, and Nick didn't dare cross her.

"Ms. Regina, we'd like some snacks to take with us down to the creek," Nick said.

"Have a seat, and I'll get somethin' fer ya." Regina motioned to the kitchen alcove.

"Make yourself at home, guys," Nick said. "I'll be right back."

Simon and Bates sat down on the built-in window seat, while Josh and Sam found a seat on the mesh chairs around the glass kitchen table.

Regina's pleasant smile turned to a scowl when she recognized Bates. She set down the pan she was cleaning and turned to him abruptly. "What's you doin' har?"

Bates folded his arms across his chest, his tone defensive. "They invited me to go swimmin' with 'em in Hound's Creek."

She shook her head with a grunt and turned to the refrigerator. She opened it, pulling out a tray of fried chicken and biscuits. Then she slammed the tray down on the marble countertop with a bang. She placed the food on a large sheet of aluminum foil, wrapped it up to go, and placed it in a paper grocery bag on the table.

Finished, she returned to Bates. "Come wit me fer a second." She motioned to the door to the garage, and he followed Regina into the garage. She slammed the door behind them.

Josh, Simon, and Sam rushed to the door and pressed their ears against it.

"Can you hear anything?" Josh asked.

"Shh. Yeah, listen."

Nick returned just in time with what appeared to be several magazines rolled up in his hand. "Hey, what's up, guys?"

"Shh!" Simon said. "We're tryin' to hear."

Simon waved him over, and together they listened to the conversation transpiring in the garage.

"Boy, whut in tarnation are ya doin' wit these white boys in this neighborhood?"

"Like I said, they invited me to go to the creek with 'em," Bates said. "I didn't know we were gonna stop here."

"You wasn't thinkin' is what you was doin'. Ya gots no business bein' here, and ya knows it. Walkin' around here likes ya owns the place. Ya ain't company here."

Bates said nothing.

Sam swallowed hard and felt bad for Bates. He felt even worse because he'd invited him to come along.

"This ain't no place for you," Regina said. "I wants ya to git home right now. And sure enough, I'll be talkin' to your mama 'bout this."

"Yes, ma'am," Bates said in a dejected voice.

Sam and his friends rushed back to their seats just in time. Regina returned to the kitchen by herself and handed the bag of food to Nick. She looked at him crossly. "Bates needed to get on home. And you gots some work to do in that room of yours when ya gets back."

"Yes, ma'am," Nick said.

Sam glanced out the kitchen window and saw Bates heading down the driveway, away from the house. He got up and ran after him.

"Bates, stop! Hold up!"

Bates didn't slow his stride. He was already halfway across the street, head bowed, hands thrust into the pockets of his jeans. He kicked a rock, and it went flying into somebody's lawn.

Sam caught up with him on the sidewalk across the street and touched his arm. "Bates, wait! I'm sorry. I heard some of what Ms. Regina said to you."

"Go on back, Sam." Bates kept walking, eyes downcast. "Your friends will be missin' you."

Sam kept pace with him. "I wish I could do somethin' to help."

"Well, you can't. There's nothin' you can do. Goin' along with you guys was a bad idea to begin with. I knew it, and you shoulda known it too." He kept walking with no intent to stop.

Sam stopped and watched him go. He kicked at the sidewalk.

Sam turned back to Nick's house. His friends were waiting for him at the end of the driveway.

"Well, that was awkward." Nick spat on the cement. "Maybe askin' Bates to come along wasn't such a good idea after all, Sam. First Dewayne and now Bates. Man, if you keep this up all summer, we're gonna stay in trouble."

CHAPTER 10

Behind the Walkers' yard lay a cow pasture. White clouds resembling wispy cotton candy floated gently over the field. The boys reached the pasture beyond the wire fence at the end of Nick's backyard by climbing a Kidron County Rural Electric box and vaulting over the fence. A warning on the box read, "CAUTION: HIGH VOLTAGE. RISK OF ELECTRIC SHOCK."

Nick led the way, and they set out across the field, carefully avoiding the plentiful cow pies. Crum crawled under the fence and joined them.

Sam gave the animals plenty of space. A small herd of Jersey cows, standing belly deep in a muddy pond, lowed and watched them warily. A nearby bull supped water. Sam stared at the only horse in the pasture, a beautiful brown-and-white pinto. Startled by their presence, it whinnied and cantered away.

A dilapidated barn stood on the other side of the field. One of the walls displayed a faded advertisement for chewing tobacco: CHEW MAIL POUCH TOBACCO: TREAT YOURSELF TO THE BEST. A rain-beaten red-and-white International Harvester Tractor sign hung askew from another corner. Beyond the barn, the ground sloped toward a ravine bordered by yellow-green willow trees swaying in the breeze.

Hound's Creek flowed beneath the trees. It rambled toward Colgate and skirted the town's northern rim. The boys climbed over yet another wire fence at the end of the pasture and marched single file down a narrow footpath along the creek, which snaked through thick hardwoods—sycamores, birch trees, and a few mature pin oaks scattered here and there. Nearby, a woodpecker hammered away, looking for a meal.

They followed the path for three hundred yards. It narrowed, and Colgate disappeared from sight and sound, as if they were entering another world.

Sam loved this place. When he lived in Kidron Heights, he often came here to read. Near the swimming hole was a spot where the trunks of two box elder trees grew together, their intertwining trunks forming a wide, sloped bough twelve feet above the ground. Sam would straddle the wide branch and set his feet on two smaller branches, pretending it was a recliner nature made especially for him.

They stopped when they reached a clearing in the woods where the creek pooled deep just below its bank. Trees encircled the pool, giving it a secluded feeling. Crum dashed down the bank to the water's edge and lapped up a drink. He wagged his tail when Josh patted his head and scratched his neck.

Glad to finish their walk, Sam slumped onto the creek's bank between Simon and Nick, letting his legs dangle off the bank above exposed tree roots. The creek meandered by, while a gentle breeze blew across the water. Sam plucked a blade of grass and rolled it between his fingers.

Maybe I should have stood up for Bates in front of Ms. Regina. I should have at least tried. After all, I was the one who invited him to go swimmin' with us.

Nick opened the bag and passed around the food. Sam's stomach growled at the sight of the cold chicken and biscuits, and he soon forgot about Bates. He accepted his portion and dug in, the chicken more delicious than he expected. Ms. Regina was a mighty fine cook.

Excited to be there and to be freed from school and away from town, the boys peered around. Beyond the water's edge, the creek was alive with little, silver fish. Two gray squirrels scampered about and chased each other in the branches above their heads. Crum foraged among the bushes, bemused by a rabbit he'd seen.

"He wouldn't know what to do with that rabbit if he caught it." Nick seized a piece of chicken between his front teeth. Then, when

Crum came back to them, he spit a piece of chicken and hit him in the eye. Nick fell into raucous laughter. "Wow, what a shot!"

"Why'd you do that?" Josh said.

Nick glared at him. "Because I felt like it, stupid. He's my dog—I can do whatever I want with him."

Everybody in Colgate knew Nick and Josh could have passed for brothers. Because both boys were together a lot, people often got them confused—and for good reason. They were the same height, taller than Sam, and their arms and legs were equally lanky beneath their jeans and T-shirts. Unlike Sam's long, dark-brown hair, which flopped down over his forehead, Nick and Josh wore their light-brown hair cut short, and similar cowlicks sprouted from the crest of their heads. Another similar feature was their small, round ears, which stuck out from the sides of their heads as if they were elves. Their thin bodies were hard with muscle and their shoulders bony and wide. Josh played tight end on the football team, while Nick played defensive end.

Nick and Josh may have looked alike, but their personalities were vastly different. Nick, whose dad owned a car dealership that made his family one of the wealthiest in town, wasn't popular at school. But he was well known, perhaps because he had the directness of a natural leader. Though always cool and self-assured, he could be wicked. In fact, his sarcastic sense of humor and acid wit often annoyed Sam. Nick teased classmates, and he had a mean-spirited habit of hitting his friends in the back or "frogging" them on the arm—his personal greeting. He also exhibited a snide way of making his questions sound like accusations.

Though Sam saw a lot of Nick, the fact was, he didn't especially enjoy his company.

Josh, on the other hand, was someone with whom Sam always enjoyed spending time. He was kind and decent, with a sunny, good-natured disposition and bright blue eyes that had a deep, penetrating quality. Josh's dad, Dr. Carlisle, worked as a physician, and his wife ran the Helping Arms Agency, which provided food and clothing for the poor as well as other services.

In the world of boys, where the typical manner of interaction was often to tear one another down, Josh was abnormal because of his encouraging personality. One of his knacks was saying good things at just the right time. He wasn't Sam's best friend if friendship was measured by how much time the boys spent together, but among Sam's friends, Josh was certainly one of his best.

Sam remembered a high-school football game last fall when Josh had invited him to spend the night at his house. While walking with Josh and his parents to the Carlisles' vehicle, Josh had nudged him and motioned toward the shadows.

"Hey, look over there."

A man and woman were strolling off together in the opposite direction. Sam's heart lifted with a sudden glimmer of hope when he recognized the couple as his own mom and dad. Whenever he saw them together, he couldn't help wishing that they'd work out their problems and get back together.

"Maybe they're workin' things out," Josh had said that night in his encouraging voice.

As it turned out, his parents didn't work things out, but Sam didn't forget Josh's hopeful words that evening.

When they finished eating, the boys scrambled up to a spring that gushed out of rocks near a cluster of blackberry bushes. They knelt and took turns cupping their hands and drinking their fill of the crystal clear water. The water was so cold that it made Sam's teeth ache.

"Check these out," Nick said. "I picked 'em up when we stopped by my house." With a cunning look glinting in his eyes, he pulled out two items from the back of his shorts. He tossed a comic book to the ground and then lifted a *Playboy*® magazine to his chest. On the alluring front cover, a curvaceous blonde smiled into the camera.

Sam blinked at the magazine in surprise.

"Where'd you get that?" Simon sounded shocked.

"From my dad's dealership," Nick said. "He keeps a big stack of 'em in the back room. I borrowed this one the other day, but he has so many of 'em, he'll never miss it."

Nick opened the magazine, and Simon glanced over Nick's shoulder, whistling at what he saw. Sam couldn't resist and joined them, stealing a look too.

Josh headed toward the creek.

"Where you goin', Josh?" Nick reached toward Josh with one hand and grabbed his T-shirt and pulled him back. Josh turned to face Nick and ducked backward at the same time, allowing Nick to pull his shirt off.

"Thanks, Nick," Josh said with a laugh. "I was gonna take that off anyhow. I don't know about you guys, but I'm goin' swimmin'." He removed his Converse Chuck Taylor tennis shoes and long, white socks.

"You wuss," Nick said.

Josh marched up to Nick. Then, before anyone expected it, he grinned and snatched the magazine out of Nick's grasp. "You don't need to be looking at this."

"Hey, give that back!" Nick reached for Josh, but Josh was quicker. He evaded Nick by leaping into the green water with a splash.

Nick cursed at him. "I'll make you sneeze red, Carlisle!"

Josh waded through the chest-high water, holding the magazine over his head. He inched the magazine toward the water and addressed Nick in a teasing voice. "Did you really want this?"

"Don't even think about it, Carlisle!" Nick poised on the creek bank.

Josh dipped the tip of the magazine into the water.

Nick cursed again and reached toward Josh with an outstretched hand. He tried a new approach. "Give it back! It doesn't even belong to me. It's my dad's."

But Josh backed farther into the creek and away from Nick's reach.

Nick scowled, his voice enraged. "Don't make me come after you!"

"Oh, no!" Josh said in mock alarm. "It's gettin' heavier. I don't know if I can hold it up much longer!" He held the magazine in both hands over his head and made his arms tremble as if the magazine weighed three hundred pounds. Then in a flash he plunged it into the river.

Nick cursed. "You're dead!" He leapt into the creek with his clothes and shoes still on.

The boys locked arms in an intense wrestling match that stirred the green water, turning it milky from the sandy depths below. Nick locked an arm around Josh's head and dunked him several times. Each time, Josh rose with a grin. Josh finally broke away from Nick's grip, laughing. The match was over.

"Carlisle, you're just lucky there are plenty more where that one came from." Nick was submerged now with only his head sticking out.

From the bank Simon and Sam grinned at each other.

"Should we join 'em?" Sam said.

Simon nodded. They wrestled out of their T-shirts, kicked off their shoes, and stripped off their long socks. Sam remembered the photograph of his dad in his pocket and carefully folded it into his shirt.

Simon also removed his khaki school shorts. He did not wear frayed blue jeans like the others, and his mother preferred that he keep his good school shorts out of the green creek water.

Josh swam to the middle of the creek and retrieved a thick, yellow rope hanging from a strong tree branch that jutted at a perpendicular angle over the creek bank. He handed the rope to Sam, who in turn passed it to Nick. Now unencumbered from his soaked shirt, shoes, and socks, Nick climbed the sycamore tree and sat on a branch twenty feet above the water.

He held on tight to the rope, pushed himself off the branch, and swung down with a holler, flying over the creek. When he reached the highest point, as if at the end of a swinging pendulum, he whooped his loudest and released the rope. He tucked his arms and legs into his body and splashed into the water—a perfect cannonball.

Everyone took their turn on the rope after that. Sam splashed Crum, who'd been half dozing on the creek bed with his nose tucked under his hind leg. He sprang to action and yelped at no one in particular. Then he shook the water from his shiny coat and lay back down, his tongue hanging out.

A good feeling came over them as they took their turns on the rope swing and filled the air with fast talk and raised voices. They tumbled about like puppies and without fear of correction from any adult. They floated on their backs and kicked their feet—talking wildly and simultaneously yet seeming to understand each other. Summer was now in full swing, and they were in their refuge.

CHAPTER 11

Simon clambered out of the creek and crept to the high weeds beyond the row of trees.

"Where you goin', Simon?" Nick asked.

"Gotta answer the call of nature, if you know what I mean." Simon disappeared behind thick undergrowth.

"You're defilin' nature!" Nick said.

"You got it wrong," Simon said. "What could be more natural than poopin' in the open air? Where do you think the bears go?"

"Bears? In Kidron County?" Josh sounded skeptical.

"Don't confuse him with the facts." Sam pushed back a strand of wet hair. "Just be glad he didn't do his business in the water."

"Ow!" Simon said as he wrestled in the thick undergrowth.

He rejoined them, and Sam swam to the bank, where Josh was soaking in the shallows. Creek water dripped off Sam's chin and ears, and wet hair plastered his chin. He plopped down next to Josh and draped an arm across his shoulder. "Did you bring the dibble dabble?"

"Dibble dabble!" Simon said.

"Yep, I've got it." Out of his pocket Josh fished a tire valve cap he'd removed from his mother's Plymouth station wagon. "I'll take it down first."

Nick joined them on the creek bank. Josh jumped in, swam to the middle of the creek, and dove to the bottom. Once there, he released the dibble dabble and swam back. Meanwhile, Sam, Simon, and Nick waited for the tire cap to emerge from the green water. The one who initially spotted it had a chance to go after it first, but the game required quick reflexes. As soon as the first spotter yelled "dibble dabble," the others could go after the cap too.

"Dibble dabble!" Simon dove into the creek but failed to grasp the tiny cap. Instead, he knocked it back under water.

"Nice job, spaz," Nick said.

The game wasn't easy. Each time the cap reappeared, Sam jumped into the water with his friends. He pushed and jostled to secure the dibble dabble. Finally, he got it. He climbed back up the bank and decided to jump off the tree swing, taking the cap back underwater. After several rounds, Josh triumphantly won the game with five grabs.

They decided that they'd enjoyed the water long enough. Sam grabbed his clothes and followed his friends. They walked barefoot fifty yards beyond the swimming hole. Then they climbed a large, flat rock they called Paradise Island.

The rock rested in the middle of the creek bed and jutted only a few inches above the surface. It interrupted the water's natural flow and divided it into two channels of white water that rippled on either side. Broader and shallower here, the creek was only a few inches deep. Even Crum made it safely across without difficulty.

Here the boys abandoned the shade of the sycamore trees and entered the sunlight, each reclining on his own spot on the rock. Sam pillowed his head on his bundled clothes and stretched his limbs, while the sun's rays flickered over the water that rambled toward Colgate. Tree branches swayed in the soft breeze, and a yellow butterfly flitted among ferns that rose from the creek bank. Bright green leaves rustled in the sunlight as Sam allowed the sun to dry him, its rays landing pleasantly on his torso.

He smiled. Yes, this was summer—warmth on his skin and creek-soaked hair. This was their sanctuary, free from the constraints of school and home. No more instructions from teachers—no more tests. He felt only the freedom and unforced tranquility of this place. Summer had just emerged from spring.

They lazed in the sunshine for several minutes until Josh interrupted the silence with a joke. "I've got one. What was Beethoven doin' when they opened his coffin?"

Sam thought hard but was stumped. Nobody else had an answer either.

"Decomposin'," Josh said.

"I've heard that one." Simon pulled himself up and sat Indian style.

"That was mildly funny—at least the first time I heard it," Nick said. "Okay, I've got a good one. Last fall at a University of Georgia football game in Athens, two old men, Bubba and Fred, sat in seats right on the fifty-yard line. By halftime, the Bulldogs were killin' their opponent twenty-eight to zero, when their marchin' band came out along with Uga, their real bulldog mascot. When the band started playin' 'Georgia on My Mind,' Uga lays down on the twenty, hikes his hind leg, and starts lickin' himself ... well, you know where. Bubba turns to Fred and says, 'I wish I could do that.' Fred doesn't say nothin' to him. But then ten minutes into the third quarter, Fred turns to Bubba and says, 'That dog a bite you!'"

Sam threw his head back and laughed hard.

"Did you know," Simon said, "that a human sneeze travels one hundred miles an hour and that you can't sneeze with your eyes open?"

"Simon, you're such a nerd." Nick shook his head.

"Well, it's true," Simon said.

"What else do you know, geekmeister?" Nick said.

"Did you know," Simon said, "that if you took your guts out and spread them out on the ground, they'd stretch twenty-two feet?"

"No way!" Sam said. "That's not true."

"It is too. I read it in an encyclopedia. And the human heart creates enough pressure to squirt blood thirty feet."

"You're a weirdo, knowing all that useless stuff," Nick said. "By the way, Puckett, how many girls did you ask out last year?"

Simon paused to think, then began counting them on his fingers. "Let's see. Erica, Michelle, Martha, Jane—"

"And they also said, 'No, no, no.'" Nick mimicked Simon by counting the no's on his fingers. Then he burst into laughter.

"Not all of them," Simon said with a smile. "Not Martha Brangers— she said yes."

"That doesn't count," Nick said. "I remember that. It was only for one hour. Then she came to her senses."

"It was still a yes." Simon said, starry-eyed. "For the rest of her life, I will be one of her former boyfriends. She can't ever deny it."

Nick shook his head and rested his head on his shoes.

"At least I don't have to lie to get a girlfriend," Simon said.

"What do you mean?" Nick said. "I don't have to lie to get girls."

"Yeah, right," Simon said. "Remember last summer at the state fair? When we met those girls from Breckinridge County, you told them you were fifteen."

"And like an idiot you said, 'Uh, Nick, don't you have to be fourteen before you can be fifteen?'"

"Well, one of us had to be truthful," Simon said, then added with pride, "I think they found my honesty refreshing."

"They ditched us, man." Nick said.

"Maybe," Simon said. "But I still think I made a better impression on them than you did."

"I'm not talkin' to you anymore," Nick said.

Simon rose to his feet, still in his white briefs. He cleaned his glasses on his underwear and peered up at the pure blue sky, reaching out both arms in an extravagant gesture. "Since we're talkin' about failed romances, I want to dedicate this song to my dear friend, Sam Cray, and his very short romance with Emily Dogan."

"No, you'd better not, Simon," said Sam.

Simon began to croon Frankie Valli's "My Eyes Adored You." Poorly.

When Simon paused for a breath, Nick said, "You sound like a ukulele in a cement mixer." But Simon pressed on, this time adding his own words in some places.

Sam's eyes adored her
Though he never laid a hand on her—Emily Dogan.
His eyes adored her
So close yet so far away.

"Shut up, Simon," said Sam, his face red.

But Nick, Josh, and Simon clapped in hearty approval.

"There's no insult like the truth," Nick said.

"You know you'd still be pursuin' Emily if Larry Bedford hadn't scared you off," Simon said.

Sam glanced away. Before Christmas last year he'd dated Emily Dogan after she'd broken up with Larry Bedford. But he had an ugly standoff with Larry during Christmas break. Larry made it clear that he'd make Sam pay if he didn't steer clear of Emily.

Though he liked Emily, Sam decided to break up with her. Besides, she was a year older, and when they talked, he often struggled to think of clever things to say. Before calling her, he would jot down various topics he thought she might be interested in. That helped for a while … that is, until he ran out of topics. Then he felt hopeless again.

Sam decided he couldn't take more of this ribbing from Simon without defending himself. He rose and wrapped Simon in a reverse bear hug.

"Let go of me, you big ladies' man!" Simon said.

Sam put Simon in a headlock and dragged him to the downstream edge of the island, where the water was deeper, then threw him in. Simon splashed into the water and stood, sputtering, water up to his chest.

"Embarrassment over your failed romances brings out the worst in you, Cray!" he said before pulling himself out.

Sam glanced at Josh, who was staring at the water as it dribbled over the rocks, his face serious.

Nick, noticing the same thing, grabbed one of Simon's shoes and threw it at Josh, hitting him in the head. Josh jerked, jarred back to the present, and scowled at Nick. He pressed a hand to his smarting head.

"Hey, whadya do that for?"

"What're you thinkin' about, Carlisle?" Nick asked.

Josh returned his gaze to the water. Then, as if to no one in particular, he said, "Do you think we're gonna run out of summers?"

"What're you talkin' about?" Nick said.

Sam puzzled over Josh's question. "Yeah, what do you mean?"

Josh shrugged. "Well, I was talkin' to my sister this mornin' about how excited I was, this bein' the last day of school and all, and with summer just gettin' started. She said, 'Yeah, I'm excited too' but she didn't look excited to me. I don't think she's lookin' forward to summer at all. She's working a job now to pay for her car insurance. She'll be a big senior next year. She's startin' to look at colleges and she's worried about gettin' in to the right school."

Sam let his words roll around in his head for a moment. "I get what you're sayin'."

"I don't." Nick shook his head. "Maybe this is all a little too deep for me."

"You get more obligated as you get older," Simon said. "It's like the legacy of becomin' an adult."

"Maybe real summers like the kind we know are just for kids," Josh said. "We gotta grow up and face responsibilities."

"You sad sacks!" Nick said. "I'm always gonna have fun in the summer, no matter how old I am. Anyway, what she said ain't true for any of us, at least not for now. We've got the whole summer ahead of us."

"Nick's right," Simon said. "This is our thirteenth summer—we might as well enjoy it."

"I suppose you're right," Josh said.

"And anything can happen during summertime," Simon said. "Anything."

CHAPTER 12

"You ready to roll?" said a familiar voice.

Dan Cray got up from the weathered wicker chair on the deck of his third-story apartment in Old Louisville. He set aside the textbook about twentieth-century music he'd been reading and peered down into the street. His friend, Alex Hedron, had pulled to the curb in his red convertible MGB Sportster and cut the engine before setting the emergency brake.

"Not yet," Dan said. "Come on up."

Dan stepped into the apartment and pressed the black button in the hallway to release the door lock on the first floor. Then he pushed his apartment door open and waited for his friend to arrive.

Meanwhile, he glanced around the apartment as a newcomer might. It was only one of five apartments in a converted Victorian mansion on Third Street near Central Park. He'd moved here six months ago and felt the same rush of freedom a teenager feels when he or she moves away from home for the first time.

His bright, roomy apartment offered nine-foot-tall ceilings. In addition to the side deck, amenities included two bedrooms, two full baths, a spacious den, and a kitchen filled with new appliances. He'd left the furniture in Colgate with Mary, so the apartment was sparsely furnished. But recent additions included some new chairs, a couple of tables, and an L-shaped, red-and-black plaid couch.

Dan was thirty-seven years old, but was one of those people who made classmates jealous at high-school reunions because he retained his rugged good looks as well as his athletic build. He was still as lean as he was when he was in high school, even though his black hair was beginning to show signs of age with touches of gray.

Alex panted when he reached the top of the stairs. He wore bell-bottom jeans and a red dress shirt unbuttoned halfway down his hairy chest. Several gold chains adorned his neck. He was shorter than Dan but carried an extra thirty pounds. His long, wavy brown hair fell almost to his shoulders.

Dan studied his friend and marveled that they'd maintained the friendship after all these years. Alex had been his best friend in high school, and they'd played football together, Alex being Dan's favorite receiver.

Now Alex slapped Dan on the back. "Hurry up, my man! It's time to party, and time's a wastin'. I can tell you this—if you were still livin' in Colgate, you wouldn't be goin' to a beach volleyball party like the one we're going to tonight."

"Hang on, all right? I gotta make a phone call first."

"What for?"

"I'm supposed to pick Sam up tomorrow. He's out of school for the summer, and he's supposed to stay with me this week."

"But that's tomorrow, and he's not comin' today. So let's get goin'."

Dan shook his head. "Mary and I haven't made the plans yet."

"What plans do you need to make? She knows you're gonna pick him up, right?"

Dan hated to broach the difficult topic. "Sam hasn't exactly agreed to visit me yet." *Does he even want to see me?*

"Make your call then." Alex brushed past Dan, heading toward the kitchen. "You got anything to drink around here?"

"Check the fridge." *You always do anyhow.*

Dan watched Alex peek his head into the refrigerator and realized that no one had influenced him more over the past year than his friend. Alex had heard about Dan's unhappy marriage in Colgate and had called frequently, telling him about how much he enjoyed the single life in Louisville after his own divorce.

"There's a happy life waiting for you here," he said, "whenever you've got the courage to grab it."

Alex suggested that he meet with Attorney Hank Gabbard, who'd been Alex's lawyer for his divorce.

"Just go talk to Hank," Alex said at the time. "Get some information—you'll feel better."

Though Gabbard was the county prosecutor, he ran a private practice on the side. Dan delayed meeting with the attorney until one day after work last fall. Gabbard made Dan feel at ease about the divorce process and educated him about a new approach.

"It started in California," he had said, "and it's the way to go. No-fault divorce is what it's called now. You just plead irreconcilable differences, and everybody moves on. No accusations, no bitterness. It's better for the adults and any children involved. Kentucky's just now getting in line with the other, more progressive, states."

This encouraged Dan, but he still struggled with the idea of being separated from Sam.

"You're no good for your son if you're not happy," Alex had told him. "You just need to take some time for yourself. Your boy will be better off in the long run if you do this for yourself right now."

When Dan decided to enroll at the University of Louisville to obtain his teaching certificate (he needed only twelve more college hours), Alex helped Dan find this apartment and a job as a waiter at an upscale downtown restaurant. It didn't pay much, but the night job enabled Dan to attend classes during the day.

Dan started to dial the telephone with a knot in his gut. Then he remembered that Alex's son had graduated from high school a year ago.

Dan glanced at his friend. "Let me ask you. Got any advice for a father-son relationship? I've had trouble talking to Sam lately."

"My son and I hardly ever talk," Alex said with a shrug. "He finished his freshman year at Western Kentucky and lives down in Bowling Green year-round. To be honest, we just aren't that close anymore. I mean, I love him, and I know he loves me, but we've grown apart—and not because of the divorce. Cheryl and I divorced when Joey was in the eighth grade, but we were already living separate lives."

He chuckled. "Come to think of it, I have a crummy relationship with my dad too. That's just the way it is. Over the years you grow apart, if you were ever close to begin with. It's the standard father-son legacy."

"Your relationship with your dad is similar to how things went with me and my dad," Dan said. "On the farm where I grew up we spent a lot of time together. But today I wouldn't say we're close—at least we haven't been for a long time."

"There you go then—don't blame yourself or the divorce. You gotta accept life for what it is. Dads and sons just grow apart over time. It's natural." Alex paused. "So make your phone call, and let's get goin'."

Mary Cray maneuvered the heavy, black telephone receiver under her blond hair. At the sound of Dan's voice, she stiffened, an involuntary reflex. She forced a pleasant tone.

"Sam's not here right now."

"When do you expect him back?"

"Probably within the hour."

"Well, have him call me—would you?"

She took a breath. "I'll let him know you called, but it's not up to me to make sure he calls you back."

"You're puttin' ideas in his head, aren't you?"

She tightened her grip on the phone. "No, I'm not."

"Sure you are."

"Let's not go there. I'm not draggin' him into our problems."

"But we have an agreement, remember?"

Her chest tightened. "Dan, I'm not violatin' our agreement. I won't force him to do somethin' he doesn't want to do. He's not a piece of furniture we can agree about in court. You've gotta consider what *he* wants."

"Well, maybe you can persuade him to do the right thing."

She paused. "I think he's old enough to decide what is the right thing. Don't you?"

"I wonder why he doesn't seem to want to see me. It doesn't make any sense."

What is there not to understand? You walked out on us.

Dan sighed. "I guess this whole thing has been a lot for him to adjust to."

"There's been a lot of adjustin' for all of us, Dan." She hesitated. "You know, it would be a lot easier to coordinate things if you lived in Colgate. I'm glad you're fulfillin' your dreams, but—"

"My dreams have nothing to do with this."

"I don't think we are gettin' anywhere here."

"Well, if you see him—"

"I'll let him know you called. Bye."

Dan hung up and leaned back in the high-backed chair in the hallway. From his chair he could see the tall oak trees lining Third Street. He mulled over this unsatisfactory conclusion to an unsatisfactory call.

He had to admit he wasn't used to living here yet. Perhaps he wasn't used to the divorce either; it still felt weird to wake up without Mary at his side.

And there I go, thinking about Mary again.

But how could he not?

Alex took a seat across from him. "So how'd it go?"

Dan rubbed his face. "I can't stop thinkin' about her and what we had."

He and Mary had observed a formal ceremony at the Kidron Valley Church right after his college graduation. Then after only one week of honeymooning at St. Petersburg Beach, he'd started working at the rubber plant.

So much of his life had become scripted for him after that, with so many dutiful roles to play. At the plant he'd exhibit the qualities of both a hard worker and a leader, and he'd been quickly promoted. After ten years, he'd climbed the ladder to what amounted to being second in charge. In that role he'd improved efficiency and set production goals for the entire plant.

Mary volunteered her time at Kidron Valley Church and stayed busy on the Christmas decorating committee and the community welcoming committee. Then, two years after their wedding, she became pregnant with Sam. She'd stayed at home with the baby while he worked longer hours at the rubber plant. Every summer they vacationed in Myrtle Beach, South Carolina, and every Sunday they'd attended Kidron Valley Church.

The rush of thoughts and emotions flooding his mind almost paralyzed him. This memory dump, he realized, occurred each time he had a conversation with Mary—as if something about their relationship was inescapable. *Would time eventually heal this wound?*

His mom thought Mary and he married too young.

Maybe she was right.

Dan's dad thought he landed a terrific job at the rubber plant, but Dan often wondered if he foreclosed too quickly on a lifelong career there. Certainly he experienced good times and good memories, but after fifteen years of marriage, he experienced a growing sense of discontentment. He tried to mask those negative emotions with self-discipline and a sense of duty, but by the time he decided to file for divorce, he lost the energy to keep up the routine and wear the mask.

He tried talking to his dad about his marriage and discontentment. One Sunday his parents invited Dan, Mary, and Sam to the farm for lunch. After the meal Dan found his dad in the basement, cleaning one of his twelve-gauge shotguns, the room thick with the aroma of soap and gun oil. Dan told his dad the short version of where his marriage was headed and informed him he was going to file for divorce.

"I think it's better that you stay together" was all his dad said to him. *He seemed more upset that I might quit my job at the rubber plant.*

Dan was discouraged. It had been hard enough to bring up his personal problem with his dad. Then, to get such little feedback.

Maybe Alex is right. Fathers and sons just didn't stay close. He wished he were closer to his dad, but the truth was, they were distant now. Dan remembered when he used to give his dad a hug and a kiss every night before bed. However, like most Southern men, that became some sort of embarrassment, and he and his dad learned to settle for handshakes and show their love without words. After his marriage fell apart, he had nobody to turn to for advice—other than Alex.

The last thing he wanted was for Mary and Sam to cling to memories of seeing him miserable and making them miserable. He felt trapped and desperate. Leaving Colgate seemed like the only logical choice for any of them, including himself, to have a chance at happiness.

Six months ago, when Dan had arrived at his 6:00 A.M. shift at the plant, he finally found the courage to make the change he had been contemplating. He felt depressed to be working another long shift at a job he could no longer stand. Most of his adult life had been about pretending—pretending to be a satisfied employee of a rubber hose plant, pretending to be a happy Colgate citizen.

He left the note for Mary and Sam and explained his desire for the divorce. Then he stayed on at the rubber plant and tried to remain in Colgate for a few unsuccessful weeks. While he lived in a motel room on the south side of town, many advised him either to "repent" or to be "ashamed of himself."

Dan recalled one such example. Simon Puckett's dad, a deacon at Kidron Valley Church, had knocked on his motel room one night. The heavyset man had been Sam's Sunday school teacher back when Sam and his mom attended the church.

"I've come to set you straight," Mr. Puckett said. "You need to man up and return to your wife and son."

Dan remembered how he felt when Mr. Puckett left him that night—not mad but perplexed. In his heart he still wanted to have a happy marriage and be a godly role model for Sam.

Even now, sitting in Old Louisville, Dan wasn't sure where his life was going. *Is this it? Is this as happy as I'm ever gonna be?*

CHAPTER 13

Sam headed home, his fingers still shriveled from his swim at the creek with his friends. The row of houses on Dixie Avenue obscured the setting sun. He glanced at the Bedford house and made out the silhouette of someone sitting inside the screened-in porch. He decided not to investigate further and raced up the sidewalk to his house, letting himself in.

"Well, boo!" his mother called from the kitchen. "Supper's ready."

The appetizing aroma drew Sam's growling stomach to the kitchen, where she was busy at the stove.

She hooked a lock of golden hair behind her ear. "I made one of your favorites—salmon croquettes and mashed potatoes. I'll fix you a plate." She studied him and swiveled her gaze back to the stove. "So, how was your last day of school?"

He leaned against the doorjamb and spied peeling white paint on the wall beside her. "It was okay, I guess. Judge Graves gave the graduation speech. He was good."

"Would you mind helping me for a minute?" she said. "I can never get this silly necklace to unclasp."

"No problem."

She took a seat and held up the necklace clasp behind her for him to see.

Sam moved behind her and gently brushed her blonde hair over her shoulders before unfastening the necklace.

Sam took a seat at the table, and Mary set the necklace on the counter beside the sink. Then she transferred the food to two plates and set them on the table. She poured two glasses of milk and took a seat across from him.

"So, what did you do after school?" she asked.

Sam shoveled food in while he talked. "Josh, Simon, Nick, and I went to Hound's Creek. Bates was gonna go, but Ms. Regina yelled at him for bein' at Nick's house, so he went home."

The salmon tasted terrific, but Sam lost some of his appetite at the memory of Bates stalking off by himself. *Why did I let him leave like that?*

Mary shook her head, her downcast eyes concerned. "That's a shame. Change sure is slow in comin' to this town." She looked at him, her forehead furrowed with concern. "Sometimes I wonder if you and I should just sell everything we've got and move on—you know, get a fresh start someplace else."

Sam dropped his fork with a clang. "Are you serious? No way. Colgate's our home, Mom!"

After seeing the alarm in his eyes, she nodded as if making an important decision. "You're right, Sam. We'll always live here. Colgate's our home."

Sam gulped a mound of mashed potatoes when the telephone in the hall rang.

"Now who could be callin' right after we just sat down for supper?" She wiped her mouth on her napkin and got up to get it.

Sam looked up just as she cut her eyes toward him.

"Yeah, he just got home."

Sam swallowed hard. *Great.* He knew who was on the other end, and he didn't want to talk to him.

"Okay," Mary said. "Hold on. Let me get him." She pressed her hand over the receiver. "Sam, it's your dad. He needs to talk to you."

Sam shook his head.

"Dan, I don't think he feels like talkin' tonight." She listened and sighed. "Okay, I'll try again."

She placed her hand over the receiver again. "Sam, won't you come talk to your father?"

He shook his head and mouthed a firm no.

Mary sighed and dropped her head before returning the phone to her ear. "Dan, he doesn't want to talk tonight. Maybe another time … We're gonna have to trust each other to make this work … I guess he's not staying at your place then … Well, I can't force him if he doesn't want to … Good night."

Mary placed the receiver back in its cradle and returned to her seat.

Sam sensed her concerned eyes probing him, but he focused on his food.

"You know, Sam, you can't just ignore your dad like that. It's not right. Besides, you've talked to him on the phone in the past."

Sam squirmed under her gaze. "I know."

"Why not now?"

He stabbed pieces of his salmon, not looking at her.

She pushed her food around with her fork, still watching him. "When he calls, does he say things that upset you?"

"No."

She ducked her head to catch his gaze. "I need you to talk to me here, okay? Tell me what's goin' on."

"When we talk on the phone," Sam said, "I always feel bad later."

She cocked her head, her eyes full of questions. "Why?"

"I don't want him to think everythin's right between us when it isn't."

She still looked puzzled, and he struggled with how to tell his mom about how awkward the situation was for him to talk about what was bothering him. As was his nature, his dad didn't talk much about these kinds of things, and Sam supposed he didn't either. Like father, like son.

"When the two of you are on the phone," Mary said, "what do you talk about?"

"I don't know. Football. School."

"You know, you haven't even visited his apartment in Louisville."

"I don't want to. Colgate's home." He hesitated, then blurted, "We're still here—*he's* the one who left."

She folded her arms across her chest. "Our divorce agreement says you're supposed to spend every other weekend with him."

"You signed it—I didn't."

"That's just the way things work, Sam. Sometimes you don't have a choice."

He couldn't hold back his temper. "Yes, I do have a choice—I live in Colgate because it's where I've always lived. He lives in Louisville because he wants to be there. I'm not goin'!"

A moment later she spoke again, her eyes weary. "I'm not gonna make you go see him or talk to him on the phone, okay?" To his surprise, she smirked. "This is bad for me to say—I'm sure it is—but I must admit that I enjoy seein' you give him the cold shoulder. He hasn't treated us very well." She glanced at her plate and tugged on an ear lobe.

Sam wiped his mouth. "May I be excused? I want to go get my bath."

"Hold on a second, Sam. I want to ask you somethin'. Overall, how are you dealin' with the divorce?"

Would you leave me alone?

Her question troubled him because he didn't like to think through how he felt, let alone express his feelings to her.

He shrugged. "Ms. Legg asked me the same thing today."

Her eyes widened. "She asked you about the divorce?"

"Well, not exactly. She asked me how I was doin', but I could tell she meant more than what she was sayin'."

"What did you tell her?"

"That I'm fine." He pushed his bangs back from his eyes.

She shook her head. "I don't believe that. Let's try this. If you could express how you feel about the divorce in one word, what would you say?"

"I don't know, Mom." Sam got up and placed his plate in the sink. "I don't want to do this."

She rose and stood at his back, a gentle hand on his shoulder. "C'mon, Sam. Talk to me. How would you say that you feel—angry, sad, glad?"

He turned to face her. "Definitely not glad."

"Then what?"

Sam hesitated, annoyed that she was forcing him to go through this mental exercise. The truth was, he had done everything he could to avoid thinking about the divorce, and now she expected him to focus on the one thing he hated to dwell on. His gaze dropped to the floor, then rose back to her face.

"Cheated," he said.

Mary nodded. She was fingering the naked spot on her finger, where her wedding band had once been.

"Promise me—" she said. "Promise me you'll always stay with me, that you'll never leave me here alone, even if your dad begs you to move to Louisville."

"I'll never leave, Mom. I'm not movin' to Louisville, okay?"

"You're my knight in shinin' armor—you know that?"

He returned her smile.

"One more thing, Sam," she said. "Did you ever find your ring?"

Last summer before the divorce, Sam's dad gave him a ring when they were vacationing at Myrtle Beach, South Carolina. The Crays had driven to Charleston and toured the World War II aircraft carrier *USS Yorktown*. Sam learned that the ship, severely damaged in the Battle of the Coral Sea, was expected to be out of commission for three months. But the *Yorktown* miraculously fought in the crucial Battle of Midway after a quick seventy-two-hour repair in dry dock.

Purchased from the ship's gift shop, the steel ring bore a raised engraving of the aircraft carrier. The ring was special to Sam because that trip to South Carolina had been their last family vacation before the divorce. But during their move to Dixie Avenue, the ring had somehow been lost.

Sam hung his head. The thought of the missing ring depressed him. "I don't know where that ring is, and I've searched everywhere for it."

"I've looked, too," she said. "But don't worry—it'll show up."

PART TWO

THE MOVIES

CHAPTER 14

Wednesday, June 4, 1975

(The next day)

The morning sunlight streamed through the upstairs bedroom window, landing squarely on Sam's bed. The sun brought stifling heat and made sleep uncomfortable. Sam stirred. He slept long and soundly. He rubbed his eye with the back of his hand, yawned, and peered out the window at the bright sky. Then he remembered. *This is the first full day of summer!*

He sat up and glanced at this clock. It was just after 10:00 A.M. Why was the house so quiet?

Then he remembered that his mom had left for work two hours earlier. He slipped out of bed. Once downstairs, he poured himself a bowl of Captain Crunch cereal and noticed his mom left him a list of chores on the counter.

Sam frowned. *Oh, well. I guess I'm not free from all responsibilities.*

He took his bowl to the den and turned on the Zenith® Chromocolor TV, which was as large as a small hippo. Like all families in Kidron County, they received four channels from their antennae—three from Louisville and one from Bowling Green. After the farm report, he watched *Happy Days* and *Laverne and Shirley*, chuckling through the funny parts.

He decided to get dressed and returned to his bedroom, which was only half the size of his bedroom in Kidron Heights. He looked around.

Where is that missing ring? He wondered if he might find it in one of the two unopened boxes in the corner, so he took a look.

Inside the first box, he found his collection of G.I. Joe army men, his Evel Knievel action figure, and his Stretch Armstrong, a muscle-man action figure filled with a syrup-like gel and covered with extra-thick rubber skin.

He smiled. *I guess I'm too old to be playin' with these toys, but I can't help it—I still love 'em.*

He moved the toys and a coffee-stained map of Charleston, South Carolina, to a shelf inside his closet, where a previous occupant had left a child's crude drawing of a dragon on the wall.

In the second box, Sam found a leather-bound toiletry case his granddad, his mom's father, had given him before he died. Inside it, he found his granddad's steel razor, a pocket watch on a fob chain, an assortment of cufflinks, and a pocketknife. On the knife, a Confederate soldier saluted in front of an exploding cannon.

Sam removed his collection of Major League baseball cards and NFL cards. He found two plastic models he and his dad had assembled together—a Ford Mustang and a Chevrolet Corvette. Sam placed the models on a shelf above his desk and the sports cards in the drawer of his bedside table. When he peered into the bottom of the box, his heart lifted at the sight of a cloth bag lying inside his replica of a Davy Crockett coonskin cap.

Hey, maybe I left my ring in there.

But when he poured the bag's contents onto his bed, his heart sank. He saw only marbles and a few miniature batting helmets.

Where's that stinkin' ring?

Sam crossed the hall to use the toilet. The bathroom didn't have a shower, but an antique tub stood along the far wall. Sam believed taking baths was for girls, and the tub had been his only complaint to his mom when they had moved in. He and his mom attempted to install a shower wand on the tub faucet, along with metal rods and a curtain for its use as a shower. But the wand leaked and the metal rod broke while Sam showered with it for the first time, snapping sharply against his hip. Sam had since resigned himself to being an adolescent boy who took baths.

Sam knew his mom wouldn't be happy if he didn't straighten his room, so he put it in order before pulling on a tank top from the clothesbasket on his bedroom floor and heading downstairs.

He sauntered into the kitchen, noticing that he left the half-full milk jug on the counter. He took a long swig before returning it to the refrigerator. Then he grabbed the chore list and sauntered outside through the den and the back sliding-glass doors.

He stood in the backyard, momentarily blinded by the sun, and read through the chore list with a frown.

Sam glanced at the empty carport, where his mom parked her mint-green Chrysler Cordoba. It had bald tires, protruding weather stripping, and a hole in the driver's door where she hit a fire hydrant. A real dump of a car.

He found the broom in the storage area under the house and began sweeping the front sidewalk, whistling James Taylor's "Fire and Rain" as he worked. Maybe he'd look for the ring again later. It had to be here somewhere.

Next door, Ray Bedford sat on a rusting glider on his screened-in porch and read the newspaper. Up at daybreak as usual, he'd already read the Louisville *Courier-Journal* and was now halfway through the local *Colgate Herald-News.*

"Don't forget," Coach Bedford hollered toward the living room, where Mrs. Bedford and Meredith were finishing a jigsaw puzzle they began the night before. "You signed up to provide three pies for the Lions Club fund-raiser. They need to be at the school by two."

"Far from good," Mrs. Bedford said in an irritated tone.

"We won't forget!" Meredith said.

Coach Bedford detected a blur of movement out of the corner of his eye and glanced out the window. Sam was sweeping the sidewalk next door.

Meredith appeared. "Do you have the comics page?"

He handed it to her, his gaze still fixed out the window.

"What's so interesting?" She followed his eyes and smirked. "Oh, let me guess—you like things run a certain way, and poor Sam isn't measuring up to your standards."

Coach Bedford scowled at her. "If it had been up to me, I would have preferred that the Crays lived somewhere else."

"You think you're the mayor of Dixie Avenue, don't you?"

He ignored her. "It's time I had a talk with that boy."

CHAPTER 15

Hot and sweaty, Sam was about to go inside for a glass of cold water when he heard someone call his name from the direction of the Bedford house. He turned and noticed Coach Bedford watching him from the screened-in porch.

"Hey, Cray!" Coach Bedford said with the wave of his hand. "Come over here for a minute."

Sam set the broom down and crossed the lawn toward the screened-in porch.

"Come on in." Hands on his hips, Coach Bedford stood just inside the screen door. "Be quick—we don't want all the flies gettin' in."

Sam entered and quickly closed the door behind him. Coach Bedford reached to shake Sam's hand. Sam tried to return his strong grip.

Coach Bedford turned and sank into the glider. "Have a seat, Sam." He motioned to two wicker chairs stationed beside the front door.

Sam accepted the wicker chair farthest from Coach Bedford. Despite the screens, the porch smelled musty—probably from the old newspapers stacked beside the glider.

Coach Bedford clutched a green flyswatter on his lap. On the table in front of him lay an open copy of William Archibald Dunning's *Essays on the Civil War and Reconstruction*. A metal letter opener bearing an insignia of the Confederate flag lay on an open page.

On the table in the corner, a small radio broadcast news from 84-WHAS in Louisville. The volume had been turned down, and Sam could hear only distant, indistinct voices.

Meredith poked her head into the porch and smiled. "Hey, Sam."

"Hey, Meredith."

With the dismissive wave of a hand, Coach Bedford motioned Meredith away. Then he turned toward Sam and stared him down, still clutching the flyswatter as if Sam were a fly and he intended to use it on Sam's head. Sam tensed.

"Sam, there are two things I want to talk to you about. First, we keep clean yards on this street. The yards don't have to be fancy, but they do need to be neat and clean."

He paused as if to make sure Sam was listening.

Sam nodded. *Clean and neat. Got it.*

"Listen, I know your dad isn't livin' with you all, and your mom's busy workin' at the grocery store. So that leaves you. Do you think you're gonna be able to handle that yard of yours all by yourself?"

Sam nodded. "Yes, sir."

"And keep it neat and clean?"

What? He doesn't think I can keep up with my own lawn? Determination layered Sam's voice. "Yes, sir."

"Well, I sure hope so. I won't tolerate an eyesore on our street, especially one next door to me, understand? I'm gonna hold you to what you just said, Cray. And your yard needs some work."

Sam didn't blink. "I understand."

"Second, we keep a quiet street. We prefer quiet mornin's and quiet evenin's around here. No loud music and no kids runnin' around unsupervised."

"Yes, sir."

"Do you think you can keep things down at your place? Keep those friends of yours in line?"

"Yes, sir."

"Good." Coach Bedford reached over and slapped Sam on the leg—a little too hard. Sam's leg was still stinging when the coach said, "I'm glad we've got that taken care of. Now, let's talk a little football, shall we?" Amusement colored his gaze. He set the flyswatter down and leaned back.

Sam had work to do, but he didn't want to be rude. He felt himself relax a bit.

"Don't you just love football, Sam?"

"Yes, sir. I like football a lot."

"But do you *love* it?" Coach Bedford's black eyes blazed with zeal. "I *love* football—I can't get enough of it. The sport's like life. It's the only sport where you can get knocked on your can, and that's just part of the game. You gotta decide if you're gonna get back up and fight for your life on the next play. It's not a contact sport—it's a collision sport."

Sam nodded. The coach's speech reminded him of a locker-room pep talk.

"I know you played part of last season as quarterback for the seventh-grade team."

"Yes, sir, after Brent Simms got hurt."

Coach Bedford's forehead wrinkled in concentration. "He broke his arm, didn't he?"

"Yeah, in our second game of the season, so I finished the season as quarterback."

"You've got a good arm—like your daddy's when he played for Colgate."

Sam's heart swelled with pride, but he gave a self-deprecating shrug. "Thanks."

Coach Bedford's eyes fixed on Sam. "I was watchin', and I saw what you can do. You earned your spurs in those games. I expect you to play quarterback next year for the eighth-grade team."

"Thank you." Sam blinked in surprise, his face warming under Coach Bedford's gaze. Maybe the coach liked him better than he thought.

"To be honest, you're better than Brent Simms," Coach Bedford went on. "I like a sure-handed and surefooted quarterback." He shook his head, displeased. "Brent throws erratically and runs like he's walkin' on eggs."

Sam wanted to say that he didn't enjoy playing quarterback, that it made him nervous. But he remained silent.

"Coach Hicks learned somethin' last season that I've known all my life. He first tried to replace that Simms boy with Dewayne Webb and learned the hard way that you can't be a championship team with a black as your quarterback. The quarterback is a leadership role, and it's gotta be reserved for those who can lead."

"Yes, sir," Sam said, though the coach's words puzzled him.

"That Webb kid didn't work out as quarterback, did he?"

"I guess not. Coach Hicks said he didn't know the plays well enough."

Coach Bedford chuckled, a secretive look in his eyes. "My observations confirm that they don't have the intelligence to play quarterback. They're just too feebleminded. And, between you and me, blacks don't perform well under pressure. Sure, they excel at runnin' back and wide receiver, but they don't have the poise to lead the offense."

Sam folded and unfolded his hands.

"Now, don't get me wrong," Coach Bedford said as if sensing Sam's disapproval. "I'm sure glad we've got our share of blacks in Colgate. We wouldn't have had the wonderful success we've had over the last few years at Colgate Junior High without them. We were good before we integrated, but now with the blacks from Booker T. Washington, we're the best around."

The disturbing monologue was running long. Sam began to get up. "I guess I'd better get back to—"

The coach held out his hand. "Now, wait—I'm not quite done here."

Sam sat back down.

"We're talkin' football right now, but some of what I'm sayin' applies to life in general too." Coach Bedford's expression was smug. "Runnin' a football team is similar to runnin' a town. What folks in Colgate don't know is that it takes people like me to keep our citizens in the right positions so we can have the kind of town we want. We gotta know where to draw the line. My dad understood that and I understand it. Do you get what I'm sayin', Cray?"

Sam nodded, but the speech puzzled him. Why was Coach Bedford telling him all this? Coach Bedford's eyes were like black holes, and Sam couldn't get away.

"You're a bright boy, and you've had a full year with 'em at Colgate Junior High. You know how they are with their unpolished manners, loud music, and uncontrolled urges—and most of them without a daddy around. But that's the problem. We all know it's the father's responsibility to set his son on the right road at the beginnin' of manhood."

Coach Bedford paused. "This is all off the record, of course, but that's part of my job at the school now that we've integrated. Some people think I'm old school—persnickety about how things should be—but that's what I do. I keep 'em in line, and then things stay the way they should. You get that, don't ya?"

Sam gave the coach another feeble nod. *How do I get out of here? Should I just stand up and walk out?*

"You know we've got written laws here in Colgate, but we also have a few unwritten ones—town traditions, if you will. The next thing for 'em is on the social front, and that's where the shoe pinches. I'll be blunt—the families in this town don't want their daughters dating darkies. Just the thought is repugnant to them. They don't want to see this town fall to that level of degradation, and the women look to us for protection."

Coach Bedford paused for a breath and continued, using his hands for big gestures. "I see it more and more at school. It's not enough that we pay 'em welfare and let 'em go to school with us. Now they want to be treated like us without ever earnin' that right. All this talk of equal rights for colored people is just plain silly."

He shook his head, spread his hands. "What about *our* rights? What about rights for Southerners? We don't have anybody payin' for *our* illegitimate births. The need is for us Southerners to protect our heritage and culture. If we don't, it's gonna be too late."

Sam rose. "Excuse me, Coach Bedford, but I really need to get back to my chores."

Coach Bedford held out his hand for Sam to sit back down. "I know you do, Sam, but I'm not done here."

Sam returned to his seat.

"You need to understand this—we're fightin' the idealists, the liberal crusaders, the ones who live neatly at their colleges and in their legislative assemblies and don't really know the coloreds like we do. It's convenient for them to dream about things from their ivory towers." He thrust his face forward, eyes locked on Sam's. "That's a luxury I don't have, Sam. I'm in the trenches, guardin' our way of life. It's the local institutions that matter most. Do you think they come to our school ready to fit in with our society? No way!"

He slammed his right fist into his left hand, his face reddening with passion. "We have to train 'em to adopt our traditions. Why, they can hardly speak English when they start school. Like my dad before me, I work to protect our way of life as best I can in this day and age. Sam, you need to remember that we're all leavin' a legacy behind us."

Just when Sam wondered how much more of this sermon he could take, Mrs. Bedford came to his rescue. She appeared on the porch with a smile. Her thin hair and frail build made Sam wonder if the next strong wind might blow her away.

"Far from good," she said in warm greeting.

"Hello, Mrs. Bedford." The interruption relieved Sam, and he let his shoulders drop.

She turned to Coach Bedford. "Far from good. Boy has things to do—far from good—this mornin'."

Anger rippled across Coach Bedford's face. "Would you go back in the house and stop botherin' us? You and Meredith need to get those pies ready anyway." He waved a hand as if shooing her away.

Mrs. Bedford turned and retreated into the house.

"You know, the blacks should thank the whites." Coach Bedford leaned toward Sam, and his speech continued as if it had never been interrupted. "It was the whites that bred 'em for strength to work the land. That's why they're physically superior. Over many generations, your average field hand benefited from this selective breedin'. Even though that's in the past, we can still take advantage of the smart breedin' to put the best athletes on the gridiron.

"You see, Sam," Coach Bedford continued. "I know I'm not the most popular person at the school. Some coaches are soft—they've got a need to be liked. In the end, though, players don't like a soft coach. They see him as a coward. Players don't mind a coach who's hard on 'em, even one who mistreats them, as long as they win ballgames. A sure recipe for disaster is bein' soft and losin' games. I don't care if I'm liked as long as I'm respected. Remember, Sam, fear is always the best motivator."

Sam stood again to leave. "I'm sorry, Coach, but I really need to go."

Coach Bedford rose and nodded. "Okay, I think we understand each other about this neighbor stuff, don't we?" He winked at Sam as if the conversation was their little secret.

"Yes, sir." Sam turned toward the door, relieved to be leaving. He opened the screen door.

"Has your mom and dad's divorce been finalized?" Coach Bedford said.

Oh, no. Sam didn't want to hear another speech, especially about this topic. He descended the steps to the sidewalk and turned. "Yes, sir."

"I hear your dad's livin' in Louisville."

"It's just me and my mom now."

Coach Bedford grimaced, as if he were more concerned than Sam expected. "That's a shame, son. A real shame."

CHAPTER 16

S am finished with his chores around noon and took the short walk to the Colgate public square. The largest in the state, the town square offered ample parking slots inside and outside the square for the downtown businesses.

In the center of the square stood the three-story, redbrick courthouse, one of three that had served Kidron County. Confederate General Hylan Lyon had burned the first in 1864 because the Union Army occupied it. After the Civil War, the county had built the second courthouse with its front to the south and its back to the north, but it burned in 1922. The county had completed the third and present courthouse, which also faced south, in 1923.

The well-kept and brightly painted cast-iron facades of the downtown businesses surrounded the square. Colgate football bumper stickers adorned parked cars and trucks.

Sam entered the square from the north. To his left and across the street stood Marc Goldman's jewelry store. The headquarters of the Kidron County Rural Electric Cooperative sat in the northeast corner. Beside it stood the Colgate National Bank, which Frank and Jesse James had robbed after the Civil War. Behind the bank stood Colgate's water tower with the words "Colgate Colonels" painted on its side.

Sam turned right and passed Bailey's Pool Hall and Jack Thompson's Barber Shop. He paused to peer into the window of Hagan's Clothing Store, where dress clothes were displayed alongside Colgate football memorabilia. In Kidron Heights, the Crays had lived next door to Burt

Hagan and his family. His building here—four stories high—was the tallest in the county.

Sam crossed the street again and passed Corbett's Hardware Store and the Good-N-Handy. His mom was probably hard at work, so he decided not to disturb her. He paused at Jack "Hog" Allen's sporting goods store and peered into the window. His mom wouldn't buy a pair of tennis shoes for Sam unless Hog Allen personally fitted them and examined Sam as he gave the shoes a test walk.

Dominating the southwest corner of the square was the Commonwealth Theater, the only movie theater in Kidron County. An iridescent marquee, pulsing yellow, red, and green lights above the entrance, announced that *Jaws* was currently playing. Dr. Louis Manfred, the theater's owner, served as a deacon at the Kidron Valley Church. A new movie arrived every two to three weeks, and Dr. Manfred allowed only G- or PG-rated movies to be shown.

After he passed the Kidron County Bank & Trust, Sam reached his destination, the Kidron County Public Library. Above the entryway, the Kidron County Historical Society had affixed a black arrow, which pointed to a Civil War cannonball embedded in the building's brick exterior.

In 1863, Colonel John Hunt Morgan's Confederate troops had taken control of Colgate Hill during "The Christmas Raid of 1862–1863." Colonel Morgan's troops initiated cannon fire at the Union troops in the square, and one cannonball crashed into the library's brick façade but failed to explode. A reminder of the town's struggles during the Civil War, the cannonball garnered much attention from visitors.

Though the town was proud of this tangible connection to its past, the embedded cannonball always made Sam feel uneasy. The historical marker said the cannonball was a dud, but how did anyone really know?

Did they take the cannonball out and examine it? Maybe it's waitin' to go off when we least expect it. What if a sudden thunderstorm or a heavy truck circlin' the square triggers an explosion?

Sam hesitated before entering the library. He adored the library and loved to read, but he didn't like to broadcast this interest to certain friends.

He opened the swinging glass door and crossed the library's threshold. The place was quiet and still on a Wednesday morning. Near the reference desk, Meredith Bedford sat at a table, reading an issue of *National Geographic*®. Her hair shimmered under bright florescent lights, and she chewed on a pencil.

Sam's mouth turned dry at the sight of her. He'd become more aware of her presence during the past school year. Whenever he stole a glance her direction, her returning smile always made his heart skip a beat.

Sam wasn't surprised to see her here. The rumor was that two bookshelves in her bedroom were stacked with books from floor to ceiling. She'd told him once that the world of books allowed her to escape her home and Colgate. He could understand her wanting to escape her dad and brother.

Meredith glanced up at his approach and smiled. "Hey again," she whispered.

"Hey." He mustered his courage. "What are you readin'?"

She showed him the cover. "A really interesting article about endangered pandas in China."

"I think you like reading more than anyone I know. You're probably the smartest girl in our school."

"I love to read. It exposes me to viewpoints that are different than anything I'll get around this town. It makes me a true cosmopolitan citizen. At least it does in my imagination, before I move away from this town, which I intend to do as soon as I can."

Sam had no idea what the word "cosmopolitan" meant, but he didn't want to appear stupid by asking her to explain.

"I want to warn you," she said without taking a breath, "that it's not going to be easy livin' next door to the Bedford clan. We can be—how do I put it?—hard to get along with."

"I think I get the picture. This mornin' your dad gave me the ground rules for livin' on Dixie Avenue."

She rolled her eyes. "The Gospel of Ray Bedford. I bet that was an enjoyable experience. Let me guess—he covered neatness, self-discipline, and somehow ended up talkin' about football."

"You nailed it." Sam grinned.

"Scintillating, I'm sure." She leaned her head toward him, her pretty eyes darting around the room as if to ensure they wouldn't be overheard. "My dad's so set in his ways—he tries to control *everything*."

"Does he try to control you like that too?" He loved the way her eyes lit up when she smiled at him, like she did now.

"Especially me."

"What would he want to change about you? You're the perfect daughter."

Her smile faded. "He likes to pick my friends for me."

"Your boyfriends, you mean."

"Girlfriends, boyfriends—you name it."

"I heard how mad he got when you and Dewayne started datin' last fall."

She shook her head. "But that's just the thing—Dewayne and I have never dated."

"Oh, I thought—"

"Yeah, you and a lot of other people. No, we've never dated." She shrugged and smiled again as if amused. "Dewayne's just a friend who makes me laugh."

"But he doesn't make your dad laugh."

"Uh, no. When Dewayne talks to me at school, it pushes all of my dad's buttons. To be honest, he's petrified that I'm going to fall in love with a black boy."

Sam didn't know what to say to that.

"Well, what about you?" she said. "Got your sights on anybody this summer?"

Sam's face warmed under her gaze. He shifted his weight from one foot to the other. "No, not me. I've got my work cut out for me just keepin' my lawn clean and neat over on Dixie Avenue."

"Oh, please." She rolled her eyes. "Don't let my dad get to you."

"What about you? Got your sights on anybody?" *If Dewayne's really just a friend as you say.*

She glanced down at the *National Geographic*®. "Well, I do have my eye on this one guy."

Sam toed the carpet with his tennis shoe and pushed his hands further into his pockets. "Anybody I know?"

Meredith was opening her mouth to reply when Monica Greenwell, the librarian, rushed toward them with the speed of a freight train. A bespectacled, middle-aged woman with frosted hair and a welcoming manner, she carried a book about photography and a pair of scissors in one hand. In her other she held various clippings.

"Hi, Sam! Hi Meridtih!" Mrs. Greenwell said at full volume.

"Hello, Mrs. Greenwell," they said.

"Whatever you do, young man, don't go into photography." She displayed the book cover for him to see before lowering her voice to a discreet whisper. "I found several *indecent* photos in here, but they're gone now, no longer a snare for innocent eyes, thanks to my trusty scissors."

Sam didn't know how Meredith did it, but somehow she managed not to burst out laughing. She pasted on a serious expression and shook her head as if she was just as incensed as Mrs. Greenwell was.

Mrs. Greenwell's green eyes twinkled at Sam. "Are you ready for your first book of the summer, Sam? We've got some new mysteries at the front desk. In fact, I ordered a few with you in mind. Why don't you check them out?"

"I will on my way," Sam said. "Thanks for letting me know."

As Mrs. Greenwell marched away, he whispered to Meredith, "She's so loud."

"I know." Meredith smiled, displaying a set of even, perfect teeth.

"I always feel like I should ask her to lower her voice—"

"—and remind her that this is a library," Meredith finished.

They laughed. "Well, welcome to our street," Meredith said.

"You were gettin' ready to tell me—"

"No I wasn't. And just ignore my dad—and my brother too, by the way. They're stuck somewhere between ages six and seven on an emotional maturity level."

"I'll try to remember that." He paused. "Interested in any of those mystery books?"

She shook her head. "No. I like books about wildlife and nature. As for fiction, my current tastes are Charles Dickens and Jane Austen. Just between you and me, I spend as much time reading books in my room as possible. Then I won't have to spend so much time with my family."

She hung her head. "I love my mom's company, but I don't like being with my dad or brother. I love them … I guess … but I just don't enjoy being around them. As for books, I simply prefer the interesting dialogue in a book by an intelligent author to the banal conversation of most of my classmates." She stopped herself. "You're excluded, of course, Sam."

He just smiled and nodded. *Banal?* He needed to look up that word too.

Meredith was definitely her own person. It was true that she didn't fit in with most girls her age. Sam didn't think she disliked them, but the obvious fact was that she didn't seem to enjoy their company.

Her talkativeness surprised him. At school most kids thought Meredith was shy, but he wondered if her apparent shyness was just a ruse. Maybe Meredith was only quiet by choice; he couldn't imagine her being intimidated by anyone at school or really anywhere else, either.

"Hey, Sam, if you're bored on Saturday let me know. I volunteer at the pound every Saturday."

"Oh, yeah?"

She nodded. "We started an adoption program for stray dogs and cats and could really use more help."

"What can I do?"

"You can help distribute our printed posters to local businesses and schools. The posters have helped reduce the number of dogs and animals they've had to put down by one third." She shook her head in disgust. "Can you believe it? They used to shoot dogs and cats after five days, but thankfully that's changed now."

She explained how she and other volunteers had applied for assistance from the Humane Society of Louisville. In turn, the county had acquired the drugs and training necessary to euthanize the animals, instead of shooting them with a rifle behind the county dog pound.

After saying good-bye, Sam perused the new mystery novels Mrs. Greenwell had referred to. He'd always enjoyed mysteries and biographies. In the third grade he'd read *Ghost Town Treasure* by Clyde Robert Bulla, one of his favorite books. He'd read the complete Boxcar Children series by Gertrude Chandler Warner and the Great Brain books by John D. Fitzgerald and Mercer Mayer. He'd also read Eventide Elementary School's full set of Random House biographies of famous Americans, including George Washington, Thomas Jefferson, Ben Franklin, Abraham Lincoln, Franklin D. Roosevelt, Babe Ruth, and Thomas Edison.

"Oh, you found those new mysteries, I see," said Mrs. Greenwell, smiling at him over the counter.

"Yes, ma'am."

"I heard about that reading award you won at Eventide Elementary." Mrs. Greenwell's voice echoed across the room, and Sam winced. "Weren't you declared the best reader in the school?"

"Uh, I guess so."

"I heard you read more books than any other student in the sixth grade."

Sam grimaced. *That was true, but I also have the distinction of being the only boy to ever to win the award.*

With that peculiarity, Sam had decided to keep the award a secret, but Mrs. Greenwell wasn't helping matters.

Maybe if I grabbed a book and got out of here, she'd stop broadcasting my accomplishment to the world.

"That's right," he said, sliding a book across to her for check out.

He blasted out of the building as quickly as he could, hopefully before any of his friends happened to pass by and see him inside. He strolled toward the square and found an empty park bench near the courthouse steps to read. He'd just gotten comfortable when he heard a cheerful voice behind him.

"What's up, Sam?"

Sam turned in time to see Bates and Dewayne sauntering toward him across the courthouse lawn. He wondered if Bates was still mad at him after Ms. Regina's talk at Nick's house.

"Hey, Bates. What's up, Dewayne?"

Both boys carried fishing poles, and Dewayne held a plastic carton of night crawlers; he removed the lid so Sam could see them writhing around inside.

"You headin' over to the reservoir?" Sam asked.

Dewayne nodded. "Gonna land the big one today."

"Good luck."

Something shiny poked out of Bates' shirt pocket. "What's that?"

"My harmonica."

"Can you play it?"

Bates shrugged. "I'm still learnin'. I do all right on a few songs, I guess."

Sam was glad that Bates didn't appear to be mad at him anymore. "I couldn't hum a tune to save my life."

Dewayne shook his head. "Me neither."

"My mom's a natural," Bates said with pride. "She can't read music, but she can play anything on the piano after hearin' it only once."

Sam squinted up at Bates. "I'd love to be able to do that."

"I'm learnin' to play the piano too. She's teachin' me."

"Who would have guessed that our class' best athlete was a buddin' musician?" Sam shook his head.

"It's more fun than football sometimes," Bates said.

"Don't let Coach Bedford hear that," Sam said. "He gave me his football-is-like-life speech this mornin'."

"God must have a plan for you, Cray, puttin' you next door to him," Dewayne said. "You must need punishment."

They chuckled.

"Well, we'd better go," Bates said.

"I was thinkin' about goin' to see *Jaws* tonight." Sam jerked his thumb toward the theater marquee across the square. "Do y'all wanna come?"

"Maybe," Dewayne said.

"I can ask when I get home," Bates said. "I'll call ya later. Well, see ya." As Bates and Dewayne began walking away, Bates played his harmonica.

Sam smiled. *He's pretty good.*

He read in the public square for an hour, trading his bench for the trunk of a vast oak, where he rested his back. Then hunger pains prompted him to return home. A chorus of bells jingled from the Kidron Valley Church as he strolled up Main Street toward his house. He was about to turn the corner onto Dixie Avenue when a recognizable voice made him freeze.

Ahead, Larry Bedford was hogging the sidewalk with two of his lackeys from the varsity football team. Larry spotted Sam and sneered.

CHAPTER 17

Both of Larry's lackeys were linemen, square jawed with thick necks, bulging muscles, and dimwitted eyes. Larry surveyed Sam from top to bottom. He swiveled his eyes to his left and right before spitting on the sidewalk in Sam's path. Sam stopped just in time.

One of the goons grinned, revealing small, yellow teeth like a possum's, but never said a word. The other lackey wore a grimy, maroon headband. He folded muscular arms across his chest, a scowl on his lips.

"Where ya been, loser?" Larry's unwashed hair glistened on his forehead. He scratched an armpit, his smile self-aware.

"Nowhere." Sam tensed but held his ground.

"Whatcha got there?"

One of the goons grabbed the mystery novel from under Sam's arm and glanced at the cover before handing it to Larry. Sam gritted his teeth, determined to wait it out.

"A book?" Larry studied the book's cover and frowned at Sam. "Haven't you heard? School's out. Are you a freak or somethin'? Only geeks like my sister read during the summer." Larry grinned at his friends for chuckles of affirmation.

"Give me that." Sam reached for the book.

Larry yanked it away from his reach. "I knew it was bad news when I heard you were movin' in next door." He held the novel over Sam's head and above his outstretched hands, muscles bulging from his flexed arms.

"Believe me," Sam said, "Dixie Avenue was not my first choice."

"Let me tell *you* somethin'." Larry took a step closer, veins bulging in his neck. "We're not gonna be friends."

"Fine with me."

Larry stepped even closer and stared Sam down until their noses were almost touching. "If you're smart, you'll remain unheard and unseen around me. Got it?"

Larry's breath stank like something had died. "Sure, whatever you say." Sam wiped sweat off his forehead.

Larry tossed Sam's book into a nearby bush. "Don't be such a pansy."

That's it! Sam rushed Larry and threw both arms around his midsection to tackle him. But it didn't work. With a deft move, Larry dropped Sam to the ground and sat on his chest.

Sam tried to squirm free but couldn't. Larry was too strong and heavy.

Sam groaned in frustration and defiance.

"Now you know, don't you?" Larry said.

"Know what?" Sam said.

"That you made a mistake—that's what." Larry's mouth parted, and a stringy wad of saliva dangled from his lips. It hovered directly over Sam's face.

Sam squirmed and tried to move his head out of the way, but he couldn't.

The warm spittle dripped onto Sam's cheek, and he felt like throwing up. Unable to use his arms, he couldn't wipe it away.

Larry let go and rose to his feet. He stared down at Sam, a smirk on his face. "Next time, Cray, I won't go so easy on you."

Sam scrambled to his feet as Larry and his friends strode away, laughing. Sam flicked the spit off his face with his shirt and retrieved his book from the bush.

He glanced back at their retreating backs, sudden ire rising in his blood. No, he wasn't going to let Larry get away with it.

He stooped, grabbed a handful of pebbles from a driveway, and threw them at Larry. The spray hit Larry's back, and he let out a yell, more in surprise than in actual pain. But by the time he whirled around, Sam was already gone.

Sam ran hard, heart knocking against his ribs, and didn't stop until he reached his house. Inside, he slammed the door behind him and locked it, chest heaving. He scanned the street through the widow, wondering if Larry might come after him. He waited one minute, two, but he saw no evidence of Larry's pursuit. His heart began to slow down.

He'd just tossed his book onto the floor when the phone rang. He went to the hall to answer it. It was Nick.

"You been sleepin' all day?" Nick said.

"No, I was …" He didn't want Nick to know about his trip to the library. "I was out." He glanced out the window. Still no sign of Larry.

"For the entire mornin'? I've called you like five times. We're gettin' a game of football together up at my house at three."

"Okay, I'll be there."

"Don't be late." Nick hung up.

Sam fixed himself a country ham sandwich, the meat and mayonnaise extra thick. He wrote a note to his mom to let her know about the game in case he wasn't there when she came home. Then he took off for Kidron Heights.

The sun was high in the sky as Sam rode his blue bicycle with its long banana seat, wide handlebars, and blue tassels on the grips. A playing card taped to the bike's frame rippled through each tire's spokes for sound effects. Going hands free allowed him to hold his sandwich in one hand and a bottle of Coca-Cola in the other. In less than ten minutes, he reached Kidron Heights subdivision. Thankfully, he encountered neither Larry Bedford nor his lackeys along the way.

Nick had the perfect backyard for football games: the grass was thick, and the lawn was flat and wide. Sam found Nick, Simon, Josh, and some other boys in the hot, sunlit backyard.

"What's up, cabbage head?" Nick asked Sam.

"Hey, Sam," Josh said.

"Hey, Josh," Sam said.

"Hope I don't hurt you today, Sam," Simon said with a devilish grin. He'd tied a green bandana around his head "Since I don't play for the school, you don't often experience my wrath on the gridiron."

Sam just smiled at him.

"We've got nine, ladies," Nick said. "We need one more player for even teams."

"I can play," said Kathy Walker, Nick's fourteen-year-old sister. She stood on the Walkers' second-story deck, where she'd been sunbathing.

"You can't play!" Nick said. "No way."

"Come on, Nick," Simon said. "Let her play. We need one more player."

"Just give me a second." She disappeared into the house.

"She kills me." Nick groaned and shook his head.

Minutes later Kathy appeared in a tight, orange T-shirt and gray sweatpants. She'd drawn two black lines, one under each eye, with mascara.

"I saw this on TV." She gestured to the black lines. She sparkled with enthusiasm and tossed her shoulder-length brunette hair over her shoulders while the boys stared at her, open-mouthed.

"I have a weirdo for a sister," Nick said in a deadpan voice. "I guess we've got no choice. Okay, Kathy, you can play."

The football game began, the sun hot and blistering. Sweat rolled down Sam's forehead and stung his eyes.

Kathy was tougher than anyone expected. On the first drive of the game, she made a catch and stiff-armed Simon for a score. Later, on a kickoff, Nick punted the ball high into the air, and Sam raced down the sideline to tackle whoever caught it. Kathy caught the ball and raced forward.

Sam hadn't expected her to catch the ball. What was he supposed to do? Was he really supposed to tackle Nick's sister?

But Kathy had no qualms about playing hard. She dashed straight toward Sam as if to run him over. At the last minute, he stood his ground and opened his arms in a weak attempt to tackle her.

She slammed into him, and they toppled to the ground with Kathy on top of him.

Seconds seemed to stretch into minutes. Sam puzzled over the strange sensation of her body pressed to his. He felt the rise and fall of her diaphragm as she gasped for breath. He even sensed the beating of her heart. Her face hovered close to his, a playful smirk on her face, as if she were amused to find herself on top of him.

Time sped up. He needed to move. His cheeks flushed, and he glanced away, intoxicating warmth flowing through him. But then the ground thudded with footsteps.

"That was the worst tackle I've ever seen!" Nick's sarcastic tone snapped Sam out of his stupor. "Sam, she ran right over you, you weenie."

Kathy rolled off him. Sam sat up, head spinning.

"That was a pitiful tackle, Sam," Simon said. "Even *I* could have done better than that."

"I slipped." Sam knew his response was lame, but what could he say? He stood and rubbed the sweat off his palms.

Nick and Simon frowned at him, but then continued the game. Two hours later the game broke up, and they finished by gulping down water from the Walkers' garden hose.

"Be here again tomorrow at one," Nick said before everyone went home.

Sam hopped on his bike, but before peddling away, glanced at the Walkers' house, wondering where Kathy was.

Later that night, and several other nights, Sam dreamt about playing this football game—and about tackling Kathy Walker in particular. In this dream he would be in Nick's backyard again. Kathy's shapely figure would rush toward him, with her arms opening toward him and a smile on her face. He would writhe in his bed and wake with a start, flooded in sweat, not knowing at first if he was asleep or awake. In this dream Nick would always be there too, to tell him he had made a pitiful tackle.

CHAPTER 18

When Bates and Dewayne arrived at the Cray home, Sam met them in the driveway and realized something he hadn't noticed before. Dewayne was shorter than he, even though his curly hair made him seem taller.

"Doesn't Meredith Bedford live over there?" Dewayne nodded toward the Bedford house.

Sam nodded. "Yep."

"I think she's a fox," he said.

"Easy, big boy." Bates pressed a hand against Dewayne's chest. "Haven't you made Coach Bedford mad enough? With that kinda talk, he's gonna kill you."

"Forget him!" Dewayne said.

Sam decided to change the subject before Dewayne caused any trouble. "This is gonna be great. Josh saw *Jaws* a few days ago. Said it was the best movie he's ever seen."

They left Sam's house and ambled across the Bedfords' lawn on their way toward the public square.

"Did I tell you boys you could cut through my yard?" a familiar voice echoed from the dark, screened-in porch.

Sam tensed. He'd assumed Coach Bedford wasn't outside. Big mistake.

Sam followed Bates to the sidewalk to get off the grass. Dewayne, however, didn't budge. He faced the porch, hands on his hips. "Bedford, it's not like it's a nice lawn or anything."

The screen door crashed open. Coach Bedford crossed the distance in an instant and thrust a forefinger in Dewayne's face. "You will address me as 'Mr. Bedford' or 'Coach Bedford.'"

Dewayne wagged his head, a mocking tone in his voice. "I ain't gonna call you 'Coach Bedford.' You ain't my coach no more."

Coach Bedford raised his right hand then dropped it, as if thinking better of his actions. "You're right. You couldn't cut it as a player on my team."

Practically nose to nose, Dewayne said, "I don't want to play for you."

Coach Bedford put his hands on his hips, as if he were correcting a player on the football field. "What a waste of talent you are, Webb! Now you've frittered it all away. You're no good to anyone now."

Sam glanced down the street and sighed. *Why did this have to happen now?* "C'mon, Dewayne," he said. "We need to go."

Dewayne ignored him. He folded his arms across his chest. "I'm better off not playin' on a stupid team for a stupid coach."

Fire flared in Coach Bedford's voice. "It's always about *you*, Webb, isn't it? People like you just can't comprehend what it means to sacrifice for a team."

"Remember, Dewayne?" Sam said, hoping to avert a scene. "The movie?"

"You mean sacrifice for you—or the school?" Dewayne said. "Why would I want to sacrifice for a coach or a school that ain't never done nothin' for me?"

Coach Bedford thrust a finger at him again. "You play on a team for the pride of your school."

"What has the school ever done for me?"

Coach Bedford shook his head. "You're hopeless, you know that? The more I'm around you, the more you confirm my suspicions. You're like that brother of yours, a real troublemaker."

Dewayne had been depressed ever since his brother, the only person Dewayne was close to, left town for college last fall.

"The town was glad to send your brother off to whatever liberal school up north took him off our hands," Coach Bedford said.

Dewayne surged forward, fists clenched. "Don't you say nothin' about my brother, old man!"

Sam's eyes cut toward Bates. They should do something. Words were going to turn to blows if something didn't change in a hurry.

"Listen, Webb," Coach Bedford said. "Even though you're never gonna play football for me, you're gonna learn to respect me." His tone dared Dewayne to contradict him. He grabbed Dewayne's chin and turned his head to face him.

Dewayne bristled and knocked his hand away. "Not me. I don't listen to no authority that ain't proven itself to me first—which you ain't."

"Son, you don't want to put your paw in this cage," Coach Bedford said. They stared each other down. "Webb, you're unbridled. Yeah, that's what you are—a colt that needs to be broken."

Dewayne ignored him. "Is Meredith home?"

Coach Bedford's face reddened. "You tryin' to provoke me?"

Dewayne glanced at the house as if he hadn't even heard Coach Bedford. "Not home?" He backed away, his face pinched with defiance. "That's okay. I'll try later."

A long line of people crowded the ticket counter outside the Commonwealth Theater. *Jaws* was playing for the first week in Colgate, and everyone wanted to see it.

After they purchased their tickets, Bates and Dewayne waited in the lobby while Sam bought popcorn and a Coke. Behind them a cardboard cutout of a cartoonish policeman held up his hand, indicating that one should stop; the sign hanging around his neck said, "Balcony Closed." For the first time Sam could remember, the cutout faced the corner, revealing the staircase to the balcony.

"Hey, look!" he said when he rejoined them. "The balcony's open. I've always wanted to sit up there, but it's usually closed."

"You're so white bread, man." Dewayne shook his head. Then in a mocking voice he said, "'I've always wanted to sit in the balcony.'" He rolled his eyes. "Don't you know what the balcony was built for? That's where they used to put the colored folk."

Sam stared at him; he'd never heard this before.

"That's the way Dr. Manfred had things until my brother and the Justice League from Louisville protested back in 1971," Dewayne said. "They encouraged all the brothers and sisters to boycott the theater and picket on Friday and Saturday nights. After two months, the doc closed the balcony and let the colored folk sit downstairs. He said he did it so his staff wouldn't have to clean the balcony, but my brother said that was a bunch of nonsense."

"Yeah," Bates said. "They only open the balcony now when the downstairs is full."

Dewayne grinned at Sam. "They say good things happen to those who wait, but you know what my brother says? Good things happen to those who agitate."

The boys took the stairs to the balcony, where the attendant, dressed in a black suit with a handkerchief and matching tie, met them at the top. The attendant, who'd worked at the theater as long as Sam could remember, directed the boys to three of the last remaining seats in the theater. Sam had never seen the theater so packed.

They sat, and Sam offered his friends some popcorn. Bates took a handful, but Dewayne shook his head. The attendant flashed his light on Sam's tennis shoes, which he'd propped on the seat in front of him, and told him to put them down. Sam obliged with a sigh.

The movie began, and the boys lost themselves in the tale of the shark's attack on a New England town. In the final bloody scene, when the Great White bursts out of the ocean and bites Captain Quint in half, Sam and Dewayne squirmed in their seats, but Bates screamed and threw out his arms. One hand hit Dewayne in the mouth while the other knocked Sam's cup of ice into the lap of the fat woman sitting beside him.

The woman screamed and smacked Sam's head with her hand. This caused Sam to toss his popcorn into the air, sprinkling kernels all over the row. The attendant appeared with his flashlight and blinded the boys in a cone of light.

Sam apologized to the woman for spilling his ice cubes and tried brushing them from her lap, but she knocked his hand away.

Dewayne combed popcorn out of his hair and muttered. "Bates, you scream like a girl."

CHAPTER 19

"Well, he's gone way down in my book," said Lillian Wurtz, Mary Cray's mother and Sam's grandmother. "Some men like your father are solid, some men aren't."

Mary sat in her mother's kitchen and watched her mother pour two cups of herbal tea. A tray of hot, fresh pastries lay between them, and a hint of cinnamon wafted through the air.

"I didn't tell you"—Lillian set the teapot down—"but I always had a sinking suspicion that Dan wasn't made of the right stock."

Mary searched her mother's face.

"If you thought that was true, why didn't you tell me?"

Lillian sipped her tea and shrugged. "Don't get me wrong—he had his positive qualities. He was a good-looking, smart young man. Everybody said he'd be runnin' that plant in a few years, but he snapped. He lost his mind." She shook her head. "I just had a bad feelin' about him from the start."

Mary couldn't shrug off the guilty feeling. "He was miserable, and somehow I didn't know it."

"Oh, pooh! He's shirked his responsibilities and is runnin' around Louisville with that no-good Alex Hedron and doin' Lord knows what."

"Mom, I'm the first to see Dan's faults, but I do think he was unhappy."

"What a shame—you're havin' to go back to work." Lillian shook her head as if this were the ultimate outrage. "He doesn't give you and Sam enough money."

"He doesn't work at the plant anymore. He doesn't make that much money waiting tables."

"Judge Graves should have made him stay on at the plant."

"The judge couldn't make him do that."

"I don't care—he should have. Then you and Sam would still be living in Kidron Heights."

Mary nibbled on her bottom lip. "Mom, we've already gone over this. We just couldn't afford the place."

"You could have if Dan had stayed at the plant—that's my point."

"Well, he didn't, we couldn't stay, and that's the end of it. There's no point in continuing to bring this up." Mary frowned at the pastries, her appetite gone. *Why does she have to dwell on things I have no hope of changing?*

"It's degrading that you had to go back to work at the grocery store—you, who only a year ago were staying at home and spending your free time at the church. Not only were you thrown out of your house—you were thrown into a low-paying, menial job."

"It was the best job I could find!" Mary heard the tremor in her voice. Tears stung her eyes. "I'm so sorry my life doesn't please you."

Lillian placed her hand on top of her daughter's, her tone softening "I'm sorry, Mary. I didn't mean to make you upset. I just get so mad when I think about what that man has done to your life."

Mary grabbed a napkin and dabbed her eyes.

"You're too good for this to happen to you. I can't help it if I get a little worked up about it sometimes. If only your father was alive—he would have straightened that boy out real quick, let me tell you."

Mary realized how much she missed her father, though he'd been dead for five years. A hardworking postal employee, he'd eventually become Colgate's postmaster. She would always see him as a sweet man who was afraid of crossing his wife. He'd worked hard and prided himself in what quiet he could find. He'd enjoyed hunting with the bird dogs he kept out back and had hunted as often as he could. Just being in this house today reminded her of him.

"Well," Lillian said as if reading Mary's thoughts, "let's talk about something else, dear."

"Yes, please. Something happy." Mary eyed the pastries; maybe she'd have one after all.

"Have you heard about the size of the house Mrs. Graves is planning to build in Kidron Heights?"

Mary shook her head. The change in topic flooded her with relief.

"Of course, her husband needs to get reelected first, but Mrs. Graves told Fanny at the beauty shop that after he wins, she's gonna build the biggest house in Kidron County."

After the movie Bates, Dewayne, and Sam used the public bathroom under the courthouse and sat on the courthouse steps, enjoying the mild summer night. They admired the cloudless sky and the way the moon shone down in bright silver hues over the rooftops of downtown businesses. The soft chirp of crickets filled the air, making the evening purr, while the courthouse yard twinkled with the green glow of lightning bugs. Teenagers in cars and trucks cruised the square, filling the air with Motown tunes.

"White people is stupid," Dewayne said, referring to the movie. "The ocean is for fish, and the land is for people. Why's that so hard to understand? You didn't see no brothers goin' out into that ocean, lookin' for no shark."

Bates laughed. "You couldn't have paid me enough money to go out on that boat."

"That was so cool," Sam said, "when he shot the oxygen tank in Jaws' mouth."

"I would've stuffed a hand grenade down his mouth," Dewayne said.

A statue of a mustached Civil War soldier stood on the monument behind Dewayne. The statue, erected in 1923 to honor the proud county's Confederate dead, was an unyielding reminder of a real, century-old conflict in Colgate. Dewayne strolled over to the statue's pedestal and read the words aloud in a mocking tone.

On Fame's eternal camping ground,
Their silent tents are spread.
And glory guards, with solemn round,
The bivouac of the dead.

Dewayne kept his eyes on the statue. "For some reason I don't feel the love for this guy the way I should. What's wrong with me?"

Sam and Bates chuckled. Dewayne spun around to face them like a professor lecturing his students. "Did you know that Kentucky refused to ratify the thirteenth, fourteenth, and fifteenth amendments?"

"Uh, what were those?" Bates scratched his head.

"Only the constitutional amendments that freed the brothers and sisters, made us citizens, and allowed us to vote," Dewayne said.

"Oh, yeah." Bates smiled to Sam. "*Those* amendments."

"Rights we got with no thanks to Kentucky." Sarcasm colored Dewayne's words.

They lapsed into silence, and Dewayne sat back down.

Several silent minutes passed.

Finally, Sam said, "You guys wanna sleep over at my house tonight? We could play board games, and tomorrow mornin' we could play baseball in the square."

"Are you sure it's okay with your mom?" Bates said.

"Sure is. I asked her this afternoon."

"Y'all go ahead," Dewayne said. "I need to run home and ask my aunt. If I can, I'll come by."

"You could call her from my house," Sam said.

"Naw, that's okay. I need to run home." He got up and strolled away.

"They don't have a phone at his aunt's house," Bates said.

Sudden realization spread over Sam's face.

Sam and Bates left the square and ambled up Main Street, passing the county jail, which looked like something out of a medieval tale. Sam admired its black-veined, stone façade; solid steel door; and crisscrossed iron bars. The jailer's house was next door.

A ruckus stopped them in their tracks. A drunk, whimpering between the bars of his cell on the second floor, hollered, "You boys, you gotta help me out. They's not been fair to me. I ain't drunk. Last weekend I wuz really tight on some 'shine, but tonight I ain't. They should at least put me in here when I's really pie faced. I've only had a few sips of Kentucky Colonel tonight. This is a miscarriage of the justice, I tell ya. If anyone knows what drunk is, it's me. I tell ya' I ain't."

The drunk entertained the boys for several minutes until the jailer trudged out of his house and hushed him.

Sam and Bates climbed the stairs to Sam's musty bedroom, and Sam opened a window to let some fresh air in. He lingered, the cool night air refreshing. The gentle breeze tousled the curtains and blew against his face. From outside came other sensations—the chirp of crickets and the scent of magnolia blossoms on the wind.

While Sam enjoyed the breeze, Bates inspected Sam's framed picture of the Thoroughbred horse Secretariat, which had won the 1973 Kentucky Derby. Other framed pictures included a University of Kentucky football poster showing Coach Fran Curci and the 1974 team. Another poster was of the University of Kentucky basketball team's new home, Rupp Arena. On the poster, beside Rupp Arena stood Kentucky's basketball coach Joe B. Hall.

On the desk were model cars and a framed photo of Sam's Little League baseball team. In the photo next to Sam stood his dad, Dan Cray, the team's assistant coach. Bates glanced at a poster from the TV series *Charlie's Angels*, then he noticed a teddy bear on the bed.

He picked up the bear with a grin. "Oh, how cute," he said in a mocking voice. "Sam still sleeps with stuffed animals."

"No, I don't," Sam said. "My mom must have put it there."

Bates grinned. "Yeah, right."

They dove into a game of Monopoly®. Sam was just purchasing Park Avenue when Sam's mom knocked on the door and came in, carrying a tray.

"Here you go, boys." She handed each boy a bowl heaped with chocolate brownies, chocolate ice cream, and chocolate syrup drizzled on top.

"I forgot to tell you." Sam grinned at Bates. "My mom's got a bit of a chocolate problem."

Mary folded her arms across her chest, her lips tugged into a playful smile. "If I do, Sam Cray, I've passed it on to you. I've never seen you turn down one of my desserts."

"No ma'am." Sam shook his head.

"Hey, didn't you say Dewayne Webb was comin' too?" she said.

"He went home to ask his aunt if it was okay," Sam said. "He said he'd drop by if he could come. I guess she must have said no."

"That's too bad." Deep creases appeared across her forehead and she turned to go.

"Thanks, Mom."

"Thanks, Mrs. Cray."

"You're welcome," she said and headed downstairs.

The boys dug in.

Ten minutes later they were back to playing Monopoly when angry voices from the Bedfords' front lawn drifted through the open window.

"Get away from my daughter and out of my yard!"

Through the window drifted the sound of the Bedfords' screen door opening and banging shut.

"Hey, somethin's up," Sam said.

He sprang to his feet and kicked the board game, scattering its pieces. He dashed to the windowsill, where he could clearly see the Bedfords' yard.

Sam gawked at the scene playing out below him. Coach Bedford charged across the lawn toward Dewayne and Meredith. Dewayne clutched a baseball bat with his right hand and held it at his side.

Coach Bedford stabbed Dewayne hard in the chest with two of his fingers, pushing Dewayne back a few steps. Sam had seen Coach Bedford use this method of persuasion in the hallways at school and on the football field, thumping the object of his displeasure in the chest. When he got really mad he would put his index and second finger together, with his thumb behind them, and thump the object of his displeasure in the chest. Once during practice he'd even knocked a player to the ground.

Then, with stunning speed, Sam saw Coach Bedford swing an open hand toward Dewayne. Dewayne raised his arm to protect himself, but he was a split second too late. Coach Bedford slapped Dewayne across the face with his open palm. Before Dewayne could respond, Coach Bedford slapped him again, this time with the back of his hand.

Sam gasped.

Meredith shrieked. Dewayne fell to his knees and dropped the bat.

"Hey, what's going on?" Bates said from across the room, setting the Monopoly pieces back in place.

Sam shushed him and turned back to the window.

Dewayne pulled himself to his feet. He grabbed the bat and gripped it with both hands.

Coach Bedford came at him again, this time with a fist. But Dewayne dodged the blow just in time. He gripped the bat with both hands.

Sam saw what was coming and tensed.

Dewayne swung the bat and smacked the side of Coach Bedford's head. The coach recoiled and crumpled to the ground.

Meredith screamed.

Sam's heart jolted. "Oh, no!"

"What?" Bates raced to the window, but was too late. He hadn't seen what Sam had.

Sam's hands shook. "We need to get down there." He bolted down the steps, only to be met by his mom at the foot of the stairs.

She held up both hands to stop the boys. "Sam, you're not goin' out there. I heard the commotion and called the police."

"Let me take a look." Sam tried to push past her, but she held him back.

"Sam, stop!"

"Please, Mom!"

She ordered them to sit in the living room and wait until the police arrived. But when the telephone rang and Mary got up to get it, Sam seized the opportunity and darted out the back door.

Trees blocked the moon, and Sam could hardly see anything. He took two strides and tripped on his beat-up bike. Back on his feet, he hustled toward a juniper bush, crouched, and peered toward the Bedford house. Meanwhile, the memory of Coach Bedford falling to the ground kept replaying in his mind.

Had Dewayne killed him?

Moonlight broke from the trees, shimmering across the lawn like a ghost. Sam sucked in a quick breath. Coach Bedford lay face up on his front lawn. Meredith knelt beside him, her face in her hands.

Sam rushed to Meredith's side and looked at Coach Bedford. Blood flowed from a nasty gash above his left ear.

Meredith shook his shoulder. "Daddy! Daddy?"

He didn't respond, but Sam saw the rise and fall of his chest.

The screen door opened, and Mrs. Bedford appeared in bare feet, hair tousled. The porch light shadowed half of her dazed face, and the breeze played with her nightgown, which danced about her in ghostly folds.

Meredith wiped her eyes and ran to her mother, putting her arms around her. Mrs. Bedford peered over Meredith's shoulder and saw the blood on her husband's face. Her thin, frail body quivered, and she bit the heel of her hand.

Mrs. Bedford dashed to her husband's side and knelt beside his motionless form. "Far from good. Dear Lord, far from good!"

A police siren wailed in the distance.

CHAPTER 20

Thursday, June 5, 1975

(The next day)

The screen door slammed shut.

"Sam, where's your mother?"

Sam looked up from the living room floor, where he and Bates were finishing a game of cards.

His grandmother, Lillian Wurtz, stood just inside the door with an indignant look on her face. She wore an expensive, black pant suit and a bright red scarf, which covered her perfectly coiffed gray hair. A triple strand of cultured pearls hung around her neck.

She regarded Bates with a cantankerous scowl and pointed at Sam. "I want a word with you in a moment, young man. But first I want to speak to your mother."

Mary appeared from the kitchen, dishtowel in her hand.

Without so much as a hello, Lillian said, "You're lettin' things get out of hand, Mary. That's why somethin' like this happened."

Mary flicked her gaze at the boys then back at her mother. "Mom, why don't you come into the kitchen? I have taken the day off. I'll get you a cup of coffee."

Lillian followed Mary into the kitchen, where Sam and Bates could hear the murmur of concerned voices.

Over the last year, Sam's grandmother had been a steady force in their lives. She visited them more now than she ever had before the divorce, and she'd been helping them financially too. A lifelong member of the Kidron Valley Church, she'd insisted that Mary and Sam continue attending church services.

After ten minutes Mary stepped into the living room. "Sam, could you step into the kitchen for a minute, please?" She gave Bates a forced smile. "He'll be right back. Can I get you anything?"

"No, ma'am," Bates said.

Sam got up and gave Bates a shrug before entering the kitchen.

"Have a seat, Sam," Lillian said from the table in her brassy tone.

Mary sat next to her with her hands clasped submissively in her lap, her chin lowered. Her body language made her look like a little girl next to her mother.

Sam slumped into a chair opposite them.

"Sam, this is a mess you've gotten your mother into." His grandmother's eyes flashed with anger. "What were you thinkin', havin' Bates and that Webb boy over here to your house last night?"

Sam didn't say anything because he knew she didn't really want an answer.

"You should've known there's no good that could come from that. This is the last thing your mother needs to deal with right now. Isn't it enough that your dad has run off and left her? Now that Webb boy has attacked Coach Bedford next door with a baseball bat, and the coach is in the hospital."

"But we don't know what happened yet." Sam's voice sounded small. "How can you say …"

"Be quiet!" Lillian said. "We all know Dewayne's brother, and Dewayne's just like him. They're both troublemakers."

Sam shifted his gaze to his mother, but her eyes were lowered.

Lillian continued in a softer tone, "Sam, you're a good boy, and I know you and your mother have been goin' through a tough time. I've tried to be here for you, but I need to set you straight on a few things."

She glanced at the door leading to the living room and turned back. "It's okay to be friends with them at school but not spend-the-night kind of friends. That's bein' over familiar with them."

Sam swallowed. "But why?"

She rubbed her eyes with her thumb and index finger, then gave him a disapproving frown. "Listen to me—it just is. Everybody has a place, and there's a place for everybody. I know what I'm talkin' about. Do your mother the courtesy of not causin' anymore trouble for her than you already have." She motioned toward the door. "It's time you asked your other friend to go home."

Sam started to speak, but Mary held up her hand. "Please, Sam, maybe Grandma is right. Mrs. Bedford might be home from the hospital soon, and havin' Bates here might upset her—you know, considerin' what happened last night."

"But Bates didn't do anyth—"

"No buts, Sam," Lillian said, her eyes flashing. "Go do it right now—and not another word from you."

Sam rose and hesitated, ambivalent about what he would do next. He recognized the strain on his mother's face and knew he had no choice. He yielded and turned, pushing open the door to the living room. To his surprise, Bates was already waiting at the front door, disappointment flitting across his face.

"Your grandmother wants me to leave, doesn't she?"

"How'd you know? Did you hear her?"

"Boy, you sure are dumb sometimes, Sam. I can read a look. I knew she wasn't happy to see me here the moment she walked in."

"I'm sorry, Bates, but with what happened last night, I guess it would be better—because of Mrs. Bedford comin' home and all—" His voice trailed off, and he wished he knew what to say. "You understand, don't you?"

Bates didn't answer him, eyes downcast. He turned and trudged out the front door without saying another word. The door slammed shut behind him.

PART THREE

THE TRIAL

(TWO MONTHS LATER)

Colgate Herald-News

(The only newspaper in the world dedicated to Kidron County, Kentucky.)

Wednesday, August 13, 1975

Webb to Stand Trial for Second-degree Assault, Wanton Endangerment

COLGATE—Today at 1:00 P.M. at the Kidron County Courthouse, Judge Albert Graves will preside over the trial of minor Dewayne Webb on assault and related charges involving an altercation with Coach Ray Bedford, an assistant principal at Colgate Junior High School. Kidron County Attorney Hank Gabbard will prosecute the case on behalf of the county.

In July, Hank Gabbard asked the court to try Dewayne Webb as an adult, but Judge Graves overruled that motion. Last week, Webb's counsel, Ted Jones, waived the confidentiality of the juvenile hearing, which will now be open to the public. This development pleased the prosecution.

"Sunlight is the best disinfectant," Gabbard said, "and the county is pleased that not only Judge Graves but the whole town will know what happened to Coach Bedford."

CHAPTER 21

"Albert, I can't believe you've put us in this predicament."

Mrs. Graves, a short, round woman with large, grayish-blue eyes and a pious face, played with the lace on her expensive dress and pushed her teacup in circles on its saucer. She carried herself with an air of distinction and was known around town for her egocentric foibles and numerous whims.

"Dear, I can't exactly pick the cases that come before me." With an amused twinkle in his eye, Judge Graves took a bite of his country ham biscuit.

She shook her head. "It's just like you to put everything we've worked so hard for at risk. If you're not firm in how you handle this Webb boy today, you'll anger the whole county. I know you always see the best in everyone, but we can't have that happening today, not with the election only a few months away."

She pushed a plate toward him. "Have some spoon bread, dear. It's very good."

He ignored her offer and took another bite of his biscuit. "This will all be behind us soon."

She spread her hands. "But, dear husband, what will people in this town think of us if you lose the election? What will I tell my family in Lexington? This is simply dreadful."

He sipped his coffee and smiled at her talent for exaggeration. "I think you're making too much of this, darling."

Her doubtful look didn't match his optimistic tone. "No, I am not! With the election this fall, this case could make or break us. It's what everyone is talkin' about, dear. And it's just our luck that the attorney running against you would be low-class Hank Gabbard, the county prosecutor." She frowned. "He's of no account. His daddy was a drunk, and he's as crooked as a snake. I don't know how on earth he became a lawyer to begin with. I suppose he must have bribed somebody."

"Now, now." He reached across the table and patted her hand. "No need to get all worked up."

She sighed, her forehead wrinkled in anxious lines. "But what'll we do if he wins and you lose? You haven't practiced law in five years. You don't have any clients."

Finished with one biscuit, he started on another. "I'm sure I could find work. We wouldn't starve."

"No, we'll not starve. And we are going to have that new house we've dreamed about—and I'll tell you why. Albert, you're going to send that boy away today."

He wiped his mouth, startled by her bluntness. "I need to hear the witnesses and then impartially apply the law—you know that."

She shook her head. "Now you listen to me—you *have to* send him away today. Darling, that's all you need to do. It's very simple. You know you're melancholy. You know that you're prone to the glooms, the dark, heavy ones where you can hardly move. You don't want that to come on you."

She paused for a breath. "He must be sent away—that's all there is to it. Everyone knows he's trouble anyway. He should go to that state home in Kimball County; that place knows how to deal with troublemakers like him. And that poor Mr. Bedford! He works so hard with all those kids up at the school."

She stared at him. "Albert, you must do the right thing. I'm puttin' my foot down, and I don't want to hear another word about it."

Weary of her speech, the judge stared out the window absentmindedly. He pulled out his pocket watch to check the time. Then he continued to open and shut it—open and shut it, open and shut it—eyes down, deep in thought.

"Would you mind stepping into my office, Ms. Cray?" Bert Fink, manager of the Good-N-Handy grocery store, extended his hand to Mary with a wide smile.

In spite of his smile, she fought a sudden spasm of panic. *Have I done something wrong? Is he going to lay me off? What will I do if I lose this job? How could I support Sam and myself?*

Mary stepped away from the cash register, palms moist, and took the small flight of stairs up to Bert's austere, stuffy office. The small room provided just enough space for his desk, his chair, and an additional chair across from him. Revenue charts and employee schedules filled two walls. The remaining glass walls enabled him to monitor the store's employees and customers.

"Please, have a seat." He motioned to the lone chair while chewing on a peppermint. He was overweight and had a comb-over.

She'd never had a problem working with him before. She sat and clasped her moist hands in her lap. "Is there a problem? Did I do something wrong?"

"No, there's not a problem—well, not really. I'll get right to it." Bert drummed his fingers on the desktop, his face apprehensive. "I received an interesting visit yesterday from my supervisor, Jim Marsh. Do you know Mr. Marsh?"

"Of course. He used to be the manager here."

"That's right, he was … until he received a promotion. He still lives here in Colgate, but he's now the district head for the chain."

She jiggled a knee and tried to force herself to be calm. "I'm sorry, but I still don't understand."

"I'm gettin' to it." Bert tapped his coffee-stained teeth with a pencil. "Last night before we closed, Mr. Marsh stopped by, and we talked about the trial of the Webb boy. He's very concerned about Sam's testimony today."

What does Sam's testimony have to do with my job?

"I still don't understand," she said.

"What he basically said is that our business is very competitive." He paused for a breath. "With two other grocery stores in town, it would be unfortunate if one of our employees—or a family member of one of our employees—were to portray someone like Coach Bedford … well … in a negative light."

She couldn't believe what he was implying. "What are you sayin'?"

"I'm not sayin' anything, Mary. I am just relayin' the conversation, for what it's worth. This trial today is all everyone is talkin' about. People around here are followin' it very closely—it's important to them. Everyone is talkin' about the fact that your son is one of the only witnesses to what happened between Coach Bedford and that boy."

That boy. She bit her lower lip. Already people were deciding the outcome of this trial, and Dewayne hadn't even been tried yet.

Bert hesitated before adding, "Mary, Coach Bedford is important to this town. That's why people like Mr. Marsh don't want to see him … well … embarrassed or contradicted."

Mary straightened her spine. "I've told Sam to tell the truth. No one can expect him to do more than that."

"Of course, I'm sure he'll do just fine," he said unconvincingly. He slapped his leg and rose. "Well, I'm sure this will all be behind you soon. Mary, I think you're doin' a terrific job here."

She stood. "That's good to hear because I need this job." She turned to leave.

"But, Mary, bear in mind that Mr. Marsh is in charge of this store …"

She turned, sudden uneasiness mounting.

A pained look crossed Bert's face. "And if he says I need to let you go, then that's what I'll have to do. Let's just pray your boy does the right thing today."

CHAPTER 22

Something startled Sam from deep sleep, and he rubbed his eyes. A noise from somewhere in the house, more than just the creaking of the old place, made his eyes fly open.

What was that? Was it the back door?

His mother was at work, and he was home alone. He tried to focus his eyes, but they were still sticky with sleep. He rose on his elbows and glanced at his alarm clock. 9:23 A.M.

Maybe Mom forgot somethin' and had to come back. That had to be it.

He lay back down and listened. The house was now so quiet it seemed to be holding its breath. But then one of the stairs creaked, and he tensed.

He sat up. "Mom, is that you?"

No response.

We need to start lockin' our doors. Anybody could get in.

In the upstairs hallway a floorboard groaned. His pulse quickened. "Mom?"

Still no answer.

Someone's creepin' down the hallway toward my room.

A prick of sweat dripped down the side of his head and his mind raced.

Should I hide in the closet? No, I should act like I'm asleep.

The footsteps drew closer. Ten feet away. Seven. Three.

Sam was too paralyzed by fear to call for help.

His door opened, and Larry Bedford stood in the doorway, a teasing smile on his face.

Sam let out a surprised yell, his heart pounding. "What are *you* doin' here?"

Larry leaned against the door frame, thrust a finger to his lips. "Shhh."

Larry entered and looked around, his eyes taking everything in. He paused at the poster of *Charlie's Angels* and jabbed a thumb toward it. "Very nice." Then he crossed the room to Sam's bed and looked down at him.

Sam still didn't understand what Larry was doing in his room. He measured the distance between him and the door.

I could try to run if I have to.

"Since we're next-door neighbors and all," Larry said in a low voice, "I figured you wouldn't mind me comin' to pay you a little visit this mornin'."

"Okay." Sam followed Larry with his eyes as Larry sat on the edge of his bed, a faint smile on his lips.

"You're gonna testify today, aren't you?"

"Yeah."

"Well, I just wanted to drop by and encourage you. That's what neighbors do, isn't it, Cray? In fact, close neighbors don't even need to knock, do they?"

"We aren't exactly close, Larry."

"What time do you have to be at the courthouse today?"

Sam's mouth turned dry. "Not until after lunch."

Larry pulled a silver Case pocketknife from his pocket and folded out the three-inch blade. The silver blade flashed in the morning light, and Sam tensed, ready to bolt. But before he could move, Larry pressed the cold blade against his bare chest.

Sam gasped, afraid to move, his arms stiff at his sides. "Hey, what—what're you doin'? Are you out of your mind?"

He began to pull away, but Larry pressed the sharp blade against his skin. Sam winced.

"I wouldn't move if I were you," Larry said, "unless you want to get blood on these sheets."

Sam froze, and Larry lessened the pressure.

Sam breathed hard. His heart pounded like a jackhammer. He fixed frantic eyes on Larry's face.

Larry's smile faded. "Now listen good, neighbor. I've heard things about you that bother me—like you told the prosecutor that you saw and heard everything."

Sweat trickled down Sam's forehead.

Larry kept his voice low, his eyes menacing. The calmness of his voice was chilling. "I don't know what you saw or didn't see the night that coon attacked my dad. I know my dad can get worked up and sometimes say things he shouldn't, especially when he's around punks like Dewayne Webb." Larry shook his head, his eyes locked on Sam's. "But whatever you say at the trial today, you'd better go soft on my dad. You've gotta back his story—understand?"

Sam wished Larry would put the knife away, but he didn't.

"Understand?" Larry repeated, his voice louder.

Sam nodded.

"We all want to see that Webb kid sent away today. Our family wants it, our town wants it, and you should want it too. It's time to be rid of him. He's of no account. He just comes to school to get a free lunch."

Sam didn't respond.

"I want to make sure you're with the program, so here's the story." Larry locked eyes with Sam. "That monkey was in our yard and attacked my dad with a baseball bat for no reason other than that he's a punk. And my dad never even touched him—got it?"

In his mind Sam could see Coach Bedford thumping Dewayne in the chest and slapping him.

Tell him what he wants to hear.

"I'm not exactly sure what—what I saw that night," Sam stammered.

Larry shook his head. "That ain't gonna cut it. Listen to me, Cray. I'll tell you exactly what you're gonna say. You heard that coon yellin' at my dad. You heard my dad talkin' real respectful and polite like, tryin' to calm him down. And then you seen the Webb kid hit my dad with a baseball bat, swingin' at his head like he was goin' for the fence.

131

And what you *didn't* see is my dad layin' a hand on him. That's your testimony. It's simple. You got it?"

"Yeah, I got it." Beads of sweat dripped down Sam's forehead. "What about Meredith? Is she gonna testify too?"

"Meredith's been taken care of. She's not gonna testify."

"Why not? She saw the whole thing."

Larry looked at Sam as if he were stupid. "County Attorney Gabbard and Webb's attorney, Ted Jones, agreed to it. They're honorin' Dad's request not to subpoena her on account that it would be too much for her. Besides, between me and you, we don't trust her. She's got some wild ideas, and she might just lie for that Webb boy."

Sam tried to raise himself up, but Larry applied more pressure to the blade. Sam flinched and lay back down. Apparently, Larry wasn't finished.

"So that just leaves you and Webb. We ain't worried about Webb because nobody's gonna believe him no ways. It'll be my dad's testimony against his, which should be enough. But with your testimony jivin' with Dad's, it'll be a sure thing that kid gets sent away for good. Do you understand me?"

Sam nodded.

Larry's eyes turned hard. "You're to blame for all this, you know. What were you thinkin', havin' him over to spend the night? What're you tryin' to do, friend? Ruin our nice little street?"

Sam glanced away. He couldn't take much more of this.

"Hey, I'm talkin' to you! Pay attention."

Sam's eyes snapped back to Larry's face.

"Look, my dad will go first. Gabbard told my dad that Webb's attorney has already agreed to let you stay in the courtroom when dad testifies. Just listen to what he says. Whatever you saw or heard, it had better be the same story as my dad's. The truth is whatever my dad says it is—you got it?"

"Yeah, I got it."

Larry grinned. "See how easy this is?"

Maybe for you.

Larry closed the blade and rose, slipping the knife back into his pocket. He got up and meandered toward the door. Sam felt his body start to relax but didn't move.

Larry turned. "I knew you were gonna be a pain when you moved in, Cray. And if I haveta come back for another visit, well"—he shook his head—"I won't be so gentle if there's a next time."

Larry left, and his steps creaked on the stairs. Sam waited several minutes before he rose from sweaty sheets. He rubbed the sore spot on his chest.

No doubt he meant every word. It would be foolish to believe otherwise. Sam shook his head and said, "What am I gonna do?"

CHAPTER 23

The Kidron County courtroom was wood paneled and cavernous. In its three-section ceiling, two outside panels angled toward the center panel, where four antique brass chandeliers hung in a straight row from the front of the room to the back. The judge's massive walnut bench, which towered over the rest of the courtroom, had darkened over the years and looked more black than brown.

Two brass lamps rested on the edge of the bench, and two identical lamps sat on the clerk's desk directly below the bench. Portraits of four dead judges in gilded frames hung on panels behind the judge's bench, two on the right side and two on the left. An antique brass lamp burned between each portrait.

Directly behind the bench hung the official seal of the Commonwealth of Kentucky, which depicted a frontiersman and a statesman shaking hands. Surrounding these two men was the state's motto, "United we stand. Divided we fall." Hanging beneath this seal was a map that depicted the Commonwealth of Kentucky when it entered the union in 1792 as the fifteenth state. On the map the state was labeled with its Indian name—"Kentucky, dark and bloody ground."

The afternoon temperature spiked above ninety degrees, and those occupying the gallery were grateful for the air-conditioning. At 1:05 P.M. Judge Graves, wearing his black robe and wide, black necktie, entered the courtroom from the back corridor with his clerk.

Sheriff Micah Brothers whispered, "Judge, we've started turning folks away. Every seat in the gallery is taken."

135

The judge nodded and ascended the bench.

Sheriff Brothers turned to the crowded room and bellowed, "All rise! The court of Kidron County is now in session. All you who have causes to bring come forward, and you shall be heard. May God save the Commonwealth of Kentucky and this honorable court. Your silence is commanded. Gentlemen, remove your hats."

Even if he was only a rotund five-seven, Sheriff Micah Brothers' presence in the courtroom was impressive. In his early sixties, he had eyes like a basset hound, and the right side of his face bore a mulberry-colored birthmark. Though his voice was rich and resonant, his speech was folksy and accented. Judge Graves had always appreciated the respect the sheriff showed all courtroom participants, even criminal defendants.

"Be seated." Judge Graves waved his hand in a downward motion before reaching his chair. He arranged his lanky frame under the bench and surveyed the gallery, certain this was the largest crowd he'd ever seen at one of his trials. He absently fingered the edge of his robe, his gaze roving around the room.

To his left sat beefy Hank Gabbard, the county prosecutor, at a table with clean-shaven, fresh-looking Coach Bedford. Mr. Gabbard wore a crisp, gray suit and freshly polished black shoes. He tapped his pencil on the yellow legal pad before him.

To the judge's right, at the defense table, sat Dewayne Webb, who stared straight ahead, looking at no one. Since the incident in June, Dewayne lived at his aunt's house under the judge's handcrafted house arrest order, which basically instructed him to stay out of public view until the trial.

Beside him was Ted Jones, the county's public defender. Ted Jones was a white-haired man of sixty-five with stooped shoulders, liver spots on his hands, and thick, untamed eyebrows. He wore bright red suspenders, a rumpled seersucker suit, and scuffed brown shoes. Though Ted Jones had an amicable personality, he'd never been successful in his law practice. Forty years ago, he'd stumbled into the legal profession while following two of his fraternity brothers to law school. Now, thirty-seven years after he began his career, he liked to joke that he didn't take himself too seriously; after all, he was just *practicing* law. His vocation afforded him a decent living and ample rounds on a golf course in an adjacent county. Though he wasn't a dishonest man, his career could best be described as altogether complacent.

Judge Graves opened the file in front of him. "*Commonwealth of Kentucky, County of Kidron v. Dewayne Webb*. Indicted for second-degree assault and wanton endangerment in violation of the law of the Commonwealth of Kentucky. I note for the record that I have previously denied the county's motion to have the defendant tried as an adult, and we are proceeding here today under the juvenile code. I note for the record that Mr. Jones and his client have waived the confidentiality of these proceedings under the code. Also, I note for the record that counsel have agreed to waive opening statements. I have reviewed the file and am familiar with the averments of the parties."

Judge Graves looked up. "Mr. Gabbard, is the county ready to proceed?"

Mr. Gabbard stood. "Yes, we are, your Honor." He strode to the center of the courtroom with a confident, tough-guy amble. "Your Honor, the county calls as its first witness Coach Ray Bedford."

Coach Bedford sauntered toward the female clerk and plopped confidently into the witness chair.

"Do you swear or affirm to tell the truth, the whole truth, and nothin' but the truth so help you God?" the clerk said.

"Yes ma'am, I do," Coach Bedford said.

"Please state your name for the record, sir," Mr. Gabbard said.

"Ray Jefferson Bedford."

"And Coach Bedford, what is your profession?"

Coach Bedford's voice was strong and clear. "I have served as a school teacher with the Kidron Board of Education for twenty-five years. I serve as the assistant principal at Colgate Junior High School, teach American history there, and am the school's head football coach."

Mr. Gabbard cleared his throat. "Okay, Coach Bedford, I will try to be as succinct as I can in order to save your time and the court's as well. Where were you on the night of June fourth of this year?"

"I was at home with my wife and daughter. My son was at a friend's house."

"And did you have occasion to have contact that night with Dewayne Webb, sir?"

"I did."

"Can you identify the Webb boy at this time?"

"Yes, I can. He's sittin' right there in the navy-blue shirt." He pointed to Dewayne, who kept his eyes down.

"Sir, would you tell us what happened on the night of June fourth?"

Coach Bedford nodded. "Yes, but first, if I may, there's some background I think the court should be aware of. May I elaborate?"

"Please do, sir."

"On June third, the final day of the school year, we—Principal Sheridan and I—discovered that someone had vandalized the school's marquee. Please excuse me, but the graffiti read, 'Bite me, Coach Bedford.' It's common knowledge that the Webb boy was responsible for this."

Murmurs echoed through the courtroom. Judge Graves glanced at the defense table, expecting a hearsay objection from Ted Jones. But the white-haired attorney sat benignly, if not indifferently, and did not reply. Dewayne just kept his eyes on the floor.

"And Coach Bedford," Mr. Gabbard said, "could you give the court a little background as to why the respondent may have done somethin' like that?"

Judge Graves raised his right knee and rested it on the bench. He looked at Ted Jones again, expecting an objection, but Mr. Jones just listened intently as if he enjoyed hearing Coach Bedford talk.

"Well, there are two reasons I suspect," Coach Bedford said. "I oversee both the seventh and eighth grade football teams. The Webb boy and I had several ... what I would call 'incidents' during last season when he was a seventh-grade player."

He looked at Dewayne and frowned. "Frankly, the boy has talent and terrific speed but a terrible attitude. As educators and coaches we try our best to mold and help young men, but some cases are beyond our help. Dewayne has such a dogged stubbornness that I'm afraid I had to address it several times during last year's season. We had what you would call a contentious relationship."

"And the second reason?" Hank Gabbard said. "You said there were two."

The coach shifted his body and appeared uncomfortable for the first time. "Well, the second reason is a bit more personal and has to do with my daughter, Meredith. See, she's in Dewayne's class at Colgate Junior High. To put it bluntly, Dewayne was makin' unwanted advances toward her. I had to talk to Dewayne about them."

The judge studied Dewayne. He didn't move, his eyes still fixed to the floor.

"I see." Mr. Gabbard plucked at the edge of his mouth with his thumb and index finger.

Coach Bedford sucked in a breath, his chest rising. "Naturally, due to those instances, I was keepin' a close eye on my family and my house. On June fourth, I saw Dewayne through the window of my house. He was standin' on my front lawn and talkin' to my daughter. Remember, I had already talked to Dewayne about his unwanted advances, but here he was again.

"I could see that Dewayne had her tied up in some conversation, so I went to my porch to rescue her. I told Webb that he needed to move on. It was at this time that I noticed he was holdin' a baseball bat. Well, when I told the kid to move on, he cussed at me and came at me like a crazy person, all the time carryin' that Louisville Slugger."

"Coach Bedford, let me ask you this to make it clear. Dewayne was in your yard when you spoke to him?"

The coach adjusted his tie. "That's right. I think he was spoilin' for a fight—I really do."

"And then he cursed at you and approached you in a violent manner?"

"That's correct."

"Okay, then what happened?"

"He charged me with that bat and cussed at me. I believe I asked him, 'Son, haven't you had better raisin' than that?'"

"Then what happened?"

"Well, he took a swing at me with that bat."

Gasps rose from some of the women in the gallery.

"Took me by total surprise," Coach Bedford said. "I wasn't expectin' it."

"What do you recall happenin' next?"

Coach Bedford threw up his hands. "Nothin'. I mean, the next thing I remember was wakin' up in the hospital."

Mr. Gabbard tapped his index finger against his lips. "And can you tell the court what injuries you sustained?"

"A gash above my left ear and a concussion."

"Are you still experiencin' any problems?"

"No, I'm fine."

"Thank you, Coach Bedford. Anything you'd like to add?"

Coach Bedford nodded. "Only that as an educator and coach, I try to give as much as I can to our students and athletes. I give of my time and attention and do my best to help the young people in our school system. I try to make a difference in their lives—I really do. Sometimes, though, you have to recognize that some are lost causes. With some, the effort doesn't seem to do any good. It's like—like throwin' your pearls before swine."

"Thank you, Coach Bedford."

"Your witness, Mr. Jones," Judge Graves said.

"No questions, your Honor," Ted Jones said from the defense table.

Dewayne jerked his eyes from the floor and glanced at Jones. "No questions?"

Ted Jones spoke softly so as not to be overheard from the gallery.

"Trust me," he whispered to Dewayne. "It would just be worse for you if I did."

CHAPTER 24

Judge, the county next calls Sam Cray." Mr. Gabbard turned toward the gallery.

On the back row, Sam was parked next to Bates, Simon, Josh, and Nick. In front of them sat Bate's mom and Dewayne's aunt. Sam glanced around the room and felt his stomach tighten when he spotted Larry Bedford sitting behind the prosecutor's table; Larry's mom and sister were absent.

Sam stood, his heart knocking in his chest. He shuffled past his friends to reach the aisle and strolled down the middle aisle toward the witness chair, jamming sweaty hands into his pockets.

His mom had insisted that he wear his best—khaki pants, a long-sleeve white shirt, and a red tie. The dress shirt hung loose on his lanky frame, and the collar was two inches too large.

As Sam passed Larry Bedford, Larry grabbed Sam's shirt sleeve, forcing him to pause on his way to the witness chair. *Remember our talk*, his eyes seemed to say. Then he let go of him.

Sam took his seat and kept his eyes focused on the floor. His head just cleared the top of the stand's frame, but the wooden box hid the rest of him from the gallery's view. He blotted sweaty palms on his pants.

The room became quiet. Sam crossed his legs, then uncrossed them.

After he was sworn in, Judge Graves offered him a smile. "Good mornin', Sam."

"Good mornin'." Sam gnawed on his lower lip.

"Sam, Mr. Gabbard is going to ask you a few questions. Answer his questions directly and to the point, and you'll soon be finished here."

Sam nodded. "Okay."

"You'll need to speak your answers. The clerk can't transcribe a nod or a shake of the head. Do you understand?"

"Yes, sir."

Hank Gabbard sauntered over to the witness stand like he was taking a stroll in the park. He gripped the railing and smiled broadly. "Please state your name for the record, son."

"Sam Cray."

"Sam, where do you live?"

"141 Dixie Avenue."

"And that's in Colgate?"

"Yes, sir."

"Do you live next door to Coach Bedford and his family?"

"Yes, sir." Sam glanced at the gallery. The sight of so many people made his mouth turn dry. *I wish Mom were here. Stupid job.*

He shifted his gaze back to Mr. Gabbard.

"Okay, where were you on the night of June fourth of this year?"

Sam raised his eyebrows at Mr. Gabbard. "Sir?"

"That's the night in question, Sam, when everything happened."

"Okay, right." Sam swallowed, "Bates Williams, Dewayne Webb, and I went to see *Jaws* that night. It was really good too."

Some chuckles came from the gallery.

"What did you do after the movie?"

Sam relaxed some. "After the movie, Bates and I walked to my house."

"And where did the Webb boy go?"

"He went home to ask his aunt if it was okay for him to come over."

"To stay overnight at your house?" Hank Gabbard's voice rang with incredulity. He pinched his chin between his thumb and index finger.

"Yeah. I mean, yes, sir."

"Okay. Did you have occasion that night to hear any commotion outside your house?"

Sam stared at him, puzzled. "Excuse me?"

Mr. Gabbard shifted his feet impatiently. "Did you hear somethin' outside your house that night?"

"Yes, sir, I guess so."

"You guess so?"

"No, I did."

"Okay. Please explain to the court exactly what you heard and saw."

"Bates and I were in my room."

"And where is your room?"

"Upstairs."

"Where exactly?"

"If you were lookin' at our house from the street, it would be in the front and left side of the house."

"Okay, and to which side of your house is the Bedford house?"

"That same side."

"Okay, please continue."

"Bates and I were inside the house when I heard Coach Bedford yellin'."

"And what did he yell?"

"He said, 'Get out of my yard and away from my daughter!'"

Chuckles erupted from the gallery.

"And you heard this when you were inside your house?"

"Yes, sir. I heard him through my open window. And then I heard the slam of his screen door."

"Is this a front window?"

"Yes."

"It faces the street?"

Sam shook his head, confused. "No, sorry. I guess it's the side window. It faces Coach Bedford's house."

"Did you hear him say anything else?"

Sam hesitated. He knew Larry was staring at him right now. "No. But I went to the window to see what was goin' on."

Mr. Gabbard gestured for Sam to continue. "And what did you see?"

"Coach Bedford rushed toward Dewayne and Meredith. They were still standin' on the front lawn."

"What was Dewayne doin'?"

"Nothin'. He was just standin' there with Meredith."

"Sam, was he carryin' anything?"

"He had …" Sam glanced at Dewayne, his mind drifting. Dewayne's face reminded him of the Bengal tiger he'd seen at last year's state fair, the one that had scared him. The trainer had told Sam that the tiger was the only animal they had from the wild; other animals had been bred in zoos and animal sanctuaries. Sam remembered the troubled look in the magnificent animal's eyes—that of being unadjusted to life in captivity and annoyed to be constrained in a cage.

Dewayne's face bore this same look of contempt.

"Sam?" Mr. Gabbard said.

Sam's mind jerked back to the courtroom. He looked at Mr. Gabbard. "Uh, sorry, sir. I remember he had …" Sam stopped.

"He had what, Sam?"

Sam swallowed. "A baseball bat."

"In which hand?"

"His right."

"Okay, what happened next?"

Sam glanced at Dewayne again, his mind racing. *If I don't say anything bad about Coach Bedford, then I'll be safe from Larry. After all, I have to live next door to these folks.*

"Sam?" Judge Graves said.

I've got enough trouble in my life without adding more here. I'm not gonna throw myself into this fire.

"Sam."

Sam's gaze flew to Judge Graves.

"Sam, Mr. Gabbard has asked you what you saw next."

Judge Graves is a good man. He'll take care of Dewayne no matter what I say.

"Sam?" Mr. Gabbard said.

Sam blinked. *Just tell them what they want to hear. You've got no choice.*

"Sam," Judge Graves said, "you need to answer Mr. Gabbard's question."

Sam sucked in a quick breath and looked at Mr. Gabbard. "I saw Dewayne"—he raked his tongue across his lips—"I saw him hit Coach Bedford with his baseball bat."

The gasps of women from the gallery drew Sam's gaze. Several clasped hands over their mouths and lowered their faces, shaking their heads. Several men glared at Dewayne as if they wanted to exact punishment on him there and then.

Mr. Gabbard sounded pleased. "Okay, Sam. What happened next?"

"I left the window and ran downstairs."

"Okay, you say you left your room. Then what?"

"My mom met me at the bottom of the stairs and told me to stay inside. She said she'd called the police."

"And did you stay inside?"

"No, I went out the back door."

Mr. Gabbard now paced as he talked, "What did you see, Sam?"

"Coach Bedford lyin' on the grass near his porch."

"What condition was he in?"

"He wasn't movin', and there was blood on his face."

"Did you see the baseball bat?"

"Yes, sir."

"Where was it?"

"On the ground next to Coach Bedford."

"Did you see Dewayne?"

"No, he was gone."

Mr. Gabbard stopped and looked at Sam. "One more question. You haven't said anything about Coach Bedford touching the Webb boy. I want us to be clear on this point." He locked eyes with Sam and paused. "Did you see Coach Bedford touch or hit Dewayne Webb in any way that night?"

Sam squirmed. *Oh, no! I thought I was done with this part. Why's he askin' me this?*

"Sam, this is very important. Did you see Coach Bedford touch or strike Dewayne that night *in any way*?"

Silence filled the court room. Judge Graves began to open his mouth to admonish Sam. But before he could, Sam blurted, "I didn't see him. I didn't see Coach Bedford touch him that night."

The room seemed to sigh, and Sam glanced at the gallery. Coach Bedford flashed Sam a relieved smile, as did Larry Bedford in the front row. Mr. Gabbard was smiling too when he said, "Thank you, Sam. That's all I have, Judge."

"Mr. Jones, your witness," Judge Graves said in a tired voice.

Ted Jones stood behind the defense table. "No questions, your Honor."

Dewayne's face dropped.

"You may stand down, Sam," Judge Graves said.

Sam left the witness stand and avoided looking at Dewayne as he passed him and retreated to his seat.

I'm going to puke.

Shame and guilt hammered away at him. In spite of encouraging nods from his friends, he felt like he might throw up.

CHAPTER 25

The county next calls Deputy Caleb Hunter," Mr. Gabbard said. Deputy Hunter ambled toward the witness stand, plenty of girth hanging over his utility belt. A tall man in his mid-twenties, Deputy Hunter had a broad chest, bushy brown hair, and a furrowed brow. He tended to jabber when he got excited. He had played offensive guard on the Colgate High School's state championship football team seven years ago, but since then, he'd put on an extra forty pounds.

"Deputy, on the evening of June fourth of this year, did you have the occasion to answer a call about a disturbance on Dixie Avenue?"

Deputy Hunter nodded. "Yes, sir."

"In your own words, tell the judge what you saw that night as you arrived on the scene."

The deputy scratched the back of his head. "Well, Maxine took a call from Mary Cray that there was some kind of fight goin' on at her neighbor's house—the Bedford residence. So I left headquarters and went over to Dixie Avenue. When I was turnin' onto the street, I saw the Webb kid come runnin' down the sidewalk. He was runnin' fast and looked scared, kind of guilty like, if you ask me."

Judge Graves glanced at Ted Jones, expecting an objection, but the attorney sat at the defense table with a glum look on his face as if bored.

"The Webb kid crossed the street," Deputy Hunter continued, "and headed toward the Bottoms."

"Okay, then what happened?" Mr. Gabbard asked.

"I reached the Bedford place, and I first seen Mrs. Bedford. She was in her front lawn and leanin' over Coach Bedford, who was lyin' on the lawn. The Cray kid and the coach's daughter were there too. I got out and rushed over to take a look. Coach Bedford was knocked out cold." He gestured to his face. "He had a cut on the left side of his head."

"Did you see anything else, Deputy?"

"Yeah, there was a baseball bat layin' at his side."

"I'm now handin' you what has been marked as the county's Exhibit A. Would you tell the court if you recognize it?"

The deputy grasped the Louisville Slugger bat and nodded. "Yeah, this looks like the bat that was there, all right."

"The county moves for the introduction of Exhibit A."

"Without objection," Ted Jones said.

"So admitted," Judge Graves said.

"Thank you, Deputy." Mr. Gabbard turned toward Judge Graves. "That's all I have, Judge. Well no, excuse me, one more thing please."

Judge Graves nodded.

"Deputy Hunter, did you check the bat for fingerprints?"

"Yes, sir, we did. We found some, all right."

"And whose prints did you find on the bat?"

Deputy Hunter smirked and pointed to Dewayne. "His."

"Let the record reflect that the witness indicated the respondent. Nothin' further, your Honor."

"Mr. Jones, your witness."

"No questions, Judge," Ted Jones said.

Dewayne leaned back in his chair and folded his arms across his chest. He shook his head and glanced at his attorney in disbelief.

"The county rests, your Honor," Hank Gabbard said.

Judge Graves gazed at the courtroom floor. His eyes paused there before shifting to the defense table. "Any witnesses, Mr. Jones?"

Ted Jones stood. "Yes, your Honor. I would like to call the defendant, Dewayne Webb." He turned and whispered to Dewayne. "Now here's your chance like I told you. You can tell your side of things."

Dewayne rose and strode to the witness chair. Judge Graves thought he looked thin and small, yet defiant just the same.

"Please state your name for the record," Mr. Jones said.

"Dewayne Webb." Dewayne studied the people in the gallery, his eyes wide.

"Well, Dewayne, you know why we're here. I just wanted to give you a chance to tell your side of things as best you can. So, go on ahead—tell us the whole story about what happened back in June."

Dewayne glanced at his attorney and at Mr. Gabbard. Then he just sat there and stared at the floor, as if contemplating whether he should bother speaking at all.

"Just in your own words, Dewayne," Mr. Jones encouraged.

I wish my brother could have come home from college.

Dewayne heaved an audible sigh as if to say "What's the use? But here goes nothin'."

"Me and Bates and Sam went to the movies that night."

"Sorry, Dewayne," Judge Graves said. "You're gonna have to speak louder than that."

Dewayne cleared his throat and increased the volume this time. "Sam asked us to stay over. We were gonna play some board games at Sam's that night and play baseball in the square in the mornin'. I went home to ask my aunt if that was okay."

Mr. Jones nodded. "Did you pick up anything while you were there—a change of clothes? Maybe a baseball glove?"

"I didn't bring no change of clothes, and we play in the square with a tennis ball, so I didn't need no glove. But I did get my bat."

"Okay, go ahead."

Dewayne licked his lips. "I turned down Dixie Avenue on my way to Sam's house. I was headin' down the sidewalk in front of Coach Bedford's house when I saw Meredith sittin' on her porch. I hollered at her, and she came out, and we started talkin'."

"Okay, what happened next?"

"All of a sudden Coach Bedford comes to the screen door and yells, 'Get out of my yard, boy.'"

"And then?"

Dewayne took a deep breath. "He tells Meredith to go inside, but she doesn't want to. He says to her, 'Meredith, the only thing that boy can give you is a reputation.' And then he comes down his steps and comes at me real quick. He says, 'We got two pieces of unfinished business, boy. First, I told you to stay away from my daughter, and second, you need to confess to me about the vandalism up at the school.'"

Dewayne's gaze roamed the courtroom. "I tells him that me and his daughter is friends and that I don't know nothin' about the vandalism at the school, like I told him a buncha times before, but he don't believe me, like always."

He swallowed hard. "He moves real close to me then. Too close, I thought. And then he says, 'I think you're lyin'.' I turn to move on, to get to Sam's place, but he grabs my arm and says, 'You know, the problem with you, Webb, is you spend too much time tryin' to change things. Some of us like things the way they are, the way they've always been.'"

"Okay, go on," Mr. Jones said.

"I turn to leave, but he grabs my arm again. He says, 'I'm not finished with you yet, boy. You know what your other problem is? You don't smile enough. You should smile more. I like it when the people I'm talkin' to smile at me. It tells me they get me, get what I'm sayin' to them.'"

Dewayne cleared his throat. "I says to him, 'You must be doin' all right if the biggest worry you got is whether I'm smilin' at ya or not.' As soon as I says this, Coach Bedford points his fingers and thumps me hard in the chest several times." He glanced at the people in the gallery, using his own finger to show how it was done. "That don't sound like much, but it hurts. Then he says, 'You're a good-for-nothin', trouble makin' nigger just like your brother.'"

Several women in the gallery gasped.

Dewayne's voice trembled with anger. "Then he slaps me twice, once with his open hand and then again with the back of his hand."

Mr. Gabbard turned his head toward the gallery and shook his head. "He's lying," he mouthed.

"So, Dewayne," Ted Jones said, "Coach Bedford struck you on the chest repeatedly that night with his fingers and then slapped you two times across the face?"

"That's right."

"And you hadn't touched him at all up to this point?"

Dewayne shook his head vigorously. "No, sir, I didn't."

"Okay, then what happened?"

"I falls to the ground, but when I looks up, I see that he's made a fist and is comin' right at me again. I roll over and he misses."

"Thank you, Dewayne. That's all I have, Judge." Mr. Jones returned to his seat at the defense table.

"Your witness, Mr. Gabbard," Judge Graves said.

Hank Gabbard stood and swaggered toward the witness stand. He put both hands on his hips. "You seem to remember quite a bit about that night, don't ya?"

Dewayne gave him a small nod, his eyes wide and uneasy.

"The problem is, I feel like I've just been to the movies like y'all did that night, 'cept the film broke right in the middle of the story. Dewayne, let's just assume for a moment that Coach Bedford did in fact tap you on the chest with his fingers." He shrugged. "That's hardly a violent gesture, in my opinion. But let's assume that he even allegedly slapped you, like you say."

He stepped toward Dewayne and drilled him with his eyes. "Now what I want to know is this. What did you do in response?"

Dewayne stared at Mr. Gabbard.

Mr. Gabbard eased closer to Dewayne, stroking his chin. "I'll ask you again. What did you do after Coach Bedford allegedly tapped your chest with his finger and slapped you?"

Dewayne broke eye contact with Mr. Gabbard and glanced out the window.

"You must answer the question, Dewayne," Judge Graves said.

Dewayne suddenly turned to the judge, fire flaring in his eyes. "I busted him upside his fat head with my bat!"

Several women in the gallery gasped. Others lifted hands to cover their gaping mouths. A pall fell across the courtroom.

"There you go then," someone said from the front row. "He's halfway to Kimball now."

Judge Graves motioned with his hand. "Would counsel approach the bench."

Hank Gabbard and Ted Jones drew near, and the judge leaned toward the men. "Where's Meredith Bedford?" he whispered. "She should have seen everything. Why wasn't she called as a witness today?"

"Well, your Honor," Mr. Gabbard said, "Ted and I agreed that her testimony wasn't necessary. It would have been repetitive and therefore would have shed no additional light on the case at hand. That's what I thought. And you know Ted here—he's a good team player."

Judge Graves studied Mr. Jones' face. "Ted, you agreed to this?"

Mr. Jones didn't hesitate. "Yes, your Honor, I did. Hank told me her testimony would be the same as Coach Bedford's. Therefore, for the sake of judicial economy, I agreed not to call her today."

Judge Graves sighed through his nose. "I'm not sure I agree with that decision, but it's your case to defend. I'm not in any position to second-guess you or to call my own witnesses." He paused, his eyes darting between the two men.

"Okay, that's all, gentlemen. If the testimony has been completed, we'll take a half-hour recess. Then I'll hear closing arguments."

"All rise!" Sheriff Brothers said.

The room echoed with the sound of a courtroom full of bodies rising from chairs.

Judge Graves exited the courtroom and ambled down the narrow corridor to his chambers, not speaking to his secretary on the way. He shut his door and hung his black robe on the hook behind his door. Then he approached his window and shoved hands into his pockets, gazing across the public square.

The statue of the Civil War soldier stood tall and resolute just as it had for so many years.

He ran fingers through his hair and paced between the window and his desk for several minutes, deep in thought. Then he sat at his desk and reached for his telephone. After a brief call, he pulled a sheet of paper from a drawer and began to write.

Twenty minutes later he rose, opened his door, and stepped toward his secretary. He set the sheet of paper on her desk. "Type this for me right away."

CHAPTER 26

You may proceed with your closing argument, Mr. Gabbard," Judge Graves said.

"May it please the court. Your Honor, it is in the best interest of this community that this adolescent be transferred to the facility in Kimball County which, as your Honor knows, has abundant experience in handlin' this kind of behavior."

Mr. Gabbard paused, as if allowing a moment for his words to sink in. "I know your Honor has listened to the facts in this case, but let me say this. I found Dewayne Webb's testimony to be muddled at best. And I want to talk a minute about his allegation that Coach Bedford touched or slapped him."

Mr. Gabbard straightened his back and rocked on his shoes. "You've heard the testimony of one of this community's leading citizens. Coach Bedford's impeccable reputation and track record at Colgate Junior High are known to all. The court will surely take judicial notice of his good reputation and integrity. You have his word against a teenage boy who has been nothin' but a troublemaker in our town.

"But even if you were to believe half of what he said, he still admits to perpetratin' a violent act upon an honorable citizen of Colgate—and that's the core of the apple. He did this by his own account. Your Honor, there is less to this case than meets the eye. The simple truth is that we've got a swaggerin' black boy here who's got an anger problem and needs help."

Judge Graves looked up and noticed the heads of many in the gallery nodding in agreement.

Mr. Gabbard turned to address the gallery. "As the court knows, you speak for the county in this case. It's the government's role to provide a safe community for our citizens to work and live. It has been and still is the county's position that because of the violent nature of this offense, this defendant should have been tried under the regular laws governing crime in the commonwealth and not under the juvenile code. But your Honor has already made his decision on that issue, and I don't want to belabor the point."

"Yes, I have," Judge Graves said, "and no, you shouldn't."

"Your Honor," Mr. Gabbard continued quickly, "there are bigger issues afoot here. To quote the Good Book, it's the 'little foxes that destroy the vineyard.' The county is compelled to take note, and ask the court to take note, of the racial unrest across our nation."

Mr. Gabbard turned to the gallery again. "The fact is, unrest could descend on our fair town if the proper safeguards are not kept in place to prevent it from doing so. I applaud the black community's struggle for equality but must call the court's attention to the fact that people like Coach Bedford stand in the trenches in a racially mixed atmosphere at our junior high school. Placin' all of our children in that atmosphere without strong and capable leaders like Coach Bedford havin' the authority they need would be in negation of the best interest of our children and this community."

He paused and strolled back to the prosecutor's table. He placed a hand on Coach Bedford's shoulder. "Let's talk about the victim here. Coach Bedford was born and raised in this town. After a tour of service in the Marine Corps and an honorable discharge, he has served this town like his daddy did before him. His daddy served our community as its sheriff for many years, and Coach Bedford has provided his service to us in the school system and on the football field. He deserves our respect. He deserves to be protected and vindicated today. The proof is not contradicted—in fact, it is irrefutable—that Dewayne Webb assaulted Coach Bedford with what could have been a deadly weapon."

He turned to the gallery. "Your Honor, this community is dependin' on you to do what is right."

Ted Jones rose to deliver his closing argument. He placed his hand on Dewayne's shoulder, but Dewayne brushed it off.

Mr. Jones edged closer to Judge Graves. "May it please the court. Your Honor, what can I say here? I applaud your decision in July to try Mr. Webb under the juvenile code. That was an unpopular decision in this town, but the right one."

He nodded. "There is anger in the community over this incident. I recognize that—Dewayne recognizes that. I don't intend in any way to offend Coach Bedford, a prominent citizen in this community by everyone's standards, by what I want to say here. But what I want to point out—on behalf of my client, that is—is that reasonable minds can differ. Reasonable minds can differ as to the proper disposition here. I agree with opposin' counsel that there are no grounds here for me to argue that the appropriate disposition is a full acquittal of my client; we realize he's made a mistake. What I would like the court to consider, however—if I may—is to suggest a disposition that does not uproot my client from his home and community."

"Do you have any specific recommendations for the court to consider?" Judge Graves asked.

"No, I don't, Your Honor … except maybe he could get some counselin' or somethin' …" His voice trailed off.

Loud murmurs rose in the courtroom.

"Coach Bedford is a respected citizen in our community, but even a self-disciplined man like Coach Bedford can lose his temper," Mr. Jones said. "He clearly lost his temper with Dewayne on the night in question and said some things he shouldn't have. Maybe he did slap Dewayne—I don't know for sure. But I suggest to your Honor that Dewayne Webb was provoked. Because of that reason, he should not be pulled from his home and taken away from his community. I submit that an alternate disposition be considered."

Judge Graves sighed. "Anything else, Mr. Jones?"

Ted Jones hesitated, as if recalling another closing argument he'd given on another occasion. "I would like to add that my client and I are grateful today that we have a judicial system in our country that works for all of us: poor, rich, black, and white. And I believe it's workin' today. Your Honor has heard the facts, and we entrust Dewayne into your capable hands."

Judge Graves longed for some aspirin; his head was pounding. Ted Jones sat down next to Dewayne. The gallery grew silent, and all eyes turned to him. Everyone was waiting for what he would do next.

He took a deep breath and held it as his eyes traveled across the many faces in the gallery. He knew what everyone anticipated. Many of the older folks, in particular, expected him to take a recess. It was true—he usually took a recess after hearing all the testimony in a case. Sometimes he announced that he would take the case under submission and issue a written order at a later time.

Mr. Gabbard leaned back in his chair, a smug look on his face. "Judge, if I may, when can we expect a rulin' from you in this matter?" He waved his hand over the gallery. "Clearly, there's a lot of interest in this community to hear your decision on this matter in a timely manner."

"Before the election is what he means," someone muttered from the front row.

Judge Graves stared at Hank Gabbard. For a moment, he didn't appear to the judge as an attorney in his courtroom but as his opponent in the fall election for the very seat he was occupying at this moment.

"The court is prepared to give that ruling right now, Mr. Gabbard."

The attorney's eyes widened in surprise.

Judge Graves took a deep breath, and his eyes roamed across the many faces. "I have considered the testimony of the witnesses and the arguments of counsel. This court finds that the respondent, a juvenile, has committed assault with a deadly weapon upon the person of Ray Bedford. Accordingly, it is the order of this court that Dewayne Webb be remanded to the county's custody for immediate removal to the juvenile facility in Kimball County until he turns eighteen, at which time he will reappear before this court."

Dewayne lowered his head and pressed his closed fists to his face.

Judge Graves allowed himself a small grin as he watched Hank Gabbard's startled and disappointed expression. Mr. Gabbard may have won the trial, but this decision hurt his election chances. He pasted a smile on his face before turning to Coach Bedford.

Not all faces were as happy. Incomprehension and disappointment dominated the faces of Bates Williams' mom, Bertie, and Dewayne's aunt.

Coach Bedford glanced at Dewayne, gloating over his victory. He whispered loud enough for Dewayne to hear him, "You're always gonna lose in my town, boy."

Dewayne Webb rose and glared at Judge Graves. "You fake!" He slammed both fists down on the defense table in front of him.

Judge Graves' face flushed.

"I thought you was better!" Dewayne said. "You's no better than any of them. Is this yo' justice?"

Sheriff Brothers barreled toward the defense table. "Sir, control your client," he told Ted Jones. Ted Jones tried to put a comforting arm around Dewayne, but Dewayne shoved it away. Then he slumped down in his chair.

"This court is adjourned." Judge Graves pounded his gavel and stood, his robe draping around him, as he fled the courtroom.

The gallery responded with loud murmurs. Several old-timers raised victorious fists in the air.

Bertie Williams and Dewayne's aunt didn't budge from their seats. They stared straight ahead with misty eyes.

CHAPTER 27

Sheriff Brothers and Deputy Hunter led Dewayne into a holding room off the courtroom. The sheriff shut the steel door behind them with a loud, reverberating clang that echoed in Dewayne's ears. Dewayne lifted despondent eyes and studied his surroundings. The room had two doors. One led from the courtroom and the other to the courthouse lawn. The room had no windows.

His eyes took in the room's dismal furnishing—a bench, a locker, and a steel toilet sitting low along the floor. Dewayne leaned against the door, and the sheriff and deputy stood in the middle of the room beneath a naked light bulb.

"Caleb, I'm gonna run over to Dewayne's aunt's house to get some of his things," Sheriff Brothers said. "You get him ready here and then take him to headquarters. I'll meet you there." Deputy Hunter nodded and pushed his thumbs under his utility belt.

Dewayne watched them, still unable to grasp what was happening to him. *I don't belong in this place.*

The sheriff left. Deputy Hunter closed the door and slid the bolt home. He turned to Dewayne and pointed to the metal bench along the painted brick wall. "Sit down."

Dewayne sat with a thud, slapped the wall with his palm, and cursed.

"Oh, yeah?" Deputy Hunter smirked, handcuffs jangling at his side. "Well, you might as well get used to it." He opened the gray locker, rummaged through bright-orange jumpsuits, and chose one for Dewayne.

He tossed it to Dewayne, and it landed at his feet. "That's the smallest one I've got. Go ahead. Put it on."

Dewayne picked up the prisoner garb and squeezed it in his hands as if to strangle the life out of it. *I guess this makes it official. I'm a criminal now.*

"I can't believe it!" Sam took a seat on the courthouse lawn next to Bates.

"'I can't believe it,'" Bates said, mimicking him. "Did you expect somethin' different to happen?"

"Yeah, I did. Judge Graves is a good guy. I thought he'd let Dewayne off. Surely he knows what a maniac Coach Bedford is."

Bates' eyes were sullen. "Man, you really don't know how things are done around here, do you? Dewayne hit a white guy—a school teacher in fact—with a baseball bat. Did you really think he was gonna get away with that? You're supposed to be as innocent as a dove, not as dumb as one."

"But you heard what Dewayne said about the stuff Coach Bedford said to him. Then Coach poked him in the chest and slapped him."

Bates narrowed his eyes at Sam. "Unfortunately, Dewayne didn't have any witnesses to back that part of his story."

Sam glanced away.

If Bates really knew what I saw and lied about, he'd hate me. How could I explain about Larry's threats? Sam, you're nothin' but a pathetic coward.

"Anyway, no matter what Coach Bedford did," Bates said, "Dewayne was gonna get sent to Kimball today, and everybody knew it."

"I guess I thought it might be different with Judge Graves bein' in charge. Everybody knows Kimball's an awful place. I hear it's like a maximum security prison for kids." He shook his head. "There has to be somethin' somebody can do about this."

"Nope. There's nothin' anybody can do. It's just the way things are."

Sam stood. "No, I don't believe it. There has to be somethin' we can do." He peered down at Bates, a faint smile on his lips. "C'mon. I've got an idea."

Sheriff Brothers entered the courtyard, where at least a dozen citizens were discussing the day's events and hoping to get a look at Dewayne in his new prison garb.

"You gonna put him in shackles, Sheriff?" asked a man in faded blue coveralls.

"Move along now. I won't have you interferin' with official business."

A half hour later, Sheriff Brothers pulled his squad car into the parking lot of department headquarters in downtown Colgate and noticed that Deputy Hunter's squad car was already there. He killed the engine and noticed Dewayne sitting in the backseat of Deputy Hunter's car in an oversized orange jump suit.

The sheriff got out and strode to the squad car, where Deputy Hunter was waiting. He handed a paper bag to Deputy Hunter, who glanced inside. The bag held a few toiletries and some clothes Dewayne's aunt had given him.

"Is this it?" Deputy Hunter sounded surprised.

"Yep, that's all she gave me."

The sheriff handed the bag to Dewayne through the open car window. Dewayne sat in gloomy solitude in the back seat.

"You'd better get goin'," the sheriff said. "They'll be expectin' you at Kimball. I radioed Maxine, and she's called 'em."

He glanced through the window and noticed that Deputy Hunter had handcuffed Dewayne. "Caleb, take those off him. There's no need for handcuffs."

"I don't take risks with the prisoners I'm transportin'," the deputy said. "It's a prudent precaution."

"Look, you probably outweigh the kid by 150 pounds." His gaze dropped to Deputy Hunter's ample belly. "Get 'em off and get goin'."

He waited for the deputy to obey, then watched Deputy Hunter drive away. Sheriff Brothers shook his head at Deputy Hunter's bullheadedness and marched into headquarters.

"Everything taken care of, Maxine?"

"Yes, sir," the redheaded dispatcher said.

"All right, then I'm headin' home."

"Uh, Sheriff, there's somebody waitin' for you in your office."

"Who?" said the sheriff.

She nodded toward his open door, a knowing look on her face.

Sheriff Brothers turned. The long legs of Judge Graves protruded from behind the L-shaped wall of his office, a Fedora hat resting on his knee.

The sheriff entered his office and closed the door behind him, his interest piqued. The two elected officials nodded to each other, and the sheriff sank into his leather chair. It had been a very long day and he was feeling his age today.

"To what do I owe the honor, Judge?"

The judge's eyes were pleasant, but something burned behind them, something serious and secretive. "Sheriff, there's been a slight change of plans." Judge Graves reached inside his suit pocket and removed a single sheet of paper.

Sheriff Brothers turned into the roadside cemetery off Hodgenville Road, where Deputy Hunter had parked on his way to Kimball County, and pulled alongside. The cemetery was only one mile from the split-rail fences bordering Abraham Lincoln's birthplace.

Deputy Hunter gave him a nod through his open window. "What's goin' on, Sheriff? I'd like to get on to Kimball so I can get home before midnight."

"You're not goin' to Kimball." He handed the deputy a manila envelope. "You're to give this to the man mentioned in the order."

Deputy Hunter accepted the envelope and stared at it, baffled.

"It's Dewayne's enrollment papers for his new school. It's all covered in the order."

Deputy Hunter stared at him. "What order?"

"This one." The sheriff waved a paper before his face. "Read it."

Deputy Hunter pawed the single sheet between his two beefy hands and began to read aloud.

Kidron County, Kentucky
County Court
Hon. Albert Graves, Presiding

IN RE: DEWAYNE WEBB

This matter having coming before the court *sua sponte*
following the disposition hearing for Dewayne Webb, a
minor. The court having heard the evidence, and finding
the minor guilty of assault with a deadly weapon, previously
remanded the boy to the state's juvenile facility in Kimball
County. That disposition is hereby rescinded. It is hereby
ordered that the sheriff of Kidron County shall proceed,
with haste, to transfer the respondent to the Canaan
Boarding School in Louisville, Kentucky. Arrangements for
Dewayne Webb's enrollment there have been made, and the
Kidron County Sheriff's Office is to deliver the enclosed
envelope to the headmaster, the Reverend Henry Klevenger.
Furthermore, the contents of this order and the placement
of Dewayne Webb at Canaan School shall be held strictly
confidential by this court's clerk's office and the Kidron
County Sheriff's Department, upon penalties of contempt
of court. The court will personally communicate the new
arrangements with the minor's guardian.

A. Graves
Judge, Kidron County Court

Deputy Hunter's mouth gaped, and he stared out his windshield.
From the back of the squad car, the sheriff heard Dewayne laughing.

"Got any questions?" Sheriff Brothers said. "If not, you might want
to close your mouth before you catch a fly."

Deputy Hunter snapped his mouth shut. "Sorry, sir. Uh, no questions."

"Then get goin'."

"But, hey. Isn't that the fancy school in Louisville?"

"What's that to you, deputy? Just follow the order."

"Guess you're not gonna have the pleasure of seein' me get locked
up, fatso," Dewayne said.

163

"Dewayne," the sheriff said with a smile, "get that prison garb off and change into your regular clothes."

"Yes, sir," Dewayne said, unbuttoning the bright orange jumpsuit.

"Albert, I'm so proud of you." Mrs. Graves handed him two platters, one with roast beef and the other with vegetables. "Today, for once, you used some common sense and did what you should have done."

For once? Judge Graves set the platters down on the dinner table before him. "I'm not so sure, dear. I'm not sure I've done the right thing."

"Of course you have. Now, you've got to look at the big picture. You can't do anything to help this community if you're no longer on the bench. The simple fact is, if you would've done anything other than send that boy to Kimball, you'd have lost the election this fall. Just too many votes against you."

She set her elbows on the table and cradled her chin on top of her folded hands. "Listen, Albert, the majority of people in this county wouldn't vote for Hank Gabbard unless you gave them a reason to vote against you. Everybody knows he's as crooked as a barrel of fish hooks."

She got up, marched over to him, and hugged him warmly across his shoulders. "I'm so proud of you."

Judge Graves just looked at his plate. *If she only knew.*

CHAPTER 28

Thursday, August 14, 1975

(The next day)

Sam and Bates sat anxiously in the front office of Colgate Junior High School. Sam's body was wound like a spring. Sweat beaded Bates' forehead, which he kept wiping. His leg bounced nervously up and down, up and down.

"You may see him now." The austere, middle-aged secretary's voice was devoid of inflection, her countenance cold. Her blonde-from-a-bottle hair was pulled back from her face, and large-framed glasses dangled from a silver chain looped around her neck.

"Thank you, ma'am." Sam stood and blotted sweaty palms on his pant legs. Bates stood as well.

She primly clutched a pencil in front of her and, without looking up, gestured down a narrow corridor with a bony finger. Her eyes seemed set apart too far, and her facial features had the same range as that of an iguana.

Sam steeled himself and made the dreadful trek toward the principal's office with Bates only a step behind. His mind raced as he considered what he was about to do in light of the possible consequences. Other fleeting thoughts assaulted him.

What will Grandma think about this? What will Coach Bedford or Larry do if they find out?

Principal Sheridan sat behind a large metal desk littered with forms and notes. Files were stacked on chairs and on the floor. Though the whole office screamed that he was a busy man, he rose and offered his hand, first to Bates and then to Sam. Then he sank into an enormous leather chair that nearly swallowed him whole.

Wow, he's smaller than many of his students.

Sam felt sorry for him for a split second. Then his thoughts returned to the reason they'd come for this visit today, and his mouth turned dry.

Principal Sheridan smiled warmly. "Hello, B-B-Bates and S-S-Sam. Have a s-s-seat."

As they accepted his invitation, Sam sensed that maybe they shouldn't have come. Perhaps this wasn't such a good idea after all. He felt his resolve melt like wax before a fire.

The principal seemed surprised to see Sam. "You had a b-b-busy day yesterday. Weren't you a w-w-witness at Dewayne W-W-Webb's trial?"

"Yes, sir."

"So what b-b-brings you two here so early in the morning? I would think this would be the last place you'd want to be on one of your last d-d-days of summer. B-B-Boys, what can I do for you?"

Sam nodded. *Only a complete idiot comes to visit the principal two weeks before the start of school.*

"We need to talk to you." Sam wiped his hands on his shorts. He looked over at Bates, who was wiping away sweat as it dripped down his face.

"I could have g-g-guessed that. Boys, I have a music teaching p-p-position to fill and class schedules to m-m-make and a hundred other things. I'm sorry, boys, but I am terribly b-b-busy today. If there is nothing that I can help you with, I'm afraid I don't have the t-t-time for a social visit today."

Something Sam didn't realize existed inside him suddenly rose up, compelling him to lean forward and open his mouth. "We want you to fire Coach Bedford."

Sam's words seem to hang in the air.

Principal Sheridan didn't seem surprised or alarmed. He simply removed his reading glasses and massaged his eyes. "I'm listening."

"Coach Bedford is a bad influence on this school, and we think you should send him packin'," Sam said.

Principal Sheridan took a deep breath and slowly let it out. "Even if I agreed with you, I need more than your opinion to do something as d-d-dramatic as firing someone."

"We've been thinkin' about that." Sam leaned back in his chair and gave Bates a nod.

Bates pulled a sheet of notebook paper out of his back pocket and handed it to Principal Sheridan.

"What you have there," Sam said, "are instances when we've witnessed Coach Bedford doing things that I don't think you'd want this school to stand for."

Principal Sheridan raised his eyebrows. "Things?"

Sam nodded. "Things he's done when other adults weren't around. Things he's said to us."

Principal Sheridan gave Sam a doubtful look over the top of the sheet. "Could you give me an example of th-th-things on this sh-sh-sheet?"

"Okay, sure," Sam said. "Coach Bedford told me in private that blacks were bred by whites to be physically superior and mentally inferior."

Principal Sheridan raised his eyebrows.

"And I have one, too," Bates said. "During one of the practices last year, I overheard him do a monkey chant—you know, 'Uuwwa, Uuwwa, Uuwwa'—toward a group of black players behind their backs."

Principal Sheridan swallowed hard.

"Another time I heard him talkin' about a black player on last year's team," Sam said. "He said, 'That coon's so dumb, he couldn't read a cereal box.' And I heard him say to our coach last year that he would like to hang his two runnin' backs from a tree."

Principal Sheridan pushed his reading glasses up his nose with a trembling finger.

Sam said, "Those are on that sheet, and there are more. There's other stuff about our football practices and how he abuses his players. We witnessed all of 'em."

Principal Sheridan smoothed the wrinkled paper on his desk and peered down at it. After reading the list, he looked up and met Sam's gaze. "Why are you d-d-doing this?"

Bates shrugged. "We just knew it was time that we speak up."

"Thank you, boys. Is it okay if I k-k-keep this?"

"Of course," Sam said. "You're who we wrote it for."

Principal Sheridan turned in his chair and held the sheet up with both hands. He studied Bates' small print, which filled both the front and back.

"What will you do?" Sam said.

The principal shook his head, eyes worried. "I don't know. Bates, you are p-p-president of your class, and you comin' in here today with Sam … well, that draws a lot of w-w-water with me. But this"—he shook his head—"this could cost me everything."

He set the paper down and stood, signaling that the meeting was over. "Thanks for coming to see me, b-b-boys."

Sam and Bates left his office and plodded down the sidewalk in silence for several minutes. "We're knee deep in it now," Bates said.

Sam nodded. "We've stepped into the breach."

"Into the what?"

"I read it in a book once. I'm not sure what it means, but I don't think it's good."

PART FOUR

THE KIDRON RIVER

(Two weeks later)

Thursday, August 28, 1975

Local Football Coach Sacked, Then Jailed

COLGATE—The Kidron County Board of Education announced last night that Coach Ray Bedford has been fired as an employee of the school system. Yesterday's announcement concerning Colgate Junior High School's football coach came as a surprise to many. A source close to the school stated that the dismissal resulted from a difference of opinion regarding racial remarks and practices associated with the football program.

"It became clear to Principal Sheridan," the source said, "that the football program had a problem with racist and abusive practices involving student-athletes."

The board's announcement has stirred strong sentiments in the community. "I am completely shocked," said George Holliday, a Colgate resident. "Coach Bedford is the best thing about that school. He's done nothin' but good for our youth and this community. He's always been the soul of integrity."

"I think we should find a way to reinstate Coach Bedford and get rid of Principal Sheridan," said Red Burris, another resident.

Asked to elaborate on the circumstances of Coach Bedford's dismissal, Principal Sheridan declined, citing confidentiality issues. He did state that he wanted to thank Coach Bedford for his many years of service to the school. When asked directly if the firing was related to issues involving race on the football team, Sheridan stated, "I will only say that there was a difference in philosophy about how things should be handled with the football program."

According to our source, Principal Sheridan recommended to the board that Coach Bedford be fired two weeks ago. However, the decision was not announced until after the board's closed-door session last night when, according to our source, it heard from two unnamed students who testified about certain alleged incidents regarding racist and abusive behavior by Coach Bedford.

At press time, Bedford was unavailable for comment. In a bizarre turn of events, he is being held in the Kidron County Jail due to an altercation with Sheridan after the board meeting.

"He will be held for a few days," Sheriff Brothers said. "The judge wants him to cool off before we let him out. We expect he'll be released on Sunday."

CHAPTER 29

Sam heard a knock on the front door and opened it to a pale, gray sky. To his surprise, Meredith Bedford sat on the front steps.

"Hey, Meredith. What are *you* doin' here?"

"I thought you might need some help plannin' your trip." She rubbed red eyes.

"Sorry about your dad, Meredith."

She shook her head, long bangs falling in her face. "I know he deserves what happened to him, even if he is my dad. You guys did the right thing. Believe it or not, I'm proud of what you and Bates did."

Sam's eyes widened. "How did you know it was us?"

"Come on, Sam." Meredith smiled. "This is Colgate, remember?"

Sam's mind spun. *If she knows Bates and I were involved, then—*

"Look, I don't want to talk about it, okay?" She swept a lock of hair out of her face. "What needs to be done for you guys to get ready for your canoe trip? I want to help."

An overnight canoe trip on the Kidron River had been a rite of summer since Sam was seven years old. For the last five years, Simon, Josh, Nick, and he had taken the excursion to celebrate the end of summer. For the first time, however, they'd go this year without an adult chaperone.

The trip would also be different because Sam had invited Bates William to go along. Over the last two weeks, he and Sam had become inseparable. After thoroughly investigating the trip and talking to all the mothers, Bates' mother had agreed to let him go.

Sam led Meredith to the storage room under the Cray home, where they stored the canoes, a canvas tent, and other needed supplies. He opened the rough-hewn door on rusted hinges and crawled under the house. Meredith helped him haul out what they needed.

Sam used a garden hose to spray dirt and grime off the canoes. Just as he finished, Dr. Carlisle pulled into the driveway in his boxy International Scout.

"Well, I gotta go," Meredith said. "Have fun on your trip, Sam. I'll see ya tomorrow after you get back."

"Thanks for your help." Sam waved and watched her cross the lawn to her house.

Dr. Carlisle, Josh, Simon, and Nick hopped out of the Scout. Dr. Carlisle smiled at Sam with his fresh, good-humored face. "Sam, I talked to your dad on the phone this morning."

Sam's heart sank. *Oh no! They're not gonna let us go on the trip by ourselves.*

"We both think it would be irresponsible of us … not to allow you all to go by yourselves this year."

Sam punched the air with his first. "Yes!" He grinned at his buddies.

"Absolutely!" Simon said.

Josh nodded. "You can trust us."

"That's what we both thought too." Dr. Carlisle grinned. "Some of the moms weren't exactly of the same opinion, but we still think you're mature enough to go solo. So, let's get goin'."

The boys loaded the canoes on top of the Scout and secured them to the bumpers with a skein of twine. Sam added his sleeping bag to the back of the already crammed vehicle before piling in with his buddies.

Dr. Carlisle turned the ignition, and the engine caught. He backed out of the Crays' driveway, and Sam noticed several day's worth of newspapers littering the Bedfords' front lawn. The Scout lurched forward and headed down Dixie Avenue with a jerk, blue smoke spilling from the exhaust pipe and into the humid air.

From his second-floor bedroom window, Larry Bedford watched the Scout drive away, a football in his hand, a scowl on his lips.

He turned and threw the football across the room. It crashed into the lamp on his bedside table.

He made fists. "Sam Cray, you're gonna pay."

Dr. Carlisle drove the tank-like International Scout south and out of Colgate. The wind whistled through the open window. "Bates, is this your first time canoeing on the Kidron River?" he asked.

"My first time canoein' anywhere," Bates said.

"It'll be a trip you won't forget, I promise." Dr. Carlisle grinned at him in the rearview mirror.

From the front seat Josh glanced back at Sam. "We watched the coolest episode of *The Six Million Dollar Man* last night."

From the back, Simon said, "Yeah, but I could have done without all the snugglin' between Dr. Carlisle and your mom. No offense, Dr. Carlisle, but don't you think you're gettin' a little old for that sort of thing?"

Dr. Carlisle chuckled. "I hope I'm never too old for that sort of thing."

"Aren't you guys a little sick of each other by now?" Simon said. "Not that I don't think Mrs. Carlisle isn't hot or anything, because I think she is—"

"What?" Josh glanced back at him with a perplexed expression.

"Well, not that I—" Simon blushed. "Oh, never mind."

"Better stop while your behind," Nick said, next to him.

"It only gets better every year, my friend," Dr. Carlisle said. "This may bore you boys to death, but I'm going tell you anyhow. There are two kinds of love between a man and a woman."

Josh rolled his eyes. "Please, Dad, just stop."

"Two kinds of love, huh?" Nick grinned. "Yeah, one with wrinkles and one without, right?"

"Or one with hair and one without it," Josh said.

"You're close." Dr. Carlisle scratched his high-domed head, which was as bald as an egg and fringed with hair around the ears. "To me there's a first love that's full of wonder. That's like when your mom and I first dated in college. Then later, when the new wears off, when you're an old man like me, there's a different kind of love. It's full of knowledge. Both kinds are fantastic, but for me the second is better."

Josh shook his head. "Whatever."

Simon said, "Yeah, sorry I brought the subject up."

"You did bring it up, Simon," said Dr. Carlisle.

"Dr. Carlisle is a total bore," Nick whispered to Sam.

Sam studied Dr. Carlisle in the mirror and couldn't help admiring him. The previous Saturday Dr. Carlisle had shown Josh and him the value of setting screens for their teammates during basketball games. He'd shown them how this act freed teammates to get open shots, and Sam never forgot the lesson, noting how few players set screens during recreational pickup games. He remembered what Dr. Carlisle had said: "Only well-coached teams play selfless ball."

Dr. Carlisle changed the subject. "Do you guys have enough food packed for tonight and tomorrow mornin'?"

"We're all set," Simon said. "Look here." He dumped the contents of a paper bag onto Bates' lap, revealing a cornucopia of Simon's favorite candies: Bit-O-Honeys®, Kit Kats®, Milky Ways®, and an assortment of sour balls.

"Don't worry, Bates," Nick said. "Ms. Regina packed another bag with real food."

"I called Frank Wiseman at the Kidron Valley Campground," Dr. Carlisle said. "He's expectin' you to arrive tomorrow around lunchtime." He glanced at his son. "Josh, call me from Mr. Wiseman's cottage as soon as you get there."

"Will do, Dad," Josh said.

Retirees Frank Wiseman and his wife, Wendy, worked full-time at the Kidron Valley Campground, a summer retreat center for youth in the southern part of the county. The river bent in a loop around a thirty-acre camp, where an old mill had once operated. Next to the old mill stood a dam, where the water tumbled twenty feet in a cascade of foam and green water. Dr. Carlisle knew Wendy well because she served as his office manager for twenty-two years before she and her husband retired and moved to the groundskeeper's cottage.

The boys fell silent as the Scout's wide tires droned against the asphalt in a low whine. Sam glanced out the window, enjoying the view. The county's southern end was easy country, sparsely populated and dominated by thick, deep woods and small ponds. They passed occasional dirt driveways and telephone lines that curved between the poles.

After driving by the Sills' farm, Dr. Carlisle slowed the Scout to cross a single-lane bridge that spanned a small creek at the Jones' Ferry junction. He turned at the general store, and they passed a small church and a graveyard enclosed by a black, wrought iron fence.

Dr. Carlisle pulled off the state road and rambled down a quiet, uneven dirt road leading to the river. Tree branches brushed the sides of the Scout as it bounced down the path, which widened near the river. Dr. Carlisle braked to a stop, then backed the Scout to within ten feet of the water.

Sam peered out the open window and smelled the air. It was pungent with the aroma of damp earth and river musk. Dust clung to the green leaves of sassafras trees standing near the water's edge.

Within minutes the boys unloaded the canoes and their gear. They carried them down a gentle slope to the river's edge. While Nick and Simon skimmed rocks, Sam watched the current carry a gray log downstream.

Dr. Carlisle helped Josh and Bates carry several heavy bags containing food supplies, sleeping bags, and drinks. Then he climbed back into the Scout and started the engine. Josh hugged him good-bye through the open window, and Dr. Carlisle kissed his son on the cheek. Then he waved good-bye to the boys and steered the Scout up the hill and out of sight.

I wonder where Dad is now? Sam thought.

Nick's acidic tone interrupted his thoughts. "Joshy poo, have fun, but be smart."

CHAPTER 30

The overnight canoe trip was popular among Kidron County residents. The contours of the Kidron River provided an enjoyable two-day paddle with a comfortable spot in between for overnight camping. From Jones' Ferry the river snaked through the countryside for eight miles before reaching the Kidron Valley Campground.

The Kidron River's source was an area north of Colgate packed with cone-shaped, rounded hills known as knobs. Knobs weren't mountains, exactly, but more like soft, green, bumpy hills covered with trees. As Sam had learned at Eventide Elementary School, the Knobs region was gentle, like the people of Kidron County. True to their name, the knobs resembled old-fashioned doorknobs or—more accurately as Simon always said—like women's breasts lined up in rows.

The Knobs region covered a twenty-mile swath of countryside across central Kentucky. Tributaries like Hound's Creek flowed through the Knobs and into the Kidron River, which in turn flowed west out of the county and eventually joined the Ohio River south of Louisville.

Sam stood at the water's edge and studied the Kidron as it flowed past, calm and slow under an overcast sky. Sam wondered about possible rain. The forecast called for rain showers, but this looked more intense.

He glanced at his friends and noted the grins on their faces. He shared in their high spirits and felt a little overwhelmed by their wealth of newfound freedom. There weren't any adults around for miles. They could do whatever they wanted to. As Dr. Carlisle drove off, Sam was aware of that familiar rush of adrenaline that always preceded adventures with friends.

Nick took charge and announced that he and Josh would take the first canoe while Sam, Bates, and Simon would follow in the second. Simon would occupy the middle as the duffer.

"Let's shove off!" said Nick as he climbed into the first canoe.

Bates agreed to paddle in the front of the second canoe while Sam paddled in the rear. At first, Sam had difficulty paddling in sync with Bates, but after they worked together for while, they fell into an easy rhythm.

A distant train whistle sliced the morning silence. They passed rolling hills, small farms with tobacco patches, and fields dotted with wildflowers.

Because Simon had nothing to do but watch, he passed the time by taking out his fishing pole, putting a spinning lure on the line, and dragging it behind their canoe. But he lacked the patience to fish for long and gave up after a half hour.

Another hour passed. Sam glimpsed a hawk perched high in an elm tree. The fragrant aroma of honeysuckle that climbed down the bank filled the air.

The canoes rounded a bend and came abreast of each other. The boys eyed each other across the water, then dug in hard, racing to see which canoe would be first. After a minute of hard paddling, their hearts pounding, Sam and Bates gave up. The race was over. Josh and Nick had captured the checkered flag.

After a few minutes of silence, Simon spontaneously stood up in the canoe and struggled to keep his balance. Then he began singing "Black Water" by the Doobie Brothers, dancing along as he sang. The boys joined in.

Well, I built me a raft and she's ready for floatin'.
Ol' Mississippi, she's callin' my name.

When the song ended, Simon grinned at the water. "Bates, how many million albums do you think I'm gonna sell?"

Bates snickered and dipped the paddle. "Not many because I think I'm gonna drown you before the day's over."

Bates complained about the heat and stripped off his shirt. Sam couldn't help noticing the veins popping out of Bates' forearms when he rowed. Sam glanced down at his own forearms and pumped his fists a few times, but frowned when he didn't achieve the same results.

Short, deep scars crisscrossed Bates' arms, and thin streaks appeared on his back where his skin had been scratched, the pigment deteriorated.

"Those scars from football?" Sam asked.

Bates examined the scars on his arms. "Yep."

Sam shook his head. "They're permanent, aren't they?"

"Guess so."

"You look like you've been branded."

Bates examined the scars again, then shrugged. During games, he carried the ball for Colgate's offense the majority of the time. When the team was on defense, he played middle linebacker and was involved in most of the tackles.

Sam stared at the marks on Bates' back. *What a crazy game that could cause permanent scars on the arms and back of a star player.*

"It's too bad you're black," Simon said.

Bates glanced back at Simon in disbelief.

Sam squinted his eyes so much it looked like his face hurt. "What did you say?"

Simon shrugged. "Because your skin's black, your scars are more noticeable."

Bates turned and looked straight ahead, his paddle horizontal on his leg, the end drip, drip, dripping in the water. An awkward pause followed.

"Simon ..." Sam said.

"Well, it's true," Simon said. "The scars would be harder to see if you had lily-white skin like mine. That's all I'm sayin'."

Lily-white indeed. Simon had removed his shirt too, and his fair skin was a target for the sun. His neck and shoulders were already turning a shade of pink, which would likely turn into painful, skin-peeling sunburn by afternoon.

Bates glanced back at Simon with a grin. "If my teammates like Sam here played a little harder, maybe I wouldn't get so many scars."

Sam chuckled. "Bates, I'd like to help more, but no can do. I hafta keep my jersey clean."

This backwoods country was dominated by hardscrabble poverty and people living mostly hand-to-mouth. As the canoes floated around another bend, they drifted under a railroad trestle. Just as Sam's nose filled with the aroma of creosote and oil, his head jerked toward the bark of two hound dogs on shore.

Beyond the dogs, a run-down house, perhaps once white but now colorless, squatted on the riverbank. Three apparently disabled pickup trucks, rusting in the side yard, were surrounded by several ramshackle sheds that looked ready to collapse. In the backyard, two children waved at the boys from a tire swing, and the boys waved back.

In the garden just beyond the house, Sam spied tall rows of corn and a few beaming sunflowers. Nearby, a couple of chickens pecked at corn in the dirt, and a cage-ribbed horse tethered to a tree gave them slight notice before continuing to graze on sparse grass. Two pigs stared at them while smacking at their food, and a goat cropped low thistles.

Josh pulled their canoe alongside and gave Sam a nod. "That's that family my dad told you about last year."

The family had previously lived a quarter mile from the river. After a heavy flood in 1969, however, this house had floated downriver from elsewhere and rested on this property. The parents had decided that this house was better than the one they lived in and they moved their family in and had remained ever since.

The canoes drifted around another bend and passed the Kentucky Colonel Distillery, one of several in the area that produced Kentucky straight bourbon for consumption all over the world. The rotten-egg smell of the strong sour mash by-product flowed out of an iron pipe and into the river.

Sam remembered his dad telling him some oddities about Kentucky's bourbon making. In Kentucky, each county had the right to allow or disallow alcohol sales. This curious provision in the law allowed for ironic results. Even though three-fourths of Kentucky's counties disallowed the sale of alcohol of any type, Kentucky distilled seventy percent of the world's bourbon. Locally, alcohol sales were illegal, so the bourbon produced at the Kentucky Colonel Distillery couldn't be purchased in Kidron County despite being made here. Also, Bourbon County in Kentucky was dry while Christian County was wet. And the first bourbon was produced by Elijah Craig, a Baptist minister.

The boys paused for lunch where a large granite rock seemed to rise out of nowhere, a stream spurting from its side and gurgling into the river. Atop the stone they ate peanut butter and jelly sandwiches and potato chips. Afterward, they took turns jumping from the rock into the river.

Near where the stream flowed from the rock, Nick led them single file down a skinny trail along the tributary for about a hundred yards, passing the crest of a hill. There they stopped, and Sam eyed a steep wall of rock to their right. He peered into a cleft in the wall where rock receded into the hillside, revealing the waist-high opening to a cave.

Sam and Simon turned on flashlights they'd brought along, and the boys crawled in. The temperature seemed to drop at least twenty degrees. Sam shone his light along a craggy ceiling and chased away shadows from dark corners. He rubbed his hands along his arms to keep warm.

Though the room was spacious and airy, flashlights set it aglow. Sam directed his light across the wall, where topaz flashed and flickered. The cave may have contained Indian artifacts long ago, but now only empty beer bottles and cigarette wrappers littered the floor. "Jack was here" and "Woody loves Lynn" graffiti covered the walls.

Simon screamed. Sam whirled.

With a shaking hand, Simon pointed his flashlight at a skeleton pinned to the wall beneath stone icicles. Bates stepped back, stumbled, and fell to the dirt floor with a groan.

Nick marched over to the skeleton and picked it up, a sneer on his face. "It's only plastic, you morons."

"Doggone it, Simon!" Bates said. "You 'bout scared me to death."

Nick shook his head. "That stupid thing's been here for years."

They descended farther into the cave, where a rushing sound filled the air. The rocky ground yielded to a clear, underground stream. Narrow, deep, and swift moving, it gushed through a trench worn into the rock at their feet before tumbling into a dark hole and disappearing from view.

Nick grinned at Simon. "This is it. I dare you."

"What'll ya' give me?" Simon said.

"I'll let you borrow my video game for a month if you go all the way in over your head."

"Your Sears Tele-Games Pong?"

"If you're man enough."

Simon eyed the stream and stepped close to the edge. He sat down on the rocky floor and swung both feet into the water. "Man, it's freezing!"

"He's not gonna do it!" Nick's laughter echoed in the cave. "I knew he wouldn't."

Simon glared at him. "Shut up, Nick! I didn't say I wasn't gonna do it."

Josh ventured close to the edge and frowned. "Maybe you shouldn't, Simon. That water's movin' awfully fast."

"Yeah, you better not, you sissy." Nick egged him on.

Simon ignored him and studied the dark, fast-moving current. "Do you think there are any eels in there? I saw on *Wild Kingdom* a few weeks ago where electric eels could paralyze a man with one sting."

Nick folded his arms across his chest. "There aren't any eels in Kentucky, stupid. Put your money where your mouth is. You gonna go in or not?"

Simon lifted himself with his arms and lowered his body into the rushing water. The wince on his face revealed the water's coldness. His feet touched bottom and he let go of the edge when the water was chest high. He kept his arms out of the water to his sides.

He whooped, his cry filling the cave. "Wow, that's cold! My nuts just froze!"

They laughed.

"Your peanuts, you mean," Nick said.

Simon eyed Nick. "Okay, sissy, your turn. Time for you to—"

But Simon didn't finish his sentence. He lost his balance and groped for the rock ledge where he'd been sitting, but he couldn't reach it. The water toppled him over and began to carry him along to where it disappeared into the earth.

CHAPTER 31

Sam and Josh reached for Simon but missed. They needed to hurry before the current pulled him into the dark hole and out of sight.

In an instant Bates vaulted across the stream to the rocky edge on the other side. He dropped to his knees and grabbed one of Simon's feet, which protruded out of the water. He pulled Simon's body toward him. Most of Simon's head was underwater now.

Josh joined Bates, and they seized Simon's other foot, heaving both legs out of the water. They arched their backs and lugged Simon's body out of the water and onto the rock.

Simon came out, flailing his arms and sputtering. Then he coughed up the water he'd inhaled and pulled himself into a ball, teeth chattering. His face and hands had turned an unnatural tinge of blue.

"C'mon," Josh said. "Let's get back outside and warm him up."

Josh and Bates lifted Simon by the armpits and helped him cross the stream, while Sam and Nick reached for him on the other side. They led him toward the cave entrance, while he coughed and shivered and muttered that he never should have accepted Nick's dare.

Once they were outside with the cave far behind them, the hot summer air was a relief to everyone. Simon collapsed on the ground and let the sun's rays bake his skin, his bluish tinge fading away.

"Well, that sure was a bright idea," Sam said to no one in particular.

"Anything I can do to entertain you guys." Simon grinned. "Nick, I'll be over to pick up that video game as soon as we get home."

The boys returned to their canoes and began to paddle downstream. Three hours later, as the overcast light was beginning to fade, they reached their campsite. The site was a small clearing, perfect for tents, at the river's edge where the water's path elbowed. Though the site stood several feet above water level, it flooded in the spring when the river was high.

A county dirt road ran adjacent to the river beyond the campsite. Others had been here before, using the natural access point to launch canoes into the river or to pull them out.

The ground was smooth and flat, dotted here and there by weeds and wiry grass. Sam crouched beside the old fire pit, where they would soon build a roaring fire and cook supper. His stomach growled at the thought.

Josh and Nick pitched the tent while Bates, Simon, and Sam searched for firewood. They ventured into the thick grove of oak trees that stood between the river and the county road.

Bates swatted at a mosquito and studied the sky. The sky had been overcast all day, but now it was growing darker. Storm clouds drifted in from the west.

"I don't like the looks of those clouds," he said. "Mama says bad things happen in cloudy weather."

"I hope Josh and Nick have the tent ready, just in case," Simon said.

Rain hadn't fallen in over a week, so the boys had no problem collecting enough dry firewood for the evening. Sam passed through a small clearing and froze. He motioned to Bates and Simon and put a finger to his lips. Several whitetail deer grazed at the edge of the woods; they hadn't yet seen the boys. But the snap of a twig under Simon's foot sent them dashing away.

They returned to the campsite and heaped their findings beside the old fire pit. Sam used several sticks to create a tepee. Then he placed birch bark and dry leaves as tinder inside and beneath. He struck a match he brought along and lit the leaves and bark, blowing gently on the flame until it flared up, crackling as it spread to the sticks. Sam grabbed a coarse log, turned black with dried algae, and placed it on the fire. A few minutes later he added another one. Flames danced along the wood, and a plume of smoke trickled upward, tickling the treetops.

Soon the blazing fire roared against the darkening night, and Simon and Bates sat with Sam on old logs.

Josh and Nick drove the final stakes into the ground to secure the tent and joined them around the fire.

The sun dipped behind the tree line. Its orange and scarlet rays spilled through the branches and shimmered across the river. The crackling of the logs increased in volume and blended with the chorus of crickets. Lightning bugs floated in the nearby woods, and grasshoppers shrilled in the thick undergrowth. From the woods came the distant, haunting cry of a whippoorwill.

"Oh, man! I can hardly wait to eat!" Sam said, his stomach growling.

Simon unpacked five large cans of beef stew, opened them with a Swiss Army knife, and set them near the fire's edge to warm them up.

Josh handed out plastic spoons and passed around cans of Coke. Sam sipped his warm soda and watched the stew, his mouth watering. At the moment he couldn't think of anything that would taste better.

"Here's to Colgate football!" Nick raised his Coke can, and they bumped their cans against his.

Moments later the stew started to bubble over. Simon scooted the cans back from the heat with a long stick, and they dug in with their spoons. The fire crackled as they licked up every drop of the rib-sticking stew. Josh sliced two apples, and the slices were gone in no time. They washed down what remained of the meal with long pulls from their Coke cans, and everyone sat back, occasional belches splitting the air.

Simon licked his fingers, which he used to reach every drop of gravy from his can. Out of the corner of his eye, something moved. "A snake! A snake!"

Everyone jumped up.

Sure enough. A long, black snake slithered out of the pile of wood Sam, Simon, and Bates had heaped beside the fire pit. It tasted the air with its forked tongue. Before anyone else had a chance to react, Josh stomped one of his Chuck Taylor's on the snake's head.

The snake's body coiled, writhed, and lay still.

"Why'd you do that?" Nick said. "It was just a little snake."

Josh used a long stick to pick up the dead snake and toss it onto the fire. "In my book there are no small snakes."

CHAPTER 32

As the last rays of daylight flickered and died, Simon pulled a bag of assorted candy from his bag. The boys pounced on the sweets like a pack of ravenous wolves. Sam felt the cool night air closing around them and edged closer to the flames. The logs hissed and popped.

"All right, I've got one." Simon popped a Bit-O-Honey® into his mouth. A spark popped, and a plume of smoke wafted into his face. He waved the smoke away with his hands.

"My dad told me that when he was little, there was a crazy man in Colgate named Burt Malone," Simon said. "Everyone called him Fingernails because he never cut his nails. In fact, they were each a foot long, and when he was angry—which was all the time—he used them as weapons."

Sam grinned and glanced at Bates, who grinned back as if to say, *Yeah, right.*

"Fingernails lived at home with his mom, but as he grew older and got bigger, she couldn't control him any longer," Simon said. "He became such a menace to Colgate that she purposely had him locked up in the county jail. But he was so difficult to handle that the county transferred him to the state penitentiary in Eddyville. Well, at the state pen, they made him cut his long fingernails every week."

Simon paused and glanced around to be sure everyone was listening. "But Fingernails was smarter than they thought. He broke one of his own fingers, so they had to put it in a cast. The problem is, while he was wearing the cast for six weeks, they forgot to cut the nail on that finger. What they didn't realize was that Fingernails was grindin' that fingernail to a point so it was as sharp as an ice pick.

"One evening when the guard brought him his dinner, Fingernails used his sharp fingernail to stab him in the heart. Fingernails grabbed the keys and unlocked his cell. Then he killed another guard with his fingernail and escaped. He stole a guard's car and drove all the way back to Colgate."

The logs snapped and crackled. Sam slapped at a mosquito.

Simon continued. "Now, they announced in Colgate over the radio that Fingernails had escaped from jail, and everyone in town was supposed to lock up their house. Well, back in Colgate, the rain was fallin' hard, and Delores, a schoolteacher, was at home. While she was watchin' TV, she kept hearin' a scratch at her front door."

The night had turned still, and the crackle from the fire seemed like the only sound for miles. Sam felt himself holding his breath. His friends seemed to be on edge too, their eyes glued to Simon. Simon had them in the palm of his hand.

"Delores looked out her living room window but couldn't see anyone." Simon lowered his voice. "Then she heard the scratch again, but this time it was at her back door. She glanced out her kitchen window, but again, she saw no one.

"She called the sheriff's office, but the deputy who picked up said, 'Lady, do you got any idea how many Fingernail sightings we've received tonight? It's just the storm we're havin'. Only call us if you see him, okay?'

"So Delores sat back down in her living room to watch TV. When she heard her back door creak open, she raced up the stairs and locked herself inside the library. She called the sheriff's office from inside the room. 'I'm all alone,' she said.

"'How do you know it's Fingernails, ma'am?' the deputy asked. 'Couldn't it have been a cat?'

"'Well, I thought I heard somebody open my back door, so I rushed upstairs,' she said.

"'Well, like I told you five minutes ago, only call us if you have a confirmed sighting of him. All of our officers are out right now.'

"Delores hung up and sat in an easy chair. Then she heard a scratchin' at the bedroom door. She got up and moved to the window. Then she opened it and looked out. The door burst open, and there stood Fingernails.

"She put one leg over the windowsill, then both, and jumped. She landed hard and broke both of her legs. She looked up through the rain and saw Fingernails swing his legs over the windowsill, and he jumped too. He landed hard, breakin' both of his legs."

Simon was talking fast now and having a hard time catching his breath.

"Delores tried to move away from him, but Fingernails used his elbows to drag himself across the lawn toward her. She glanced back and felt Fingernails grab her around the ankle. He reached out and pointed his long fingernail at her calf. She felt a flash of pain ... then ... then the next thing she knew, she woke up in the hospital.

"Sittin' beside her bed was the same deputy she'd talked to on the phone.

"'What happened?' she asked, 'Where is he?'

"'He's back in Eddyville, ma'am,' the deputy said, 'and this time he'll never get out. The boys in Eddyville State Prison put him in isolation after they ripped out all of his fingernails.'

"Delores pulled the covers up to her chin. 'Did he hurt me?'

"'No ma'am,' the deputy said. 'We got there a few minutes after you talked to me on the phone. Don't worry—we stopped him.'

"'I don't understand. How did you know he was really in my house?'

"'You told me you were alone in the house, and when you called the second time you said you were upstairs in the library. I could hear the TV in the background, just like I did when you called the first time. But when you hung up, I stayed on the line and could still hear the TV. Then the second person hung up. That's how I knew he was in the house.'"

"Ooooooh," Josh said.

Bates nodded. "Good one."

"Yeah, I liked that one," Sam said.

"Simon, I've heard your dad tell that story before." Nick belched. "It's just a made-up story, but I've got a true one for you."

"All right," Sam said. "Let's hear it."

"Did you hear about what happened to Mrs. Turner, who used to live on Maple Street?" Nick said.

The others shook their heads in unison.

"Okay, one night several years ago she came home from choir practice and knew somethin' was wrong. Her dog, Max, a German shepherd, was coughin' and havin' trouble breathin'. Mrs. Turner called Dr. Townsend, the vet, who lived across the street from her. He asked her to bring Max over, and he'd take a look at him. She walked Max across the street to Dr. Townsend, left Max with him, and returned home. She settled into her easy chair and started watchin' *Hee Haw*.

"Dr. Townsend called her a few minutes later. 'Mrs. Turner,' he said, 'I want you to get up and meet me on your front lawn right now.' Mrs. Turner was upset because she thought for sure Max had died, but when she opened the door, Dr. Townsend was on her front lawn with Max. Without explaining, Dr. Townsend grabbed her arm and pulled her across the street. About that time, a Kidron County Sheriff's patrol car came flyin' down the street with its lights flashin' and its siren screamin'.

"'What's happenin'?' Mrs. Turner yelled. 'Why is the sheriff here?'

"'Did you hear?' Dr. Townsend said. 'Last night an inmate escaped from the mental hospital over in Raywick.'

"'Why no, I didn't,' she said.

"'Well, he's in your house,' Dr. Townsend said.

"A few minutes later Mrs. Turner watched in horror as a deputy sheriff led a deranged man with wild hair out of her house in handcuffs.

"'But how did you know he was in my house?' Mrs. Turner asked.

"'I found out what was wrong with Max,' Dr. Townsend said. 'I found this stuck in his throat.' And he pulled out a plastic sandwich bag, which contained a bloody ear with a long earring attached!"

"Oooooo, nice," Sam said.

"I don't get it," Simon said.

"You're as dull as ditch water," Nick said. "It was the deranged man's ear."

"Oh, I get it now," Simon said. "But did the dog get sick?"

Josh and Sam exchanged glances and shook their heads.

Bates, however, just gazed at the fire, not listening to them. The orange light flickered off his somber face and black eyes.

CHAPTER 33

H ey, what's the matter, Bates?" Josh said. "You don't seem like yourself."
"Yeah, what's wrong with you, dude?" Nick said. "Lighten up. You're rainin' on our parade."

Bates shrugged. "Sorry, guys. I guess I've got a lot on my mind."

"Like what?" Josh asked.

"Oh, I don't know. Lots of stuff."

"C'mon," Simon said. "Spit it out."

"Well, for one I've been thinkin' about Dewayne and wonderin' how he's doin' at the juvey home in Kimball."

"This may sound crazy," Nick said, "but my dad doesn't think Dewayne's even at Kimball. He thinks Judge Graves did somethin' sneaky that he doesn't want anybody to know about until after the election. My dad's tryin' to find out more about it."

"How does your dad know this?" Sam said.

Nick grinned. "My dad's a car dealer—he talks to everybody and knows everything in this town." He shrugged. "Well, wherever Dewayne is, he brought the trouble on himself—always causin' problems, tryin' to date Coach Bedford's daughter, and then spray-paintin' the school's sign."

Bates shook his head. "Nick, you don't know as much as you think you do."

"What's that supposed to mean?" Nick glared at Bates from the other side of the flames. "What don't I know?"

"Bates, what's botherin' you?" Josh asked.

"You-all don't really know me," Bates said in a low voice, eyes studying the flames. "Lots of things in my life stink."

"Like what?" Sam said.

Bates hesitated.

"C'mon, Bates," Josh said. "We're your friends. You can talk to us."

Bates finally began to open up, perhaps because he felt like he was with friends and away from town and the adults in his life. Gradually, he began sharing the heartache lurking just beneath the surface, his voice thick with emotion.

"My whole life stinks. Homework, exams, football practice, basketball practice, class president—my routine's a burden."

Sam glanced at his friends, and their eyes met. "Bates, how can you say that?" Sam said. "You're the most successful kid in our school. You're the best athlete and the star of the football team. You make all A's on your report card, you're the president of our class, and the teachers love you."

Bates shook his head. "They love the Bates Williams they've created. They don't even know the real me. I spend so much time pleasin' my mom, pleasin' my teachers, and pleasin' my coaches that I don't even know who I am sometimes. I feel like an actor." He paused. "No, I feel like a fraud. I don't know how to find my place in this town. I walk around most days feelin' like I'm carryin' a rock in my gut. I hate my life."

Josh thrust a stick into the coals, and sparks danced.

"I'll tell you somethin' else," Bates said. "Dewayne didn't put that graffiti on the school marquee … I did."

Everyone looked dumbstruck.

"*You* did?" Simon sounded confused.

Nick shook his head. "No way! You're out of your mind!"

"I know it sounds strange," Bates said in a low voice, "but I think I've always hated Coach Bedford. The weird thing is, I can't stop thinkin' about him. I can't stop playin' over and over in my head the things he says to me."

Sam shook his head trying to sort out these revelations.

"I just can't believe that *you* vandalized the school's sign," Nick said.

"Well, you better believe it," Bates said. "Coach Bedford's always talkin' to me about the football team and what we're gonna do next year. Sometimes I get stuck in his office, and he just talks and talks, and I have to just sit there and listen to all the terrible stuff he says. He doesn't really care about me. All he cares about is the stinkin' football team."

Bates wet his lips. "I've always been too afraid to cross him, so on the night before the last day of school, I snuck out of the house and went to the school with some spray paint."

Sam digested his words and then said, "Bates, we've been friends for a while. Why haven't you told me any of this stuff before?"

"Friends?" Bates' eyes drilled into Sam, his voice husky. "You think you're a true friend?"

Sam just stared at him.

Bates was grateful for the dark as the words gushed out of him like a mountain stream. "You're the worst because you think you're one of my best friends, but you're only pretending."

Sam cringed and glanced away. But Bates wasn't finished.

"Were you a good friend to me when your grandmother got mad because I stayed the night at your house? Did you stand up for me then? I don't think so. I remember you tellin' me it was best that I go on home."

Sam's face burned, but not from the heat of the campfire. Bates' words hit him like physical blows, leaving his conscience bruised. He couldn't help feeling ashamed when he remembered how he'd given in to his grandmother's wishes.

But what else could I have done at the time? She's my grandmother, after all.

Bates pressed on, his voice thick with passion. "And what about at Nick's house, when Ms. Regina told me I couldn't stay and go swimmin'? Did you stand up for your friend then? I remember walkin' home all by myself while the rest of you went swimmin'. What do you know about bein' my friend?"

He ran his forearm across his face, trying to hide the tears rolling down his face. "Man, this smoke is stingin' my eyes."

A tight spot swelled in Sam's stomach, and he hung his head.

I hate hearin' this. But I have to admit he's right.

"This is stupid!" Nick said.

"It's called being honest," Josh said.

Sam spoke up. "You're right, Bates. I should have stood up for you. I wanted to, but something held me back. I don't have any excuses."

A long moment of silence passed.

Sam sighed and made an important decision.

My friends might as well know the rest.

"I might as well come clean too." Sam swallowed hard. "I'm even worse than you think. I doubt any of you will want to stay my friends after I tell you what I did."

Bates was still looking at him. "What do you mean?"

"It's okay, Sam," Simon said. "You can tell us."

"Yeah," Josh said. "We'll still be your friends."

Nick rubbed his hands together with a devious chuckle. "Oh, I guess this is gettin' good. Okay, Sam, you might as well tell us your deepest, darkest secrets too."

Can I really do this? Should I really do this?

He found his voice and blurted what he needed to say before fear won the battle. "I didn't tell the truth at Dewayne's trial. In fact, I flat-out lied."

"What!?" Josh said.

Sam's face burned again as all eyes turned to him. He shoved his foot down into the dirt, wishing for a place to hide.

"How'd you lie?" Bates asked.

Sam sucked in a breath. "Do you remember that part when Hank Gabbard asked me if I saw Coach Bedford hit Dewayne?"

"Yeah," Simon said. "You said you didn't see anything."

"Like I said, it was a lie." Sam shook his head. "I saw it all. Coach Bedford poked Dewayne in the chest just like Dewayne said. Then Coach slapped him across the face—not once, but twice."

Bates swore.

"I can see the slaps. I see them over and over again in my mind like an endless loop."

"But why, Sam?" Bates said. "Why on earth did ya lie?" He flung his Coke can into the fire, and a shower of sparks leapt into the night sky.

"To protect myself, that's why. You guys don't understand. I've gotta live next door to those Bedfords—you don't know what that's like." He paused for a breath. "Then the morning of the trial, I woke up and Larry was in my room with a knife. He told me to keep my mouth shut—or else."

"Are you serious?" Simon asked.

"I'm not lyin'."

"Man, if he was here right now"—Nick drove his right fist into his left hand—"I'd punch him to kingdom come."

Sam cleared his throat. "I felt bad about decidin' to lie, but I didn't think what I said would make any difference. I mean, Judge Graves is an honest man, right? I figured, you know, that he'd do the right thing for Dewayne, no matter what I said. I've written a letter apologizin' and given it to Dewayne's aunt to get to him. But I don't think he'll ever forgive me, and I don't blame him."

He hung his head, not really expecting them to understand.

The silence after Sam's confession lingered for what seemed like an eternity for five thirteen-year-olds.

Finally, Bates broke the silence. "One other thing I need to tell you guys. I'm not gonna play football this fall."

"Now you're just talkin' foolish, Bates," Nick said. "You're the best player in our school. You'd really throw all that talent away? How can you *not* play?"

"I don't think I'll miss it one bit." Bates scratched his puffy eyes, which were irritated from his tears and the smoke. "I'm gonna join the jazz band, and I might even play in the marchin' band."

Nick stood. "Let me get this straight. Instead of bein' on the football field with cheerleaders yellin' your name and the band playin' for you, you're gonna join the geeks in the band and play music for the football team?"

"Hey, watch it," Simon said. "I used to be in the band."

"My point exactly!" Nick beat his fist against his leg with a scowl, eyes darting from one boy to the next. "What a bunch of pathetic drips! I don't feel sorry for any of you guys. Quit your whinin', for cryin' out loud."

He stared at Bates. "Bates, the fact is, your life ain't nearly as bad as you think." He turned toward Sam. "And Sam, Dewayne's a trouble-maker who had it comin' either way. Forget about that stupid trial. It doesn't make any difference to me. In fact—"

The crunch of gravel cut through the night air and silenced him. It was the sound of a car inching down the country road just beyond the woods. A hush fell over the boys as the engine's roar invaded the silence. The vehicle turned toward their campsite, its headlights cutting a ghostly swath through the dark and resting on stark, tree branches, turning them white as bones.

The headlights winked out. A car door opened, then slammed shut. In the darkness beyond the fire, someone approached in the shadows.

CHAPTER 34

The crunch of footfalls on fallen leaves sent a tingle of fear down Sam's back. A flashlight flicked on, and two figures crept through the dark like phantoms. Something about their shapes didn't feel friendly. The orange glow from the fire was now casting ghoulish shadows into the trees.

"Well, what have we found here?" A familiar voice sliced through the shadows. "Must be the latest meetin' of the Jackass Club."

Larry Bedford and one of his goon friends stepped into the light. They drew close to the fire, devilish grins on their faces. Larry's friend wore a grimy maroon headband.

Sam stiffened. *What is Larry doin' here?*

Nick cursed.

"Look what the cat dragged in," Simon muttered under his breath with a shake of his head.

In a flash, Larry grabbed a thick log from the firewood pile and tossed it onto the fire. Everybody leapt back as flames and embers exploded into the air.

The closest to Larry, Sam stood and drew his fingers into fists, angry at Larry for disrupting their gathering. "What do you want, Larry?"

"What do I want, Cray?" Larry chuckled. "I've given that question lots of thought over the last two weeks, neighbor boy."

Larry stepped closer to Sam, eyes hard. "You didn't think you could ruin my dad's life and get away with it, did you? I know all about your meetin' with stu-stu-stutterin' Sheridan and your secret talk with the school board."

Larry spat into the fire and edged closer until he and Sam were practically nose to nose. Sam's face flushed, but he held his ground.

"You know, Cray, I tried to warn you," Larry said. "I told you about the trouble you'd get into if you talked too much. Well, guess what? You didn't listen, did you? I saw you packin' for this trip and knew I had to come and teach you a lesson."

Sam heard the threat in his voice and tensed. Without further warning Larry leapt onto him and tackled him to the ground. Sam landed hard on his back, the impact knocking the wind out of him. Larry landed on top of him, his eyes livid. He raised his fist, ready to slam it into Sam's face.

Sam saw the blow coming and turned his head at the last second. Larry's fist glanced off his cheek and caught his left ear, splitting the skin around the lobe.

Searing pain blossomed from the wound. Sam felt hot blood trickling down his neck. He tried to wiggle free, but Larry was bigger and heavier.

In the light of the flickering flames, Larry grinned when he saw the pain he'd inflicted. He drew his fist back a second time. Sam winced, expecting the blow. But then a figure, like a ferocious wildcat, lunged at Larry out of the shadows, knocking him clean off Sam.

Bates had come to his rescue. He rolled with Larry on the ground close to the fire, fists flying.

Sam stood, chest heaving. The other boys edged closer for a better look.

Still on the ground, Larry swung at Bates but missed, his right hand landing on the fire's embers. He cried out and sucked in a lungful of acrid smoke. His face twisted, and he writhed in the dirt, coughing. After the coughing fit passed, he pulled himself onto his elbows and glared at Bates, who now stood beside Sam, breathing hard.

Larry rose to his feet and reached into his pocket, pulling out a pocket knife. He faced Sam, the single blade shiny in the reflection of the golden flames.

It was the same knife Larry had used to threaten him in his bedroom.

Larry's face twitched with rage. He thrust a finger at Sam's face. "Sam, you're not gonna make it back to Colgate."

When he took another step, Bates leapt forward. With a deft kick, he knocked the knife from Larry's hand, and it went flying into the brush. Larry howled and clutched his hand.

Simon ran over and foraged for the knife. Finding it, he flung it toward the river, its splash echoing into the night.

Larry's friend made his move. He rushed toward Sam. But Bates seized his arm with one hand and planted his huge fist in the middle of his chest with his other so hard that it knocked him to the ground.

The goon scrambled to his feet, backing away and wheezing for breath.

"Look, we just came for Sam." Larry's friend faced Bates, lifting his hands as if in surrender. "We didn't know you were gonna be here. I got no beef with you, man."

"You do if you're hangin' out with this dude." Bates motioned toward Larry.

Larry nodded toward his buddy. "C'mon, let's get out of here." The two backed away from the campfire, still facing the boys. "You guys have a good night now!" Larry said. "I hope you sleep well."

Larry's friend laughed hard.

Moments later an engine started, and Larry gunned it. The El Camino spun its tires on the gravel, and the car roared away. Sam watched as the vehicle's red tail lights headed down the road and vanished from sight.

"Are you all right?" Josh asked Sam.

"I think so." Sam touched his ear tentatively. Josh offered his T-shirt to wipe away the excess blood.

"We can't stay here tonight," Nick said. "Larry and his friend will be back with reinforcements."

"Yeah," Simon said, "let's not sit here and wait to be waylaid by more goons."

"Where we gonna go?" Josh said. "There's not a house for miles."

Nick frowned, thinking hard. "I guess we might as well get started down the river. With any luck we should reach the youth camp in a couple of hours."

Simon nodded. "That beats stayin' here and waitin' to get attacked by Larry and half the varsity football team."

Thunder rumbled in the distance. Dark, menacing clouds drifted across the horizon from the west and overtook the quarter moon. Cooler air swept across the campsite, carrying the scent of rain and snapping the canvas of the tent.

A rain drop fell on Sam's cheek, and he peered up at the clouds in dismay. The sprinkle quickly turned to a steady rain, rattling the leaves on the trees, sizzling the campfire, and watering the parched ground.

Sam shook his head. *That's just great.* Now they needed to abandon their campsite and canoe down the river in the rain. *All because of stupid Larry Bedford.*

CHAPTER 35

In less than fifteen minutes, the boys took down the tent, put out the fire, and stowed their gear in the canoes—all the while working under a steady drizzle. As they launched the two canoes and paddled into the night, thunder boomed again, this time closer and with more intensity.

"That doesn't sound good," Sam said to Bates and Simon. They were back to the same positions in the boat with Bates in front, Simon in the middle, and him in the back.

"Maybe the storm will just drift on by." Simon sounded hopeful.

Sam felt a sense of relief. *I'm glad to put some distance between us and the campsite. Nick's right. Larry'll be back with more guys.*

"At least we won't have to worry about bumping into Larry and his goons again tonight," Simon said.

"Yeah, eat our dust, losers!" Nick said from the other canoe.

A jagged fork of lighting streaked across the sky, illuminating the night behind them. The night sky crackled as if a tree branch had snapped.

Bates glanced back. "How's that ear, Sam?"

"I'm good." Sam pressed his hand to his ear and was alarmed to see it covered with blood.

As they progressed downstream, the sky opened up and rain drove down in sheets, pelting them with stinging cold. With the heavy clouds obscuring the moon, they had little light by which to maneuver down the river.

"Can you see?" Sam had to shout over the clamor of wind and rain.

"Not very well," Bates said in a worried voice. "Even with the flash-light, I can't see two feet in front of my face."

Simon nibbled on his fingernail.

Nick and Josh's canoe was practically neck and neck with theirs. Then it pulled slightly ahead.

"I can't see the rocks!" Nick said back at Josh from the front of the canoe. "I can hardly see anything."

Sam remembered the big rocks downriver and stiffened. *If we can't see them coming—*

Something slammed into the bottom of Nick and Josh's canoe.

"We hit a boulder," Nick said. Then he swore.

Sam peered ahead and braced himself; they were in the same path. Seconds later, sure enough, something large and unseen scraped the bottom of their canoe. Hung up on the rock, their canoe tipped slightly as the river pulled them to one side.

"We're gonna tip over!" Simon said in a panic.

Bates dropped his paddle.

"No, just hold on!" Sam said.

By keeping their weight low and steady, they avoided flipping over. The canoe groaned as the rock slid beneath them.

"Bates, you've gotta tell me what's ahead!" Sam hollered above the pounding storm. "If you see rocks, you've gotta let me know."

"I'll try!" he said.

Just when Sam thought the rain might let up, it came down even harder, lashing at the trees and pounding down on the river. Sam had heard of flashfloods, but he'd never experienced anything like this, let alone from the middle of a river and at night.

He turned his face toward the night sky. The cold rain beat down hard against it and streamed down his neck.

Sam studied the river around them and knew the water level must be rising. Bates' flashlight still worked, and he shone it on shore as they raced past. Swollen, brown tributaries overflowed the river's banks and cascaded in rushing white water to join the swollen river.

Thunder exploded, making Sam start, as their canoes raced along. The rising water level helped them avoid some rocks, and they sailed right over many that might have been a problem. But then Sam realized that the canoes were racing so fast in the white water that they had lost control.

Only I have a paddle. Can we steer at all?

Waves slammed into the side of the canoe, splashing in from both sides. Bates aimed his flashlight at the bottom of the canoe. Several inches of water covered the bottom. If the river and rain kept coming in, it would swamp them in no time.

Over the din of the storm, Bates yelled at Simon to help him bail water with their hands. Due to the speed of the current, Sam realized there was no longer any need to paddle; he just tried to keep the canoe going in the right direction.

Bates' flashlight began to dim. Despite the heavy rain and the presence of water all around, Sam's mouth turned dry.

The canoes were practically side by side now.

Josh sensed their dangerous situation. "Should we stop?"

"No! There's nowhere to stop!" Nick shouted back. "We've gotta keep goin'!"

"With the river runnin' so fast, we should be there soon!" Josh said.

The canoes glided even faster now. The shore flashed by them.

"How much farther?" Sam asked.

"Can't be far," Josh said, "but I can't make out anything along the bank to know for sure."

Simon straightened. "Wait! I see some lights ahead."

"Those must be the lights of the campground!" Josh said, his voice excited. "We're almost there!"

"All right," Nick said. "Let's steer the canoes toward the bank."

A wave of relief washed over Sam at the sight of pale light shining through the trees. The rain refracted its light, giving the scene a mysterious, foreboding feeling. But his heart lifted at the thought of getting off the raging river and out of the rain.

Sam dragged his paddle behind him, steering the canoe toward shore, when a rushing sound sent a jolt of fear through him. The sound grew louder, joined by a low, rumbling, ominous sound.

Simon heard the sound too. "What's that?"

Sam's breath caught in his throat. "Oh no! The river's so high it's rushin' over the dam!"

"We're dead!" Simon said.

"Paddle to the bank. Now!" Sam yelled.

Everybody dug in. Nick, Josh, and Sam paddled as hard as they could against the fierce current. Bates and Simon tried to use their hands.

Even in the rain, sweat dripped down Sam's forehead and ran down his cheeks as his arms and shoulders strained against the current. Nick and Josh's canoe was about fifteen feet ahead; they both paddled and made good progress. But Sam paddled by himself, and their canoe wasn't keeping up.

The roar of the river plummeting over the dam was deafening. The cascade was only twenty feet away now.

Sam strained to pull the canoe closer to shore—disaster was about to strike. But regardless of how hard he paddled, the canoe remained in the middle of the river about thirty feet from the bank.

"Hurry!" Simon screamed at Sam, eyes wide with fear. "Get to the bank!"

A shiver snaked up Sam's spine. Nick and Josh were almost to the bank, but he, Simon, and Bates weren't going to make it.

"We're gonna go over!" Sam braced himself as he stared downriver. In the glowing campground lights, the rushing water turned from green to a menacing, murky gray.

Ahead, Nick and Josh were within ten feet of shore, but their canoe was edging toward the dam. Sam realized Nick and Josh weren't going to make it either.

Ahead, white water rushed toward the dam's edge, then poured over it. Sam couldn't see what awaited them on the other side. Then he remembered seeing the dam from the other side and recalled the big rocks below. His pulse spiked.

Nick and Josh's canoe turned sideways as it reached the lip. They were heading toward the rocks.

"No!" Sam shouted.

CHAPTER 36

Their canoe's bottom flashed silver as it teetered on the edge. Then it toppled over the brink, rushing into darkness. Wails from Nick and Josh made Sam shudder. He could only imagine the canoe slamming into the rocks twenty feet below.

Five second later, it was their turn, but they were hitting the dam from the middle of the river instead of near the bank.

"Here it comes!" Simon gripped the sides of the canoe, his knuckles white.

Sam's stomach sank as if he were on a rollercoaster and cresting a hill before the big plunge. The canoe rushed toward the lip, then toppled over the edge. He leaned back, yelling, as it plunged down into blackness.

Sam felt himself being tossed from the canoe. Then his body hit a cold wall, and the river enveloped him.

For a moment, the undertow pulled him to the river bottom, and the wound on his ear burned. He didn't see any rocks. There was nothing but water, and Sam swam hard against the current.

He burst from the surface and treaded water, looking around, glad to be alive. In the glowing lights from the campground, he saw that the current had already carried him twenty feet from the dam.

Ten feet away, Simon popped out of the water like a bobber wrenched free from a large bass. "My glasses!" he yelled. "I lost my glasses."

Who cares about your stupid glasses? We've almost been killed. Where is Bates? Are Nick and Josh okay?

Sam heard sputtering and turned to see Bates taking a mouthful of water. Sam came alongside and wrapped an arm around his middle.

Simon complained that he could hardly see and followed the sound of Sam's voice. Soon they were all together, treading water as the current swept them downstream.

"I can't hold him, Simon!" Sam kicked hard to try keeping both of them afloat. "Help me. I think I'm gonna pass out! My head's spinnin'!"

"I've got him." Simon grabbed Bates' arm, and Sam felt some relief.

They struggled to reach the bank. Finally, the river widened and grew shallower. Sam could touch bottom and told the others. They stood chest high and struggled to steer their exhausted bodies toward shore.

Sam reached the bank before Simon and Bates and looked around. They were at least one hundred yards south of the dam. On the opposite side of the river, a dented canoe, caught by reeds, bobbed in the water.

Sam cupped a hand to his mouth and turned his head upriver. "Josh! Nick!" he yelled, his hollow-sounding voice swallowed by the night.

No reply.

He touched his ear and saw that he was bleeding again. The pain was excruciating, and blackness began closing around him. Before his legs gave way, he sat on the muddy incline, trying to clear his head.

Simon helped Bates out of the water, and they collapsed in the mud next to Sam.

"Sam, stay here with Bates." Simon struggled to his feet. "I'm gonna check on the others."

Simon found strength he didn't know he possessed and scrambled up the slope, his shoes sinking into mud up to his ankles. Everything was blurry without his glasses.

On the embankment he cupped his hands around his mouth. "Josh! Nick!" he shouted.

No response.

A faint path ran parallel to the river, and he followed it, pebbles crumbling beneath his feet. He tripped on an unseen tree root and toppled to the ground, his hands shooting out to catch himself. He scrambled back to his feet, rubbed his aching wrists, and called Josh's and Nick's names again.

Again, only the rushing river met his ears.

Why don't they answer?

He needed help.

To his left stood the campground's bunkhouses and cafeteria. He followed the trail toward the dam. Security lights from the campground flooded the bank, and he stumbled toward them. The rain lashed his face, and the wind howled like a wounded animal. He cupped his hands to his mouth, shivering in his wet clothes.

The howling wind seemed to snatch his voice away. He squinted and tried to see beyond the shadows clogging the bank, but he didn't see anyone. He stared into the sky, the rain coursing down his face.

"Josh! Nick! Why don't you answer me?" he shouted.

"Frank." Wendy Wiseman sat up in bed and jabbed her husband with her elbow. "Frank, wake up. I hear somebody outside."

Frank rolled over with a groan and wished she hadn't woken him. "It's probably just a stray dog. Go back to sleep."

"No, I heard a voice." She elbowed him again, this time harder. "Frank, do you hear what I'm sayin'? I think somebody's in trouble."

Frank sat up and rubbed his bleary eyes. "Okay, okay. I'll check it out." He reached for his trousers, reminding himself that these occasional inconveniences were just par for the course as groundskeeper at the Kidron Valley Campground.

He lumbered to the kitchen and pulled on rubber boots and a yellow rain slicker.

Things aren't so bad. Where would you rather be? Out in the great outdoors, or behind a desk at the bank?

He knew the right answer. Both he and Wendy loved the outdoors and had served as volunteers at the campground for years. Five years ago he retired as president of the Kidron County Bank & Trust and moved to the campground full time. At the same time, Wendy stepped down as Dr. Carlisle's office manager. This simpler life was exactly what they'd been looking for.

Summers were pretty hectic, but they enjoyed serving together and doing what they felt was important work. Their busy season had ended just last week at the conclusion of an elementary school camp for children from Metcalfe and Adair Counties.

Frank checked his watch and winced. 2:23 A.M. *The coldest part of the night.*

He grabbed a flashlight and exited through the back door. He pulled up his hood and headed into the driving rain toward the dam, pausing once to glance back at the cottage. Warm lights glowed from window panes in bumblebee patterns of black and yellow, making him wish he were dry and back in his bed.

Their cottage was nestled deep in the woods near the waterfall that cascaded from the dam, which had originally served as a working mill. The night before, he and Wendy, who ran the campground's dining hall, had sat on lawn chairs overlooking the falls. They chatted about their grandchildren and their upcoming trip to Venice, Italy, until a late summer thunderstorm chased them back indoors.

Near the dam he heard the rushing river long before he saw it. He shined his powerful flashlight back and forth along the path and stopped. *What was that?*

His beam illumined the back of a boy.

"What're you doin' out here?" Frank asked.

The boy turned, squinted into the light. "Who's there?"

"It's Frank Wiseman." Frank stepped closer, his eyes widening. The boy was soaked to the skin, but he recognized the grimy face. "Simon Puckett, is that you?"

Simon nodded, his face anxious. "You gotta help us." He grabbed the sleeve of Frank's raincoat with quivering hands. He shivered from head to toe, hair matted with mud, his lips colorless.

"You look like a walkin' ghost," Frank said. "What're you doin' here? You weren't supposed to be here 'til mornin'. Where're the other boys?"

"We got spooked and decided to canoe to the camp tonight."

"During a storm like this? Are you crazy?"

"We didn't know it was going to be so bad. Then the current was so fast that we couldn't stop. Our canoes went over the dam."

Frank's breath hitched in his throat. "You did what?"

"Sam and Bates are on the bank downriver a ways—they're okay. But I can't find Nick or Josh anywhere. They were in the other canoe that went over near the bank."

Frank's chest tightened. "You mean, *this side* of the bank?"

Simon nodded.

If that's true, Nick and Josh went over the dam where it's littered with jagged rocks.

Frank stepped to the lip of the bank and surveyed the river from where the ground plummeted down a steep hill. Near the water's edge, milkweed rose taller than his head. Water gushed over the dam's rough-hewn stone wall where the mill had once stood, frothing and foaming in swirls of white.

Closer to the river now, Frank aimed his flashlight at the dam's base and sucked in a quick breath. Two bodies lay on the rocks fifty yards away.

CHAPTER 37

Frank Wiseman's hands began to shake. "I think I see 'em."

Simon craned his neck for a look, but Frank lowered the flashlight, not so sure he wanted the boy to see.

Frank ignored the small, tight place in his stomach and descended the slope, with Simon just a step behind. He reached the river's edge, amazed at the rush of the swollen river. He kept the flashlight beam low and surveyed the path across flat rocks to where Nick and Josh were sprawled near the dam's base. Neither boy moved or made a sound.

He was unsure what he would find. "You better stay here." His voice trembled.

Oh, God, please let them be okay.

With a booted foot, Frank tested the first rock in the stream. He found it secure and stepped over the rushing current to the next rock. He slipped on slick algae, and almost fell, but continued toward the dam.

Simon ignored his instructions and stayed right behind him. Frank decided it was probably useless to protest.

Twenty yards from the dam's base, he aimed the flashlight at the first boy, who was sprawled on a rock face up. Frank directed his light to the second boy, who lay face down on a higher rock. Neither boy appeared to be conscious, nor were there obvious signs of life.

Fear clawed at Frank's heart, and he tried to keep the flashlight from shaking.

He stepped gingerly from one rock to the next, reached the closest boy, and hovered over him. The boy's face, which was covered in blood, must have absorbed the impact of a powerful blow. A large, bloody gash ran across his forehead and disappeared into his hairline. His left arm was bent in the wrong direction.

A cold, numb sensation spread across Frank's chest. He leaned closer and put his ear to the boy's nose and mouth.

Please, give me a sign.

"He's breathing!" Frank said in relief. "It's shallow, but steady. Which one is this?"

Simon stepped closer and crouched, leaning his face within inches of the injured boy's. He squinted. "It's Nick."

"Now, Simon, I want you to stay here with Nick. I'll go check on Josh."

"Hurry." Desperation squeezed Simon's voice.

The second boy lay face down ten feet away.

Frank took a tentative step on another rock and slipped. He caught himself by grabbing a sharp rock with his right hand, cutting his palm. He glanced at his bleeding hand in a daze, hardly caring, and pressed the burning palm against his pant leg.

A woman's voice rang out from the bank above the roar of the dam. "Frank, is everything okay?"

He turned and glimpsed Wendy above.

"What's wrong? Do you need me to do anything?" She clutched several wool blankets in her arms.

"Call an ambulance!"

"What's happened?"

He fumed. Each wasted second could mean the difference between life and death. "Just go! Josh Carlisle and Nick Walker went over the dam in their canoes."

Her face blanched. "Good heavens!"

"Simon Puckett's here with me. Downstream you'll find Sam Cray and Bates Williams—they're fine. Nick Walker's hurt but alive. I'm gonna take a look at Josh Carlisle now."

She lingered.

"Go, Wendy!" he said.

She disappeared.

Frank turned to Simon and placed a firm hand on his shoulder. "Son, I want you to go up to Mrs. Wiseman. She needs your help. Stay with her until the ambulance gets here, then show the paramedics where Sam and Bates are. Okay? I'm gonna stay here with Nick and Josh."

Simon didn't budge. He just stared down, wide-eyed.

Frank chided himself for letting the boy get so close. "Go on now, Simon. Go help Mrs. Wiseman. Besides, Sam and Bates need you now."

Still Simon lingered.

Frank couldn't hold back the anger. "Simon, I need you to go now. Do what I say!"

As if in a daze, Simon turned and began his trek up the slope to Wendy. Frank waited until he reached the top before turning back to the two boys. He whispered a prayer. "Please let Josh be okay."

His stomach tightened when he took a closer look. The boy lay face down over the end of a straight, flat rock that jutted out of the river at a forty-five-degree angle. His arms were raised over his head, the rock's edge at his middle, his feet dangling down toward the dam's base.

Frank imagined the canoe flying over the dam. He could almost hear the crunch of the aluminum shell as it smashed against the rocks. Whether the boys had been inside or outside the canoe at the moment of impact, he didn't know. Nor did it really matter at this point.

Frank edged closer, hands shaking. Blood dripped from the boy's head, and the only visible part of his face, angled to one side, appeared to be made of wax. The rest of his face, obscured by rock, had probably been smashed beyond recognition by the impact.

The body gave no clue that life remained. His back didn't rise or fall.

He felt a pale wrist for a pulse.

He felt nothing, but maybe he was wrong.

You can't trust yourself in this heavy rain. Maybe Josh's pulse is just weak.

I shouldn't move the body, but what if Josh is alive and needs help? Just think of all the people Dr. Carlisle has helped over the years.

Frank knew he had to try something.

He placed both hands on the boy's shoulders and pulled him toward him. But the body didn't move, didn't budge. He pulled again—still no good. He took a closer look and saw where the rock's tip had pierced his abdomen. Blood covered the rock at his midsection.

He gently pushed and pulled until the body finally slipped off the rock and slid into his arms. Frank lowered him so he lay face up on the rock where Frank stood.

Frank knelt beside him and used his flashlight to see what camp security lights couldn't reveal. Josh's mouth and eyes were open in a grimace of shock. His pupils had rolled up into his skull, and white orbits stared back at him. A tangle of broken blood vessels dominated his right eye.

He pulled up the boy's torn, soaked T-shirt. A gaping puncture wound just above his stomach revealing where the sharp rock had penetrated his abdomen.

Frank's stomach turned at the sight. He paused to clear his head before pressing his ear to the cold, damp chest. He heard only silence.

The boy's curled fingers were stiffening, fingernails already turning gray-blue.

Josh is dead.

Frank realized he was looking at a corpse and shuddered. He slumped to a sitting position beside the body, his strength gone. The roar of the falling cascade filled his ears. Normally, it was a peaceful, soothing sound. But right now he hated it.

Finally, the sobs came. He let himself cry, his whole body shaking.

On Friday morning at 5:00 A.M., Sheriff Micah Brothers sat in his cruiser at the end of the driveway to the Carlisle's home in Colgate. He'd pulled onto their street at 4:30 A.M. but hadn't been able to bring himself to wake the family. Now it was time.

"Come on, Brothers," he said. "You gotta do this."

He got out of the cruiser and followed cobbled steps to the front door. The Tudor-style house was modest for a physician's residence, with a low, sloping roof, wooden shutters, and a detached, two-car garage. Thick wisteria wove through the front terrace, and a privacy fence shielded the backyard.

He took a deep breath, rapped on the door, and waited.

Soon Dr. Carlisle opened the door and appeared in a bathrobe. "Good mornin' Micah," he said.

"I'm sorry for havin' to wake you at this hour."

"Please come in." Dr. Carlisle opened the door wide to allow the sheriff to pass. "Could I get you a cup of coffee?"

"No thanks. Already had some." Sheriff Brothers stepped into the foyer and removed his hat, holding it stiffly in front of him with both hands.

Dr. Carlisle studied his face with a baffled look. "Is there somethin' I can do for you?"

The sheriff hesitated. "I'm afraid I have some bad news."

Dr. Carlisle waited.

"There was an accident early this mornin' on the river. We don't know all the details yet, but it appears that the boys tried to canoe to the camp in the dark."

Anxiety crept into the doctor's eyes, but still he said nothing.

"Well, it rained harder south of here than it did in Colgate, and the river was runnin' high and hard." The sheriff swallowed, his mouth dry. This was going to be harder than he expected.

Dr. Carlisle gave him an expectant nod. "Yes?"

Sheriff Brothers cleared his throat. "Well, both canoes went over the dam."

Dr. Carlisle pressed an open hand to his mouth and pulled hard on his lips.

"The canoe Sam Cray, Simon Puckett, and Bates Williams were in went over toward the middle of the river, and they landed in deep water. They're fine. But your son and Nick Walker were in the other canoe that went over close to the old mill. Doc, you know about the big, sharp rocks down there."

The sheriff paused again.

The doctor spoke through his fingers. "Please, Micah, just say what you need to say."

"Josh is dead."

Dr. Carlisle's hand tightened over his mouth, knuckles white. He dropped his chin.

"From all indications, your boy died instantly—a hard knock to the head on those rocks." He omitted what paramedics had told him about the wound to the abdomen.

Dr. Carlisle collapsed into one of several high-backed chairs lining the foyer and dropped his head into his hands. All was quiet except for the ticking of the grandfather clock in the corner.

"Nick's been hurt, but he's gonna make it."

The sheriff placed a hand on his shoulder. "I'm sorry, Doc. So sorry. I wish it weren't true."

Dr. Carlisle gripped the sheriff's arm and stood. "Thanks, Micah. I appreciate it being you who came to see me."

The sheriff nodded. "Dr. Mason's been called in to meet the—he's been called to the hospital."

"Ah."

Sheriff Brothers placed his hands behind his back and clutched the hat again. "Should I call your pastor? Ask him to come over and sit with you?"

Dr. Carlisle considered. "No, Micah. I think we're going to need some time by ourselves. My daughter's over at a friend's house, but I ..." He gripped his unshaven face with his right hand as if to steady himself. "I need to wake Mrs. Carlisle." His hands began to shake.

The sheriff stepped back. "That's fine."

Tears ran down Dr. Carlisle's face. Sheriff Brothers struggled to meet his gaze and the anguish he saw there.

"But would you ask Brother Billy to do me a favor? Dr. Mason is going to need someone to identify Josh's body." Dr. Carlisle glanced away. "I—I don't think I can do it, Micah, and I know Beverly can't. If Brother Billy could do that for me, I'd be very grateful."

"Of course, Doc. I'll ask him right away."

Grieving silence lengthened between them.

The sheriff backed toward the door. "Anything else I can do to help?"

Dr. Carlisle shook his head, eyes lowered to the floor.

"I'm very sorry for your loss."

"Thank you, Micah."

Dr. Carlisle closed the door behind the sheriff. In his mind, Sheriff Brothers saw Dr. Carlisle plodding up the stairs to wake his wife with news no mother wants to hear.

CHAPTER 38

Dr. Jake Mason didn't feel like his usual chipper self and dreaded what needed to be done today. He parked his raspberry Stingray Corvette in his reserved parking spot at the Kidron County Memorial Hospital and exited the car. He paused and placed his right hand on his forehead, rubbing his temples with his thumb and index finger.

Dr. Mason knew he was good-looking. When he smiled, people saw indented commas appear on each cheek of his twenty-nine-year-old, handsome face, but he wasn't smiling this morning. Too much drink and too little sleep the night before had replaced his typical stamina and clear-headedness with a pounding headache. The truth was, he'd rather be in bed right now, but duty called.

Dr. Mason, the youngest of three doctors in Colgate and the only one still possessing his hair, had a mixed reputation in Kidron County. Many knew him to be a knowledgeable, insightful family doctor—and his practice was certainly busy—but patients saw him as neither friendly nor unfriendly. He was simply indifferent.

Being the youngest doctor in the county certainly had its perks, but it also had one big drawback: he was obligated to serve as the county coroner. The position paid him a lump sum of four hundred dollars per month "whether no one in the county kicked the bucket or a whole bushel full did," the county treasurer had told him with a chuckle. Four hundred dollars didn't seem like nearly enough to induce him to report to the hospital this early on a Friday morning.

He entered the hospital through its main entrance.

"Well, good mornin', Dr. Mason," the receptionist said in a cheerful voice. "I'm not used to seein' you here this early. Come to think of it, I don't think I've *ever* seen you here before lunch."

"Mornin', Margaret." He was in no mood to bandy words with her today, so he didn't. He took the stairs to the basement and pushed through a door marked Kidron County Morgue.

The familiar aroma of formaldehyde greeted him, and the garish lights caused his headache to throb even worse. To his left, beefy-faced Deputy Caleb Hunter sat on a stool and examined a Styrofoam cup filled with black coffee.

The deputy cast a playful glance in Dr. Mason's direction and drained the cup dry. "What's the matter, Dr. Mason? Ain't the playboy doc of Kidron County used to bein' up this early?"

Dr. Mason ignored him. He grabbed a clean mug at the coffee station, filled it to the brim, and stirred in powdered creamer.

"I've been takin' a look around," Deputy Hunter said, "and I'm impressed. You run a tight ship down here, Doc. I was struck by the neatness of everything." He chuckled. "Why, it looks like everything unimportant is in order."

Dr. Mason took a long sip and sighed. At least the coffee would help. He fixed his expressionless gaze on the deputy. "I have no idea what *that's* supposed to mean, and frankly, I don't care." He gestured to the walk-in refrigeration unit. "Is the Carlisle boy in there?"

The deputy sobered and nodded. "What a shame. Brother Billy from the Carlisles' church should be here anytime. Dr. and Mrs. Carlisle didn't want to identify the body, so Sheriff Brothers said the pastor could do it."

Dr. Mason combed fingers through his thick, sandy blond hair that he knew was too long by Kidron County standards. He set down his mug and crossed to the refrigeration unit, pulling on one of the metal handles. The drawer slid open and revealed the white-sheeted shape of a body. The profile didn't seem large enough to represent a human body.

He began pulling back the sheet, then stopped. *No, not yet.* He strode back to the coffee station and refilled his mug. He cradled his coffee in both hands, feeling its warmth in his fingers.

"I simply can't believe it." He shook his head. "The kid was how old?"

"Only thirteen. The sheriff says he was a really good kid too. Did you know him?"

Dr. Mason's eyes lingered on the outline of the slender body. "Josh wasn't a good kid, Caleb—he was a *wonderful* kid."

He recalled his dinners at the Carlisle home over the last few years. His mind flooded with memories of the well-mannered boy at the dinner table. Josh grinned shyly when Dr. Carlisle teased him about girls. Dr. Mason helped Josh paint the Helping Arms Agency building after Dr. Carlisle talked him into giving up one of his free Saturdays. He and Josh enjoyed such a good time together that day and talked about all sorts of topics. He remembered talking with Josh so openly that he could not believe he was only a teenage boy; he seemed much older and more mature.

Now, he'll never grow into a man. He'll never know what it's like to see his dreams fulfilled.

The coffee soured in his stomach, and he set the mug down, deciding he'd had enough.

"Well, I guess I'll be movin' on." Deputy Hunter rose from the stool. "The sheriff told me to stay here with the body until you arrived. Now that you're here …"

"See ya, Caleb."

No sooner had Deputy Hunter left than the door opened.

"Good mornin', Dr. Mason," Brother Billy said.

Dr. Mason turned. "Good morning, Reverend. I'm sorry both of us have to be here this morning."

"I just don't know what's happened here." Brother Billy's voice wobbled. He ran a shaky hand through thinning, black hair. "For the life of me, I can't figure it out. If you ask me, there wasn't a better boy in all of Kidron County. Why the good Lord would want to take Josh—"

"Listen, Reverend." Dr. Mason locked eyes with him.

"Please, call me Billy or Brother Billy."

"Listen, Billy. Let's not get all philosophical or religious here, okay? I've got an unpleasant job to do. I just want to get it done and go home." Dr. Mason marveled at the antagonistic sound in his voice. He hadn't intended to come across so cold, but given the circumstances—

"Forgive me." Brother Billy bobbed his head, not meeting the doctor's eye. "This is difficult enough for you without me ramblin' on."

Dr. Mason crossed to the shrouded body.

"Have you seen him yet?" Brother Billy took a tentative step closer, hands wedged together.

"No, I was waiting for you." Dr. Mason pulled the sheet back to reveal a body that hadn't been cleaned since the accident.

Brother Billy gasped and appeared as if he might be sick.

The boy's head was covered in blood, which had dried on his face and in his hair. A ragged wound trailed from one side of his head to his hairline. A mass of dried blood also covered his T-shirt from the puncture wound to his abdomen.

Brother Billy turned his head, his voice shaking. "That's enough. Please, put the sheet back."

Dr. Mason obliged.

"If that's all you need me for, I'll be goin' now." Brother Billy hurried toward the door.

"Wait, Billy. It is the boy, isn't it? I need you to verify his identity."

Brother Billy turned. Tears drowned his eyes. "What?"

"It *is* Josh Carlisle, right?"

Brother Billy nodded. "Yes, but I wish it weren't." He left.

Dr. Mason's headache wasn't letting up. He sighed and grabbed a bottle of aspirin from a nearby shelf. He popped three pills into his mouth and washed them down with another gulp. Time to get down to business.

Every death in the county has to have a cause.

Dr. Mason returned to the body and pulled off the sheet.

All right. Let's get this over with, Mason, so you can go home and get some sleep.

He pulled on a fresh surgical gown and a pair of latex gloves from a box on the counter. Then he removed the boy's tennis shoes and muddy socks, pitching them into the utility sink beside the tray.

He sighed. *Don't think of him as Josh Carlisle. Think of him as "the deceased," not Dr. Carlisle's son. Just answer the question: how did the deceased become the deceased?*

Cause of death—that's all he needed to determine. Then he could get out of here.

He used surgical scissors to cut the boy's clothes and pulled them free, placing them in the sink with the socks and shoes. He eyed the skin's waxy hue and summoned his courage. He shook his head and tried to focus. Someone else should have been doing this autopsy. Not him.

Must preserve clinical detachment, Doctor. Doesn't matter if you knew him. He's dead.

He poured rubbing alcohol on a clean cotton cloth and rubbed it across the boy's forehead, then his torso. He examined the gash on the forehead, then readied a scalpel, preparing to make an incision down the boy's abdomen. Though the line would start small, it would open like a hungry mouth.

He broke into a cold sweat. *I'm a family doctor, not a coroner. I shouldn't even be doing this. I hate this rural backward county.*

He pressed the scalpel to the boy's skin and made a small cut.

Blood rushed to his head, and his throat tightened. He hurried to the sink and vomited once, twice, three times. The retching was so strong that he thought he might expel his intestines.

Cold and clammy, he grabbed a hand towel and pressed it to his mouth. He gripped the sides of the sink and waited for the dizziness to pass. Then he lifted his head and studied his pasty, sweaty face in the mirror. He ran some cold water and splashed his face.

I can't do this. I just can't.

He retrieved a large plastic bag from under the sink and placed the soiled clothes and shoes—now covered with his vomit—inside. He removed his gown and gloves, tossing them in too, before dropping the bag in a plastic container marked Hazardous Waste.

He crossed to the metal desk, studied the standard autopsy form—"Official Register of Death, Kidron County"—and picked up a pen. His job was to maintain the accuracy of the official register of deaths in Kidron County. Proper protocol required that he obtain a copy of Josh's medical records.

Oh, brother. Why not just cut to the chase?

He glanced over, let his eyes roam over the body again. Josh had obviously died either from the blow to his head or to the puncture wound in his abdomen. The laceration could have very well punctured his liver.

Massive trauma to the head or puncture to the side. Could be either or both.

He turned back to the form and scribbled, "Massive trauma to the head above the right ear." Yes, he could state with a reasonable degree of medical certainty that Josh Carlisle had died from massive trauma to the brain.

Dr. Mason returned to the body, covered it, and pushed the drawer back into the refrigeration unit. He picked up the telephone. "Margaret, this is Dr. Mason. Please call Green's Funeral Home and tell them they can come get the Carlisle boy."

"You're done?"

An impatient sigh. Why was this woman always questioning him? "Yes, I'm finished."

"That was quick."

"Yes, it was. Got a problem with that?"

He hung up and was back home in bed a half hour later.

PART

FIVE

THE

HOSPITAL

(Two days later)

Colgate Herald-News

(The only newspaper in the world dedicated to Kidron County, Kentucky.)

Sunday, August 31, 1975

Obituary Notice: Carlisle Boy Laid to Rest

COLGATE—Few deaths, if any, in this community have so sincerely impacted the people of Kidron County as that of Josh Carlisle, age thirteen. Burial services for Josh occurred Saturday. Josh was buried with a closed casket due to the nature of his injuries, which were sustained in a canoeing accident on the Kidron River early Friday morning.

We don't pretend here to write Josh's epitaph. He had been writing it himself for years. Josh amounted to something much earlier in life than most people ever do. We must have buried the richest boy in Kidron County yesterday. More than eight hundred persons paid their respects at Green's Funeral Home, and it seemed fitting that a thunderstorm broke out during the graveside service. Two people fainted, and everyone present wept openly. Members of the Colgate Junior High football team were honorary pallbearers.

Why all of this attention for one thirteen-year-old boy? Here's why. By all accounts, Josh Carlisle had never been corrected by his teachers, coaches, or principal. Josh served with his parents as a volunteer at Helping Arms Agency in downtown Colgate; he worked Saturdays sorting canned goods for the food pantry and clothes for the clothes closet. He also tutored elementary-aged children in the evenings as part of the agency's mentoring program. He was a good athlete on the junior high's basketball and football teams and a straight-A student. In sum, the finest tribute that could be paid to Josh might be in the words of H. H. Milman, who said, "It matters not at what hour the righteous fall asleep—death cannot come untimely to him who is fit to die."

CHAPTER 39

The aroma of fried bacon filled the air at Jerry's Restaurant—a testament to the thirty years of fine home cooking at the restaurant. Dan Cray and Sam sat at a table with a sticky top—an inevitable fact of life given the number of bottles of maple syrup the restaurant went through on a regular basis. Sam's eyes were heavy with sleep, his hair looking like a bird's nest. A bandage covered his left ear.

Dan pushed the ketchup toward Sam. He said something to him, but Sam wasn't really listening. He fell into watching his dad's hands. Veins rippled from his wrist and ran to thick fingers. Sam watched as they rose and fell across from him.

"Sam, are you even listenin' to me?"

"Yeah."

"Like I was sayin', I don't know anybody else who likes ketchup with his eggs."

Sam shrugged. "Everything's better with ketchup—well, almost everything. Not cake or ice cream, I guess."

Dan grinned at him, then turned serious. "About Josh's funeral yesterday … I was wonderin' if … you know … if you wanted to talk about it."

"Not really." Sam made shapes on his plate by pushing ketchup and hash browns around with his fork.

"Well, if you ever want to talk, just let me know, okay?"

"Okay."

"And you can call me collect any time. You know that, don't you?"

Sam nodded.

"Thought any more about visitin' me in Louisville? You know, the whole summer's gone by, and you still haven't seen my new place."

"Yeah, I want to. Maybe sometime soon. Just not right now ... not with what's happened and all."

"Maybe when I drop you off, I could talk to your mom. We could pick a weekend for you to visit."

"I don't know, Dad."

"Are we okay, Sam—you and me?"

Sam looked up from his plate and met his dad's concerned brown eyes. For an instant he considered sharing some of his dark worries and raw frustrations, but instead he said, "Yeah, sure."

"Just makin' sure. Sometimes us dads aren't as clued in as the moms are." An awkward silence followed. Dan cleared his throat. "Well, you ready to go back to your house?"

Sam paused. Still odd to him that that it was not *our* house.

"I'm ready." Sam dropped his fork with a clatter and drained his glass of orange juice.

They piled into Dan's green Ford pickup and reached Dixie Avenue in minutes. His grandmother's car was in the driveway.

Sam pushed the truck door open and began to exit when his dad's hand gripped his shoulder. Sam glanced back.

"I'll call your mother later and try to set up a time when you can visit me in Louisville." His eyes flicked to the grandmother's car. "I'd go in, but I'd rather not, not with her here."

Sam didn't answer. He just stared out the windshield.

"Sam, you may not feel this way right now, but there's a lot goin' for us. I think things are gettin' better. I'm settlin' into my routine a little more, and you and your mom seem to be gettin' along just fine. Once I get my teachin' certificate, why, I'll be able to make more money, though not as much as I used to at the plant."

He pushed Sam's floppy, brown hair out of his eyes. "I'll make sure you have all the clothes you want—and all the best stuff, okay?"

Sam reflected on how little his dad really knew him—his thoughts and feelings, what he wanted in life. But he knew he was partly to blame. Since the divorce, he found it difficult to talk to his dad, to express his frustrations and anger. A wall stood between them, and he didn't know how to break it down. He wanted to tell his dad many things but was afraid to say what was really on his mind—that he hated him for leaving his mom, for moving away from Colgate, for leaving him fatherless in his hometown, and now his deep sadness over Josh's death.

He wanted to tell him he didn't want to play football in the fall. He wanted to tell him about the horrors of living next door to the Bedfords, about his hopes and fears, about everything in his heart. But he knew he would never say any of those things.

Instead, he said, "Thanks, Dad."

Sam heard the truck backing out of the driveway when he entered the house. His grandmother, Lillian Wurtz, was waiting for him in the doorway, an impatient look on her face.

"Hurry up, Sam. You need to go upstairs and change clothes." She peered out the screen door at his dad's retreating pickup. "Your father decided not to come in, huh?"

"Uh, no. He had to go." Sam decided not to mention that his dad had wanted to come in until he'd seen her car. "Why do I need to change?"

She squeezed his shoulder. "Why do you think? It's Sunday mornin', and we're all goin' to church together. It's time you and your mom got back in the habit."

People all dressed up in dresses and suits—church would only remind me of Josh's funeral. Sam frowned. "Not me."

"Yes, most certainly you, young man."

"But I don't want to."

Lillian pressed her lips together. "Follow me into the kitchen, Sam. We're talkin' to your mother about this right now." She nudged him forward.

Mary was at the breakfast table, sipping her coffee while perusing the newspaper. She glanced up and met his glance with a smile. She looked pretty in a fancy yellow, flower-print dress he hadn't seen before.

He'd never forget how hard she cried when he returned home from the canoe accident with only a bloody ear.

Lillian crossed to the sink and leaned her back against it, arms folded across her chest. "Mary, I was just having a discussion with Sam here about church. Now, Sam, why don't you want to go? All good, decent people like to go to church."

"What different does it make?" Sam folded his arms across his chest. "I just don't wanna go."

His grandmother came closer until they were practically nose to nose. "Now you listen to me, young man! You're gettin' a little big for your britches."

"Come on, Sam," Mary said in a sweet voice, though her eyes were pleading. "Why don't you wanna go? It'll make you feel better—I promise."

"There's nothin' there that's gonna make me feel any better."

Lillian sighed. "So what are you gonna do then—just sit around here all mornin'?"

"I don't know."

The truth is I don't care where I go as long as I don't have to go to church. I need to find a place where I can think. Then he knew. "Down to Hound's Creek, probably."

His grandmother perched her hands on her hips. "I want you to go with us. I don't think—"

"Mother, let's let him be," Mary said.

Lillian shook her head in disapproval. "I'm very disappointed in you, young man." She glanced at Mary. "I'll be in the car." She stormed out of the room.

After the storm had passed, Mary said, "Sam, did you and your father discuss you visitin' him?"

"Yeah, he wanted to talk to you about it, but then he saw Grandma's car and—"

"Listen to me, Sam." She rose and placed her arm across his shoulders. "I think you *should* visit your dad. Over the last few months, I've said some things about him to you that … well, I shouldn't have said 'em. I'm not gonna do that anymore, okay? That's not good for you."

She sighed. "It occurred to me at Josh's funeral yesterday that life's too short to be bitter. I think you need your dad right now and should be spendin' more time with him. He really does have his good points. After all, I married him."

"Okay. Thanks, Mom." Sam grabbed his library book on his way out the door and left without saying another word.

CHAPTER 40

O n Sam's way to Hound's Creek, the air was crisp and clean, the sidewalks freshly washed by the recent rain. It was as pretty a morning as anyone could hope for, but Sam kept his head down, barely aware of his surroundings. The sun's brightness contrasted with his dark mood, his mind occupied by a confusing tangle of disconnected thoughts, worries, and a deep sense of loss for Josh Carlisle.

Just get to the creek. Maybe you can sort things out there.

When Sam crossed Kidron Heights subdivision, Crum darted out of a bush near the Walker home and fell in step with him. As if sensing Sam's grief, Crum cocked his head at Sam and whimpered. Sam paused to scratch his neck before he headed toward the fence behind the Walker home and clambered over it. Crum scooted under the fence and raced after Sam.

Sam crossed the pasture, followed the cow path along the creek on the other side, and strolled toward the swimming hole. He passed a spot where a tree had fallen, knocking down part of the wire fence.

An enormous black-eyed crow sat on the low branch of a sycamore, which was charred from lightning. The bird cocked a cynical eye at Sam and fluttered its wings. Sam thought it might swoop down on him, and he fought an impulse to run. Two more crows as large as Crum landed on a higher limb and fluttered their wings.

Sam quickened his step to the swimming hole, glanced at the far side of the creek, and froze. To his shock, a dead heifer from the pasture lay in the green water, black tongue protruded, eyes bulging at him.

The cow must have wandered to the creek through the smashed fence, waded into the creek, and gotten stuck in the mud.

Sam cringed at the thought of how the cow must have struggled to free herself. A chill shivered down his spine.

He turned and made the short walk to his favorite reading place. He'd climbed the branches of the intertwined box elder trees so many times that he didn't need to look for handholds. When he found his spot twelve feet up, his body molded into the banana-shaped seat the trees provided. Then he gazed up at the branches around him, the foliage dark and lush like a green velvet curtain all round, the leaves diffusing the sunlight into splintered rays.

Nearby he spotted squirrel nests in the trees. Above him a vibrant, red cardinal preened its feathers, and the cries of mockingbirds provided a melancholy chorus.

He sighed. Everything here was familiar. Quiet. Safe. He studied the motionless trees surrounding him. Even the long-feathered branches of the willow tree across the creek were still.

Below him the green waters of the swimming hole shimmered, and to his right lay Paradise Island. Behind him the spring gurgled as it gently fed the creek. Below and to his left ran the footpath leading to the cow pasture and, farther on, the town. Crum circled the long grass at the base of the two trees before lying down and tucking his nose between his paws.

Usually Sam enjoyed the tranquility here, from the water to the silent woods. The place renewed him, reminding him that the world made sense. But not today. This morning the setting failed to provide any peace.

Sam opened his library book and tried to lose himself in the story—without success. Today he longed to leave Colgate and Kidron County. He wanted to forget, to be somewhere else, to *be* someone else.

I can't believe Josh is gone. I just can't believe it.

Sam shut the book and inspected the cover.

The best person I've ever known is dead. He's gone forever. I'll never see him again. He died on the river. Killed by rushing water and sharp rocks.

The air was oppressive, and his chest felt tight as if it were being squeezed in a vise.

I lied on the witness stand and sent Dewayne to a horrible place. I've been a terrible friend to Bates too. Josh shouldn't be dead; I'm the one who should be dead.

Guilt overcame him, and he couldn't shake the feeling that he was trapped in a terrifying dream. If only someone would wake him up … his life had become unmoored, and his hope for a good life seemed to be slipping away.

My dad moved away and doesn't even know me anymore.

He tried to make sense, some order, out of the events of the last six months, but he failed. The happy days he had experienced when he'd lived with both parents in Kidron Heights seemed like a distant memory now.

He began to cry—softly at first. Gentle sobs shook his shoulders, then began to tear through his whole body. Tears ran down his face that he didn't bother to wipe away.

Sam took a deep breath and whispered to the blue sky, "God, if you're really out there, I need you right now. I wish I were dead. Everything in my life has gone wrong, and I don't know where I'm goin'. If you're really out there, could you do somethin' … can you just show up?"

Sam lowered his head and scoffed at himself for praying. Whatever truth existed in heaven was surely closed to him. What could anyone do to help his world make sense again? It was too far gone to be fixed. It was too messy to be cleaned up, too disordered to be ordered again.

Nothin's gonna change. Nothin's ever gonna get better.

Then, as Sam reclined in the tree, wishing for a sign, something strange happened. A gentle breeze rustled through the trees and gusted along the creek from Paradise Island, pushing a blast of cool air down the creek toward town. The gust grew stronger, and a sudden whirlwind scurried the leaves into the air, up the trees, and around Sam.

Startled, Crum stood and barked upstream.

More leaves swirled and dappled the surface of the creek. Some landed on the dead heifer across the stream, and then a broad, golden shaft of sunlight cut through the trees and touched Sam's face. He shaded his eyes, the light almost too bright for him to bear.

At Kidron County Memorial Hospital, Regina, the Walker family's housekeeper, sat in a recliner beside Nick's bed, knitting. She'd arrived at 7:00 A.M. to relieve Nick's mother, who'd stayed beside her son overnight, sleeping in the chair. Regina glanced over to the unconscious boy.

And only thirteen years old. She shook her head. *What a shame, and his friend Josh dead.*

A young, blonde-haired nurse entered and gave Regina a cheerful hello. She began the laborious process of changing the bandages covering the boy's arms and face.

The nurse removed a blood-soaked dressing from his right arm.

Regina straightened in her chair and inhaled sharply. Something wasn't right.

She stood. "Waits a minute, nurse."

The nurse stepped aside, and Regina approached the bed, gently lifting the rest of the bandage off the boy's arm. Her heart began to beat in her chest like a drum.

"It ain't there!" Her voice sounded shrill in the small room. "It ain't there!"

Concern wrinkled the nurse's brow. "What's not there, honey?"

"His birthmark! Nick gots a birthmark on his right arm, and I'm tellin' ya', it ain't there!" Regina pressed her hands to her face. *Dear Lord.* "Take them bandages off of his face."

"I was gonna change the bandage on his arm first and then—"

"Do it now. Please."

"Okay, I can start with his face." The nurse shrugged and complied. When the process reached the point that Regina could recognize the boy's face, she gasped and covered her open mouth with both hands.

"Dear Lord. Go gets Dr. Carlisle right away!"

CHAPTER 41

A blue butterfly bearing yellow dots on its wings fluttered above Sam's head. He read the same page for the fourth time and sighed in exasperation.

Coming to Hound's Creek today was a stupid idea.

He closed the book in frustration and tossed it to the ground twelve feet below. It slammed into the dirt, waking Crum, who'd been dozing peacefully at the foot of a tree.

Sam thought he heard a voice and turned his head toward the sound.

"Sam! Sam? Where are you?"

Meredith?

"Over here!" he said.

He peered down at the creek. Meredith and Bates appeared in the distance. They spotted him in the tree and ran hard.

Sam's chest tightened.

Why the urgency? Has something else happened?

He climbed down and faced them as they bridged the distance. "What're y'all doin' here?"

"You won't believe what's happened!" Bates' face was flushed with heat, excitement, or both. "Everybody's talkin' about it at Immanuel Temple this mornin'."

Sam stared at him, confused.

Meredith said, "Sam! You haven't heard, have you?"

"Heard what?"

Bates gasped. "You aren't going believe it."

Sam prickled with annoyance. "Believe what?"

"Josh is alive!" Meredith said.

He scowled at her. "Ya know, Meredith, that isn't funny."

"She's not jokin'," Bates said. "It's true—I swear. Josh isn't dead."

Sam's gaze darted from Meredith to Bates and back. "I don't understand what you're sayin'. How could Josh be alive? We just buried him yesterday. He's dead. Gone forever." *The doctor has even done the autopsy. How could this be anything but a joke?*

Meredith shook her head, her face sincere. "No, Sam. Josh is alive. Nick's the one who's dead."

Questions throbbed in Sam's head. "You're not makin' any sense. You're just makin' me mad. If this is somebody's idea of a sick joke, I'm gonna—"

"Just listen to me." Meredith grabbed his arm. "I know it sounds crazy, but listen. It was all a mistake. Remember, Simon lost his glasses in the river. When he saw the bodies, he got them mixed up. Besides, Josh's and Nick's faces were so swollen that it was hard to tell them apart."

Sam stared at her, his thoughts picking up speed. *Even without swollen faces, Josh and Nick always looked alike, more like brothers than friends. And everybody knows how blind Simon is without his glasses.*

She went on. "Then the ambulance crew wrote down the wrong names because that's what Simon and Mr. Wiseman told them. In the dark and with their injuries, everybody got mixed up. Dr. and Mrs. Carlisle were too upset to view the body, so they asked Brother Billy to do it. But he could hardly look at the body because of the injuries, so he just repeated what Simon had told them. On top of that, Dr. Mason had such a hangover from the night before that he didn't even do the autopsy."

"Ms. Regina made the discovery this mornin'," Bates said. "Nick had a birthmark on his arm, but the birthmark wasn't there. My Aunt Margaret, who volunteers at the hospital, called the church with the news. I ran to your house as soon as I heard and bumped into Meredith on the way. Nobody was home, so we decided to look for you here."

Sam just stared at them, the enormity of what he'd been told sinking in. It wasn't a joke. Sadness gripped his heart when he realized Nick was dead, but the irrepressible joy that swelled at the revelation that Josh was alive overshadowed his grief.

Without thinking, he gave Bates a burly hug. When he pulled away, Bates looked startled. He felt like hugging Meredith too. He took in the sweet curve of her mouth and her tan cheeks, a light wind playing in her hair. She'd never appeared so beautiful to him.

Without thinking, he leaned toward her and kissed her on the lips.

When he pulled back, she stared at him, perplexed but not annoyed. He studied her, unsure if this sudden impulse to show her affection was due to his feelings for her or because Josh was alive.

Stop it. You can figure that out later.

He was wasting time. "C'mon!" he said. "Let's go."

He left Meredith and Bates behind, sprinting down the path toward the hospital. Crum gave chase, and Bates and Meredith pounded the dirt behind him.

Kidron County Memorial Hospital was a long, two-story, tan-brick building. Sam, Bates, and Meredith slowed to a jog when they reached its front entrance at about 11:00 A.M. Everybody was winded from the run. Even Crum's tongue hung out of his mouth.

Sweat soaked through Sam's shirt and dripped down his face. His hair had matted to the side of his face, and his ear had begun bleeding again. He slowed and gulped down some air.

About two dozen people, many with familiar faces, lingered outside the hospital entrance.

Judge Graves and his wife chatted with Colgate's mayor and a city council member. Principal Sheridan talked to several students. Mrs. Legg, there with her husband, rushed over to Sam when she recognized him. Her clothes were fancier than he remembered seeing at school; she wore a bright blue dress, matching high heels, and cherry-red lipstick.

"I've nearly worried myself to death about you, Sam," she said. "Would you look at your ear?" Mr. Legg handed her a handkerchief, and she used it to dab away the dripping blood.

"How are you? I just want to squeeze you," she said and did just that.

Sam pulled away. "I'm fine, Mrs. Legg. Thanks for askin'."

"I'm so sorry about Josh—" She stopped herself. "I mean Nick. It's all so confusing, isn't it?"

Sam began moving away. "Please excuse me, Mrs. Legg, but I want to see if they'll let me in to see Josh."

The crowd was getting larger by the minute. The news about Josh and Nick had spread across town that Sunday morning with a speed that only terrifically good news, or terribly bad news, can spread. Most wore their Sunday finery and must have heard the news at church. Sam scanned the parking lot, where Simon Puckett's family was pulling into a spot with their station wagon.

As they plowed into the hospital, Sam realized that Crum was still following them, his tongue hanging out of his mouth.

Bates grabbed his collar and pulled him back. "We'll stay out here with Crum. You go ahead, Sam."

Sam darted inside toward the female receptionist, who was dressed in a pink uniform and matching cap. "What room is Josh Carlisle in?" he asked.

"Well, let me see." She flipped through several papers in front of her. "We don't seem to have a Josh—"

"Nick, I mean. Nick Walker."

The receptionist studied the papers again. "Of course, I knew that. Nick Walker. I guess that's Josh's room now. I'll have to make that correction on my sheet. Sorry."

"What room is he in?"

"Room 282." She smiled at him. "Go down this hallway and take the stairway on your right to the second floor. I don't know if they'll let you—"

He was already running.

"Son," she said, "your ear's bleedin'."

Sam didn't slow. He found Dr. Carlisle in the second-floor hallway; he was talking to a nurse, his eyes were small and weary with fatigue. Mrs. Carlisle beside him. She waved Sam over. She looked as tired and yet happy as her husband.

Dr. Carlisle saw Sam and motioned to a nearby nurse. "Would you please get me some gauze to put on his ear?" The nurse nodded and left to do his bidding.

"Oh, Sam," Mrs. Carlisle said with a broad smile. "It's so good to see you. You've been through such a frightful ordeal." While she spoke, Dr. Carlisle examined Sam's ear, his capable fingers moving with efficient purpose.

The nurse arrived with gauze. While Dr. Carlisle began cutting away Sam's old bandage, Mrs. Carlisle said, "When did you find out about Josh?"

"Just a little while ago. Bates and Meredith told me."

"Our prayers are with the Walker family," Mrs. Carlisle said. Dr. Carlisle nodded in agreement.

"This is an ugly wound you've got here, Sam," he said. While the nurse held the medical kit, Dr. Carlisle cleaned Sam's ear and placed a clean bandage over it.

"Would you like to go in and see him now?" Mrs. Carlisle said.

Sam nodded. "I sure would."

As Dr. Carlisle finished with the new bandage, Mrs. Carlisle gripped Sam's shoulder for a moment, her eyes tender. "This has been a rough time. He's going to need a good friend like you, Sam." She pulled him toward her and hugged him.

Sam held on, tears springing to his eyes. "I just can't believe it. I feel terrible that Nick is dead, but I missed Josh so much."

"I know. I know." She rubbed his back and released him.

"Why don't you go in and see him now," Dr. Carlisle said. "But you can only stay a few minutes."

The two occupants of the El Camino watched Sam enter the hospital twenty-five feet away. Larry Bedford, his right hand wrapped in a white bandage, glanced at his dad and studied his hangdog expression.

Coach Bedford looked as if he'd lost ten pounds in the last week. Three-day stubble bristled from his cheeks, and his hair was unkempt, his eyes bloodshot. Larry had never seen his dad look so shabby.

He'd been released from the county jail at sunrise, and Larry had been there to pick him up, instantly noticing a change in his father. A deep, dark depression had replaced Coach Bedford's usual air of efficiency and order.

"Yeah, I guess we scared 'em off." Larry chuckled. "When I came back, I had almost the whole offensive line with me. We were ready to give those boys a beatin' they'd never forget. I guess they were smart to move on down the river."

Coach Bedford stared at the hospital as if he hadn't heard him.

"You sure you're okay?" Larry asked.

"Stop askin' me that! That's the third time this mornin'."

Through the window Larry watched the crowd that gathered outside the front door. "It must be true. The Walker kid must be dead, and the Carlisle kid must be alive."

Coach Bedford remained silent, his gaze never straying from the hospital entryway.

Larry chuckled. "Some people really messed up—I mean really. They buried the wrong kid? How could that have happened? Somebody really oughta pay. You think the Walker family's gonna sue?"

"Sue who?"

"I don't know. The coroner, the sheriff, the funeral home. Everybody, I guess."

Coach Bedford cursed. "I can't believe it. Look who's here."

Larry studied the hospital entrance again and saw Bates and Meredith ambling over to a bench near the flagpole. They took a seat while a small dog sat panting at their feet.

"What's *she* doin' here?" Larry said.

Meredith took Bates' hand in hers, and they faced each other, smiling. Meredith released Bates' hand, and he put his arm around her, giving her a brief hug before dropping his arm.

Coach Bedford's face reddened. "I can't believe it. What else could possibly happen?"

Larry shook his head and smacked his mouth like he had a sour taste in his mouth. "That stupid girl!"

Coach Bedford sighed. "Okay, I'm goin' in through the side door. After I'm in, go get your sister and take her home."

"But Dad—"

"Just do as I say and take her home! I don't need any lip from you right now."

"What're you gonna do?"

Coach Bedford opened the door. Before he exited, Larry grabbed his arm. "Dad, please don't do this. I don't want to lose you. I just want things to go back to normal."

Coach Bedford glared at his son and threw off his hand. "But that's the problem—nothin' can go back to normal ever again." He shook his head. "I thought things over in that jail cell as much as I intend to. I know what I need to do. Sam Cray played me false, and he's gonna pay."

CHAPTER 42

He really is alive.

Sam grappled with the unbelievable truth. It was like a miracle, living and breathing in this room. He wasn't quite sure how to respond.

Shades were drawn, the lights dim. The room was silent except for the whirl of machines and the rhythmic beep-beep of the monitor tracking Josh's vital signs. A transparent bag hanging from the IV tree dripped clear saline and an analgesic into his right arm. With the aid of the analgesic, Josh was breathing deeply and evenly.

Sam crept toward the bed and peered down at his friend, his throat tight.

Josh lay on his back, his eyes closed. A thin, pastel blue gown covered his body, and oxygen tubes were in his nose. Josh's pale, drawn face was still swollen and puffy. Bandages on his head and arms couldn't hide all the bruises. Dried blood covered the gauzes on his face.

I hope he'll look the same and be able to walk and run like he used to.

Sam winced at the memory of Josh's and Nick's last cries as their canoe went over the dam.

A cast covered Josh's left arm; he suffered a greenstick fracture just above the elbow, Dr. Carlisle had told him. Sam touched Josh's right hand. Feeling the warmth in Josh's hand lifted Sam's spirit. For the first time since the tragedy, he felt a little better.

Josh was recovering. He was going to be okay.

Sam sighed, internal voices accusing him because he hadn't spent more time with Josh, hadn't been a better, more constant friend. He'd wasted so many opportunities to be his friend on other things. Well, no more. They had more opportunities to be better friends now. Realizing what he'd almost lost made his friendship with Josh even more special.

Sam smiled. "Your parents said you're gonna need me," he whispered, "but the truth is, I need you more than you know. It took somethin' like this to help me see that."

The door opened, and Sam turned. Mrs. Carlisle stepped into the room and edged to his side, a relieved look on her face.

"Sam, you'd better go now. It's time for the nurse to change his bandages."

"Thanks for lettin' me visit."

"You're welcome." Her hopeful eyes were fixed on her son. "It'll be all right. We'll get through this together."

"Is it okay if I come by tomorrow and every day he's here?"

She put an arm around him, giving him a squeeze. "I wouldn't have it any other way."

Sam closed the door to Josh's room and strolled down the hallway to the stairwell. He opened the door and stepped inside. The heavy door swung closed behind as he turned to begin his descent.

"We've got unfinished business, neighbor."

The hair rose on the back of Sam's neck. He knew that voice.

Coach Bedford emerged from the shadows, a resentful scowl on his face. He'd changed so much since the last time Sam saw him. His hair was disheveled, his clothes wrinkled. He'd never looked so haggard, so much like a man who'd come undone.

Sam's mouth turned dry. Fear intertwined with disbelief. *How is this possible? Wasn't he in jail?*

Before Sam could think, Coach Bedford rushed him with surprising speed and backhanded him.

Sam's head jerked to the left. Sizzling pain burned the corner of his mouth, and he cried out, the taste of blood fresh in his mouth.

He lunged toward the door to the corridor, reaching for the handle. But he wasn't quick enough.

Coach Bedford grabbed Sam from behind and placed him in a head-lock with one arm while the other pressed his hand over Sam's mouth.

Desperate to be free, Sam clawed at Coach Bedford's forearm. But the coach tightened his grip. Sam breathed hard through his nose, trying not to panic.

Coach Bedford used his body weight to jerk Sam toward a metal door. He kicked it open, revealing a broad, flat, asphalt roof that extended over a one-story section of the hospital. A large, forest-green cooling unit stood directly to their left.

Sam struggled as Coach Bedford dragged him across the threshold. Heat hit Sam like the blast from a furnace, and heat waves shimmered over the asphalt roof.

He tried to kick him, but his feet missed.

The coach's hot breath battered Sam's ear. "You didn't think you could pull a stunt like that and get away with it, did ya?" He released Sam and shoved him onto the roof.

Sam stumbled forward into the heat and the blinding sun. He whirled. Coach Bedford stepped toward him, an angry scowl on his face. Two veins stood out from his neck.

"I've got nothing to lose now," he said with both arms extended. "When I think about the time and effort I've put into that school." He shook his head in disgust. "It's all gone now. I'm finished—my family is finished. Look at me, Cray. You've bled me white."

Sam eyed the door behind the coach. *If I could somehow get around him …*

Coach Bedford lunged toward Sam. Sam tried to back away, but he couldn't.

Coach Bedford used both hands to grab Sam by his shirt, hoisting him to his feet. He pulled Sam's face up to his. With a malevolent smile he said, "Is common sense a stranger to you, Cray? Did you think you were gonna lead the parade for my demise without me retaliatin'? I've got too much pride to allow you to do that."

The coach's breath smelled foul. Sam turned his head away. He tried to reconcile this embittered man with the man he'd known before—with the school teacher, the football coach, and the authority figure.

But this man was devoid of any honorable leadership qualities the coach had once exhibited.

The coach carried Sam for several feet while Sam tried to wiggle free. "I know all about your meetin's with stu-stu-stutterin' Sheridan and the school board. The day Sheridan fired me, he was stutterin' so bad, I yelled at him, 'Spit it out, Bob!' He's pitiful. Is that pipsqueak the kind of leader they want at that school?" He laughed hoarsely to himself.

Coach Bedford glared at Sam in frustration, a wild glint in his eyes. *He looks insane.*

"You've caused me a lot of grief, boy, and now you're gonna pay."

The coach unleashed his rage. He released Sam and drove a fist into his stomach.

Sam crumpled to his knees in pain, unable to breathe. He tried to yell, but no sound came out.

Just as he caught his breath, Coach Bedford kicked him, and pain exploded in his side. Face pressed to hot asphalt, he tried to think of something persuasive to say, something to bring Coach Bedford to his senses. But nothing came to mind.

I have to get away. I have to escape somehow.

"I couldn't believe it—my own neighbor!" Coach Bedford said. "I've tried to understand why you would've turned on me."

Gotta get up. C'mon, Cray, get up.

Sam pushed himself to his knees and thought he might pass out from the pain. He glanced at the coach.

Coach Bedford edged closer, chest heaving, fists clenched and ready at his sides. "Sam, you've been sailin' under false colors. You're a counterfeit, a regular Laban. Tell me this—was it Bates' idea to turn me in to Sheridan? Did he talk you into it? Maybe he forced you to do it."

Sam rose to his feet and faced him. He glimpsed back to see how much roof he had left. He had some space. The tall steeple of Kidron Valley Church loomed a quarter of a mile away.

"No. It was my idea." He was surprised by how feeble his voice sounded.

Coach Bedford stepped closer. "Didn't you consider what would happen to you?"

Sam glanced around, eyes frantic for a way of escape.

Sweat streamed down Coach Bedford's maddened face. "I told myself I don't need that job, don't need to be with a bunch of ungrateful students and ignorant teachers, don't need to bust my gut for a football program when people don't appreciate me."

He paused for a breath, took another step. "But, Sam, the honest truth is, I don't think I can live without it. I don't know what else to do with myself. Sittin' in that jail cell is when I really started to hate you."

The wind blew, lowering the temperature by a few degrees. Without knowing why, Sam felt his fear slipping away. Courage stirred in its place—along with a desire to fight.

Anger bubbled inside Sam. His voice cracked. "Remember what you taught me, Coach? We're all leavin' a legacy. So what legacy are you leavin', huh?"

Sam didn't wait for Coach Bedford this time. He charged him low and leveled his shoulder, knocking his feet out from under him.

The coach went down, cursing.

Sam rolled away and scrambled toward the door.

But Coach Bedford sprang to his feet. Grabbed Sam by the back of the shirt. Slammed him against the cooling unit with a loud *bang*.

Pain streaked down Sam's arm. Coach Bedford grabbed him and threw him down.

CHAPTER 43

Dan Cray, a late arrival at the hospital, searched the crowd for Sam. Almost a hundred people were gathered outside Kidron County Memorial Hospital. He saw that Mrs. Legg and her husband were there, as were Simon Puckett and his family. Bates and Meredith sat on a bench and were trying to keep Crum out of everyone's way.

Dan joined Judge Graves, Sheriff Brothers, and Deputy Hunter near the flagpole under the American and Kentucky flags. They greeted him.

"I hear you're comin' back to Colgate," Judge Graves said.

"Wow. News travels fast," said Dan, nodding. "Possibly."

"Got your old job back at the rubber plant?" Deputy Hunter said.

"No."

"Then what're you gonna do?" Sheriff Brothers said.

Dan smiled. "Sorry, guys. I'm afraid I can't say just yet. It's top secret. I need to talk to Sam first. Have you seen him?"

Judge Graves shook his head. "Nope. Can't say that I have."

Concern was etched on Sheriff Brothers' face. "Dan, we need to talk to you about Ray Bedford."

"What's up? I thought we were through with him."

"We're concerned he's not gonna take his firing peacefully. Caleb's been keepin' an eye on him since he got out of the county jail this morning and followed him here."

Nearby, Crum pulled free from Meredith's grasp and scampered over to where the men stood. He raised his nose, sniffed the air, growled, and began barking at the roof. The men glanced at Crum.

Meredith and Bates rushed over and tried to catch him, but Crum evaded them, darting back and forth. He barked frantically at the roof.

Sheriff Brothers talked louder to be heard over Crum's barking. "Caleb followed Coach Bedford here. He knows we're tailin' him and hasn't tried to lose us."

"What do you think he might do?" Dan asked.

"We don't know exactly." The sheriff shifted his weight from one foot to the other. "We figure he bears watchin' right now. He's got a lot of stubborn pride and is still reelin' from being canned. We think he may have revenge on his mind."

"Revenge against who?"

The sheriff's eyes shifted to the judge and then back to Dan. "Do you know anything about the meetin' your son and Bates William had with Principal Sheridan or their meetin' with the school board?"

"No." Dan stared at him, baffled. "I don't know anything about either of those meetings."

Dan noticed Larry out of the corner of his eye. Larry was sauntering toward Meredith and Bates, who'd given up on Crum and sat no more than twenty feet away.

Crum continued to bark toward the roof.

"Hey, look. There's Larry Bedford," Dan said. The men turned to watch.

Larry and Meredith began arguing. Larry grabbed her arm and pulled her toward the parking lot. She broke free from his grasp and rejoined Bates.

"Didn't Larry show up with his dad?" Deputy Hunter said.

The sheriff nodded. "Something's not right here."

A loud bang from high above alarmed Dan.

"What was that?" Judge Graves looked up and studied the hospital roof.

Movement caught Dan's eye, and he gasped. "Look!"

Coach Bedford and Sam stood on the roof, facing each other. They watched as Coach Bedford grabbed Sam and threw him down before both of them disappeared from their sight.

Common sense told Sam this couldn't be happening, but it was. *Coach Bedford is gonna kill me!*

Coach Bedford straddled Sam's chest with his knees. His hands closed around Sam's throat and squeezed, cutting off his air.

Sam tried to pry the hands off his neck, but Coach Bedford was too strong.

Sam couldn't breathe. His eyes bulged. His lungs screamed for oxygen, and the blood in his brain pounded against his skull. He flailed his legs, trying to find a way to break free.

Coach Bedford displayed a mad grin on his face. A drop of sweat dripped off his face and landed on Sam's cheek. "I'm afraid, boy," he whispered, "that you won't be gettin' back up this time."

Sam tried to roll him off, but the coach was too heavy. He struck at him with both fists, but to no avail. The wasted effort only reminded him of how badly he needed to breathe.

Coach Bedford squeezed Sam's throat tighter. Sam clawed at the hands painfully compressing his windpipe. His racing heart pounded in his ears.

Darkness nibbled at the edges of his vision. He was starting to pass out.

Sheriff Brothers and Deputy Hunter jogged toward the hospital entrance. Dan Cray raced past them, panic and anger spurting adrenaline into his veins. He slammed through the front doors, ignoring the front desk and the shouting receptionist. He sprinted down the hall and flew up the stairs, taking them three at a time.

Dan reached the top and burst through the door to the roof, breathing hard. The sight froze him in his tracks.

Coach Bedford was on top of Sam, choking him. Sam's face was red, eyes bulging, arms flailing.

With three long strides, Dan covered the distance between them before launching himself into the air. He hit Coach Bedford with body-slamming intensity that sent both of them reeling to the roof floor. Dan landed on top of the coach and could hear the air rush out of his lungs. He pinned Coach Bedford to the roof before glancing at Sam, almost afraid to look.

Sam had both hands to his throat and was gulping large breaths.

Dan's heart lifted. Sam was going to be okay.

Dan glared at Coach Bedford beneath him. He placed his fingers around his neck and began to tighten his grip.

Larry Bedford stomped the accelerator to the floor, and the El Camino fishtailed around a corner, then raced toward Dixie Avenue. He spotted the Cray home and twisted the steering wheel to his right, aiming the car's right fender at their mailbox. He hit it, splintering the mailbox into a thousand pieces.

The inside of the car rang with his maniacal laughter.

"That'll show you, Sam Cray!"

The Chevrolet bumped the curb and lifted on two wheels before thumping down again with a jerk that rattled Larry's teeth. He steered toward the public square and hit the gas again yelling as loud as he could.

He swiped an arm across his rage-filled eyes, trying to wipe the sweat away. He blinked, unable to see the road clearly. The El Camino shot into the square.

Too fast!

Larry realized his mistake too late. He gritted his teeth and wrestled the steering wheel to his right. But the car was sliding, burning rubber, out of control. It careened toward the courthouse on squealing wheels. Slid sideways. Rammed a parked car with a sickening crunch.

The El Camino bounced off the car and kept going. Larry gunned the engine, and the powerful engine roared. The car leapt forward.

The car raced across the square on a collision course with the library.

Eyes wide, Larry turned the steering wheel.

But nothing happened, and he realized …

Panic swelled in his chest. His fingers gripped the steering wheel.

No way to turn. Too fast to jump.

Larry Bedford screamed.

The El Camino collided head-on into the library's redbrick façade. The crunch of metal squealed in his ears. Glass shattered.

Larry's body lurched forward. His head hit the steering wheel and then bounced back, smacking the headrest.

Then, amazingly, silence.

Bricks tumbled and slammed into the already crushed hood. Gray smoke plumed from the wrecked engine and poured into the morning air. Larry moaned.

More bricks crumbled, broke apart, and fell from the library wall until the bricks holding John Hunt Morgan's cannonball in place loosened. The weapon, held in place by the brick wall for so many years, rolled from its historic resting place. Three inches it rolled until it ran out of momentum and rested against a solitary brick which hung halfway off the wall.

Larry was amazed to be alive. He lifted his head and blood dripped from his temple.

He peered out the pulverized windshield and assessed the carnage. What he saw made him lightheaded.

Oh no! Dad's gonna kill me.

He slumped forward and swung his forehead down against the steering wheel with a thump. The El Camino's powerful horn blared one continuous drone throughout the square. But Larry didn't care.

Vibrations from the horn traveled through the wrecked frame, shook the crumbling brick wall, and jostled the last loose brick holding the old cannonball in place. The brick vibrated out of place, tumbled, and joined the pile of bricks on the car's hood.

Now free, the cannonball rolled free. It teetered on the edge of the remaining brick wall and paused for a second when, as if fate had breathed on it, it plummeted to the pile of bricks on the El Camino's hood.

Then, the hundred-year-old Confederate cannonball exploded.

CHAPTER 44

Sam lay on his back, coughing and gasping for breath. His throat hurt. He glanced over to where his father had pinned Coach Bedford on his back.

Sheriff Brothers and Deputy Hunter stormed onto the roof. The sheriff marched over to Dan Cray, who still straddled Coach Bedford. "Dan, let us take him from here."

Reluctantly, Dan obeyed the sheriff and rolled off Coach Bedford. The coach lay prone, staring vacantly into the cloudless sky with eyes that seemed to glimpse something beyond reality.

"Look at him, Sheriff," Deputy Hunter said. "He's snapped."

Deputy Hunter pulled the coach to his feet and spun him around.

Sam heard the crisp clank of handcuffs in the deputy's hands. Coach Bedford didn't resist as the deputy pulled his hands behind his back and snapped the cuffs around his wrists. Then the coach's face crumpled, and from his lips came the most pitiful, broken cry from a grown man Sam had ever heard.

"Caleb, just get him out of here," the sheriff said in disgust.

As the deputy scuttled him away, Coach Bedford mumbled something just loudly enough for Sam, Dan, and the deputy to hear. "Far from good."

A distant explosion made Sam's body jerk. Everybody turned and looked. Smoke billowed into the sky from the direction of the library. Nobody knew what had happened and were too busy with the events at hand to pay it any attention.

Paramedics and various sheriff's deputies arrived. The deputies led Coach Bedford away. His lips continued to move, but he emitted no sound.

Dan stood back as paramedics helped Sam to the shade of the green cooling unit. There, stunned and exhausted, he leaned against it and allowed paramedics to check him out.

When they were finished, Sam drew his knees to his chest, clasping his hands before him. He was breathing easier now. Just a few more seconds with Coach Bedford's hands around his neck, and … he didn't want to think about what could have happened.

Dan found an empty milk crate and pulled it next to Sam before sitting down. He ran his fingers through his son's hair.

"What're you doin' here?" Sam whispered, wiping his eyes. His tongue was thick. "I thought you were headin' back to Louisville."

"After I dropped you off, I stopped by to see Principal Sheridan."

"Why were you meetin' with Principal Sheridan?"

"I didn't want to say anything until I knew for sure, but given the circumstances …"

"What is it?"

Dan cleared his throat. "Well, you might as well learn now rather than later. Sam, the principal and I were talkin', and he's offered me a teaching job at the junior high school this fall. He's going to let me pick up the last few credits I need next summer. I plan to take it—that is, if it's okay with you."

Sam studied his face, confused. "What?"

"Principal Sheridan invited me to be the new music and band teacher at the junior high school. In fact, I was with him when Sheriff Brothers called him about the mix-up between Nick and Josh. I've been lookin' for you ever since."

Sam swallowed hard.

"You don't mind do you—if I teach at the junior high?" Dan said.

"No, I don't mind. In fact, I think I know who one of your new students will be."

Dan raised his eyebrows. "Oh, yeah? Who might that be?"

"Bates Williams."

"Bates?"

"Yep. He's not playin' football this year. He wants to be in the band instead."

"The sheriff told me about the danger you and Bates were in," Dan said. "I can't believe that you all were willing to risk that. I am really proud of …"

"I'm sorry, Dad, really sorry," said Sam, interrupting him.

"What do you mean, you're sorry? What have you got to be sorry for? It sounds to me that you and Bates did a very brave thing. Something that needed to be done a long time ago. There are not many people in this town who are willing to stand up to …"

"I'm sorry for hatin' you."

"What?"

Sam lifted his head, but still couldn't look at him. "I've hated you ever since you left Mom. Ever since you left Colgate … left me."

Dan said nothing for a few seconds. He draped his left arm over Sam's shoulders. "Actually, I can't say I blame you. The truth is, I feel like a failure in so many areas of life. That includes bein' your dad."

He sighed and rested his head against the metal wall. "Every dad wants to appear perfect in his son's eyes. I'm not sure why you got stuck with somebody like me. All I can say is, I'm sorry for being gone. I never meant to walk away from you."

Sam nodded. He grasped the back of his dad's hand as it hung over his shoulder. Lookin up, he said, "Can I stay with you today? Go back with you and see your apartment in Louisville?"

Dan's voice was thick with emotion. "That's what I was hopin' you'd ask. But I also need your help findin' a place here in Colgate, because I'm movin' back, remember?"

Father and son sat in silence, taking in the moment. Finally, Dan said, "Hey, you'll never guess what I found in my shavin' stuff this week. I forgot to give this to you at breakfast this mornin'." He dug into his pocket and pulled out a cotton cloth. He handed it to Sam.

Sam opened the cloth. Inside lay a steel ring bearing the engraved image of the aircraft carrier *USS Yorktown*.

Sam gasped. "You found it!" He slipped the ring onto his ring finger and then covered it with his other hand before drawing both of his hands tight against his chest.

As he clenched the ring, the weariness and frustration of the last year seemed to fade away, his fears melting into nothingness. A strange sense of calm took their place.

The roof was crowded with dozens of people now, but Sam felt like he was watching a silent movie. Mouths were moving, but he couldn't hear their voices. He leaned his head back against the metal wall and closed his eyes.

A nurse approached him and said, "Let's go inside and let the doctor take a better look at you."

But Sam didn't hear her.

His head remained back. His eyes still closed. His dad leaned forward and watched as a contented smile spread across his face.

EPILOGUE

Saturday, September 13, 1975

(Two weeks later)

S am rolled the dice across the game board and frowned in disappointment at his number. He scooted his racecar piece forward.

"Yes! That's Boardwalk, Sam!" Bates rubbed his hands together. "Let's see, with a hotel, that'll be two thousand dollars please."

Sam groaned. Crum lay beside him, his head between his paws as if analyzing the game.

"I don't think he's got it. What do you think, Bates?" Josh grinned. He studied Sam's remaining Monopoly money in an effort to count it.

Sam hid his money. "Hey, mind your own business!"

Josh, Bates, and Sam sat cross-legged on the living room floor of the Cray home on Dixie Avenue. Three empty ice cream bowls lay next to them. Josh's arm cast was crammed with signatures from dozens of well-wishers, and the yellow bruises around his neck and face were beginning to fade.

Mary Cray meandered into the room. "Would you put this on for me, Sam?" She handed him a string of pearls.

Sam stared at her, stunned. She'd changed into a red dress that fit snuggly around her waist and a white halter top that accentuated her chest.

"Gosh, Mom!" he said. "That dress looks like it's painted on."

She ignored him.

"And why all the gook pancaked on your face?"

"Pancaked?" She tilted her head with an amused grin.

Sam stood and draped the pearls around her neck and worked the clasp. The scent of perfume drifted up to his nose, and it occurred to him that his mother was going out on a date. A flash of anger spread over him. "Hey, where you goin' anyhow?"

She turned. "I'll be home in a couple of hours. Bates and Josh, I'm glad you could spend the night with Sam."

"We are too," Josh said.

"Are you feelin' okay, Josh?" she asked. "Do you need anything before I go?"

"No ma'am, I'm just fine," Josh said, smiling.

Sam faced her, hands on his hips. "Where are you goin? Aren't you even goin' to tell your own son?"

She pinched his cheek. "Can't you tell when somebody's goin' on a date?"

Another spark of anger jolted him. "But—"

She walked away.

"Sam, it's still your turn," Josh said.

"Do you got the money, or don't ya?" Bates said.

Sam slumped back down on the floor, frustration ebbing through him. "I don't have the money—I'm done." He flipped his property cards into the game box and handed his money to Bates.

"Aren't you even gonna mortgage your properties?" Bates said.

"Didn't you hear me? I said I'm done."

Bates whistled a happy tune and added Sam's money to his own.

Sam lay on his back and stared glumly at the ceiling.

So that's why she asked Bates and Josh to come over—to babysit me. Should've known.

The doorbell rang.

"Bye, boys," Mary said. "Sam, you-all don't leave the house while I'm gone, okay?"

"Okay." Sam rolled his eyes.

Her heels echoed down the hallway.

He crawled a few feet on his belly so he could see around the corner and glimpse the front door. Crum followed at his side. The salon hair dryer partially obstructed his view, but at least he could see below it.

The front door opened. At the sight of a man's tan slacks and brown dress shoes, resentment rose inside Sam. He crawled some more for a better look.

Just past the edge of the hair dryer, to his surprise, Sam saw his father's profile appear.

He watched as Dan's hand moved to Mary's cheek, gently pushed her blond hair behind her ear, and kissed her.

Reading Guide Available at
www.farfromgood.com